The

LOST SUMMER

of

LOUISA MAY ALCOTT

The

LOST SUMMER

of

LOUISA MAY ALCOTT

Kelly O'Connor McNees

AMY EINHORN BOOKS
Published by G. P. Putnam's Sons
a member of Penguin Group (USA) Inc.
New York

æe

AMY EINHORN BOOKS
Published by G. P. Putnam's Sons
Publishers Since 1838
Published by the Penguin Group
Penguin Group (USA) Inc., 375 Hudson Street, New York, New York 10014, USA •
Penguin Group (Canada), 90 Eglinton Avenue East, Suite 700, Toronto, Ontario M4P 2Y3,
Canada (a division of Pearson Penguin Canada Inc.) • Penguin Books Ltd, 80 Strand,
London WC2R 0RL, England • Penguin Ireland, 25 St Stephen's Green, Dublin 2,
Ireland (a division of Penguin Books Ltd) • Penguin Group (Australia), 250 Camberwell Road,
Camberwell, Victoria 3124, Australia (a division of Pearson Australia Group Pty Ltd) •
Penguin Books India Pvt Ltd, 11 Community Centre, Panchsheel Park,
New Delhi–110 017, India • Penguin Group (NZ), 67 Apollo Drive, Rosedale,
North Shore 0632, New Zealand (a division of Pearson New Zealand Ltd) •
Penguin Books (South Africa) (Pty) Ltd, 24 Sturdee Avenue,
Rosebank, Johannesburg 2196, South Africa

Penguin Books Ltd, Registered Offices: 80 Strand, London WC2R 0RL, England

"Amy Einhorn Books" and the "ae" logo are trademarks belonging to Penguin Group (USA) Inc.

Library of Congress Cataloging-in-Publication Data

McNees, Kelly O'Connor.
The lost summer of Louisa May Alcott / Kelly O'Connor McNees.
p.   cm.
ISBN 978-0-399-15652-6
1. Alcott, Louisa May, 1832–1888—Fiction.   2. Alcott, Louisa May, 1832–1888—Homes
and haunts—New Hampshire—Fiction.   3. Alcott, Louisa May, 1832–1888—Family—Fiction.
4. Walpole (N.H.)—Fiction.   I. Title.
PS3613.C58595L67   2010   2009046024
813'.6—dc22

Printed in the United States of America
1   3   5   7   9   10   8   6   4   2

Book design by Meighan Cavanaugh

This is a work of fiction. Names, characters, places, and incidents either are the product of the
author's imagination or are used fictitiously, and any resemblance to actual persons,
living or dead, businesses, companies, events, or locales is entirely coincidental.

While the author has made every effort to provide accurate telephone numbers and Internet addresses
at the time of publication, neither the publisher nor the author assumes any responsibility for errors,
or for changes that occur after publication. Further, the publisher does not have any control over
and does not assume any responsibility for author or third-party websites or their content.

For my family

Don't laugh at the spinsters, dear girls, for often
very tender, tragical romances are hidden
away in the hearts that beat so quietly
under their sober gowns.

—*Little Women*

BOSTON, MASSACHUSETTS, TO WALPOLE, NEW HAMPSHIRE

October 25, 1881

Louisa May Alcott approached the ticket window of the Boston passenger station clutching a large case and a black parasol. She asked for the tickets on hold under her name—she'd written a week before to reserve them. The clerk's forehead gleamed, wet in the heat of his cramped booth. He held her gaze a moment longer than was proper and began to ask a question, then stopped. He seemed to decide that if this well-dressed woman *was* who he thought she was, he probably shouldn't ask for confirmation. He took the money she offered and gave her back the change.

It was a brisk autumn day and the platform was blustery. Louisa felt the skirts of her slim black dress swirl around her ankle boots, the pair she'd had for years, the pair she'd worn in Rome in the cathedrals, in Nice, in the parlor of the Paris inn where she'd shared wine with a Polish revolutionary as he described the deaths of all his friends. The boots were sturdy but the leather was cracked. She could afford to buy new ones—she could afford to buy just about anything she wanted now, though it hadn't always been that way. In her childhood poverty she had looked with breathless guilty glee at the fashion plates in

Godey's Lady's, memorized every ruffle, collar, and bow the Paris girls wore. Now that she finally had the money to dress like a proper lady, she felt she was too old to do it. At forty-eight, she'd grown accustomed to her spinster's garb: black dresses, white lace collars fastened high around her neck. Corsets, bustles, scarlet French-heeled boots that buttoned up with pearls—those were for the younger set, still upright, with color in their cheeks, anticipating life instead of looking back on it.

She expected a smooth journey, provided they did not encounter engine trouble or problems with the track. Winter ice sometimes pried rail ties loose, but by May all the damage to the track had been repaired. Now fall was upon them once again, the destructive ice not far away, and anticipation of the looming chill filled her with weariness.

Once in the rail car, she glanced around at her fellow travelers. At the front of the car two little girls sat together, their spindly legs swinging in time with the rocking train. One girl held her doll in the crook of her elbow and stroked its carefully braided hair of gold yarn. She turned to the side and whispered something in her sister's ear. The girls broke into a shrill giggle before their mother turned to them and thrust her index finger to her lips. Quiet now, they grinned at each other, their eyes dancing.

A few men sat at the other end of the car, reading the newspaper and smoking while they watched trees and cranberry bogs replace Boston's dusty, crowded bustle. She didn't recognize anyone and they didn't seem to recognize her, which helped relax the tightness in her chest. But only a little.

It had been twenty-six years since she had seen the tidy houses and storefronts lined up along Washington Square in Walpole, the lilacs buzzing with honey bees. Twenty-six years, but the place was seared in her brain. The tracks curved through a dense stand of white birch and she realized she was wistful, an emotion in which she rarely allowed herself to indulge.

Louisa reached inside the case at her feet and pulled out the thick envelope of folded paper. She ran her fingers along the irregular edges of the letters she had tried so many times but never quite managed to destroy. Before she could restrain them, images flooded her mind and something cinched tightly around her heart. It was all right to think about it one last time, she supposed, as she unfolded the letters on her lap. Very soon these letters would be nothing more than embers. Her intention that day, the very reason for her journey, was to ensure the letters, and all other traces of that long ago summer, were destroyed.

In Bellows Falls, Vermont, she would hire a Rockaway to take her the rest of the way to Walpole, where Joseph Singer would be waiting.

For now, the train swayed on.

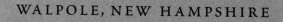

WALPOLE, NEW HAMPSHIRE

July–November 1855

Jo . . . was eager to be gone, for the homenest was
growing too narrow for her restless nature.

—*Little Women*

Chapter One

It didn't take long for the Alcott sisters to finish unpacking their clothes. Anna, Louisa, Lizzie, and May didn't have many bonnets or dresses, both because they couldn't afford them and because their father, Bronson, believed a penchant for lace and silk revealed a weakness in one's character.

"It feels so nice to put things away," Anna said as she smoothed a worn quilt at the foot of her bed. The narrow wardrobe at her back contained six dresses Louisa and Anna shared between them, though the fabric stretched a bit across Anna's slightly wider shoulders. "Should we not find something to dress these windows?"

Anna and Louisa would also share the stuffy attic room that ran the length of the borrowed house. The sisters' small beds were nestled opposite each other in the cozy—or constrictive, depending on the mood—corner made by the steep angle of the roof. On stormy nights Louisa and Anna would be forced to raise their voices over the wind whistling through the poorly insulated walls. This room would be uninhabitable in a New England winter, but for the mild summer months it would do, and they were happy to have a room of their own away from the others. Near the head of each bed, a cushioned perch in the twin dormers provided just the right amount of light for reading or sewing.

Anna twisted up her mouth. "Oh, I forgot—Marmee put the drapes from Hillside up in Lizzie and May's room." She swung open the lid of her trunk and bent down to dig through the pile of folded fabric. A moment later she stood upright and turned to her sister. "Louisa, are you listening to me?"

"Hmm?" Louisa turned her body toward the direction of Anna's voice, but her eyes remained fixed in the book she held in front of her face. It was Longfellow's *Hyperion*, a tale of a man's travels through Germany. Mr. Emerson had urged her to borrow it for the summer. Louisa knew that Longfellow admired Goethe, as she did—her ostensible reason for wanting to read the book. She also knew that the book's romance came from Longfellow's real-life fumblings with love. Something about that fact made the story all the more sensational and impossible to put down.

Anna scoffed as she tipped the trunk's lid closed. "You read too much. Sometimes I think I can't remember what your face looks like from the cheekbones down."

Louisa looked up, finally, and lowered the book. She registered the question that had so far failed to penetrate her mind, as if it were a bird colliding with a windowpane. The mention of Hillside called up an image of the cozy house in Concord where they'd lived for three whole years until she was fifteen and financial woes had forced them back to Boston. The memory of it made her glum.

"I'm sorry, Anna. I *did* hear you." She felt her flushed cheek with the back of her hand. The attic room was unbearably hot and it was only ten in the morning. "If the Hillside drapes are in use, we may have to make some new ones."

Anna nodded. "Singer Dry Goods—Margaret Lewis said we might try there for the things we need to get settled. They'll have fabric. I believe it's across from the post office."

Louisa retrieved their bonnets from the top shelf of the wardrobe. They fastened them as they descended the stairs, calling out clipped good-byes in the hopes of escaping the house before May heard about the outing and insisted on tagging along.

But they weren't quick enough to thwart their youngest sister, who had lost "the whole of society," as she put it, when the family left Boston, and was desperate for a little adventure.

"Louy, I'm coming along with you," May cried from the parlor as she threw down her needlework. "Just give me a minute to arrange my hair."

Louisa sighed as May dashed toward her room. Louisa loved her sister, but she sometimes felt May came by that love in spite of herself. It was hardly her fault. May was only fifteen, and the time before she was born had been the most difficult for the family. Bronson's determination to live out his philosophies—transcending material pleasure, developing the soul through tireless self-examination— had never been stronger, and consequently the Alcott women lived without many domestic comforts. Over time, Bronson was forced to concede that some of his beliefs worked better in the abstract than on the ground. May was born after the family had overcome the worst of its poverty and privation, and Louisa resented that the youngest Alcott walked through the world with the posture of a girl who hadn't known true sacrifice.

"May," Anna called after her, anxious to be on their way. "Another day—tomorrow. I promise. I'll take you with me into town tomorrow."

They closed the heavy front door against May's shrill protests and made their way down the path. Louisa thought about how she missed the familiar woods of Concord. As a girl, she ran there every day, darting through the narrow spaces between the trees on a path Henry Thoreau had shown her years before, when he'd taken her to see a family of whip-poor-wills he'd discovered at dusk. She ran, she said, to keep up her strength, but in truth she was desperate to escape the crowded house and chores that always waited for her. Washing, knitting, mending, baking, weeding. She longed for quiet so that she could read and spin her tales, but sometimes even that required more concentration than her vibrating brain could muster. Running calmed and focused her thoughts. While she thudded along, her skirts rustled the leaves at her feet, picking up burrs and spiders she'd later have to shake off before going into the house. Louisa felt a pang as she thought back on those carefree days. A girl of twelve could be odd and sullen and race through the woods without fear of reproach; a woman of twenty-two had to concern herself with matters of propriety.

The family hadn't wanted to leave Boston and Concord. Bronson liked living near Emerson and his Transcendental friends, like Theodore Parker, the Boston minister, and the provocative abolitionist William Lloyd Garrison, and the girls had finally managed to make friends after years of moving from place to place. But they could not stay. Bronson had not earned a regular income in sixteen years, so he and Abigail May—"Abba" to her husband and friends and "Marmee" to her daughters—depended on the charity of family and friends.

The Alcotts worried most about how Lizzie would adjust to another upheaval. One summer five years back, Abba's ever-present charity work brought her into contact with an impoverished family suffering from smallpox. She and Bronson became desperately ill. The girls' infection had seemed mild in comparison, but this consolation was short-lived. Though the other three bounced back after a few days, Lizzie never fully recovered her strength and had since suffered from a weakened constitution. Any stress was enough to send her to bed for a week. Though moving was sure to be a trial, Bronson and Abba knew they had little choice and only prayed they could find a suitable situation.

Financial mercy came when Abba's brother-in-law Benjamin Willis offered the use of a house he owned in Walpole, a New Hampshire town of fifteen hundred souls, and Bronson did not have the luxury of refusing. The house was known in town as Yellow Wood. Originally a saddler's shop, it was admired for its lilacs and golden autumn maples. Yellow Wood sat on a hill at the top of Wentworth Road, which snaked a quarter mile north and bisected the town center. Uncle Willis filled the shed with firewood and wrote to the family promising they could stay until Bronson's fortunes changed.

The first meager supper the night before had not satisfied bellies hungry from a long day of travel and unpacking, but they had to make do with the hard rolls and preserved vegetables in the pantry. When Louisa was writing, she could forget about every worldly thing, including food. The previous night she had begun a new story about a woman named Natalie, rejected and cast out by her lover when he discovered she had worked as an actress and could bring shame to his wealthy family. She filled her pages with ink late into the night, when her rumbling stomach finally broke her concentration.

Soon Abba would visit the orchard they'd passed on their way into town and establish a line of credit for food. They had no money to pay for it now, but Bronson had promised to embark on a new tour of conversations, his name for speeches he made in parlors across New England about famous philosophers. He refused to sell tickets to the events, as he was morally opposed to all acts of commerce, but he had in the past been unable to refuse donations. So a new tour held the tenuous promise of a little income. Abba knew better than to count on it, though. She knew all too well that her husband's lofty aims rarely deigned to find their way down to earth. His philosophies were concerned with ideals and symbols but rarely realities. Two winters ago he had set out for a tour of New York and Ohio, promising to earn enough to pay off their debts and finally provide a comfortable life for his family. Six months later he returned home with only one dollar.

It was true providence that Mr. Emerson had been their neighbor in Concord. He and Bronson were friends and intellectual equals, but Emerson was shrewd in pecuniary affairs. It was well known that he received a fortune when his tubercular first wife died at the age of twenty, and he and his second wife, Lidian, did not want for money. Though Bronson was proud of his refusal to sully himself with base economic affairs, he accepted Emerson's assistance with a surprising lack of protest. And the Alcott women thanked God for that small mercy.

Louisa had been to Walpole only once before, when she was quite young, so she tried to notice each storefront and memorize its contents to report back to her mother. The sisters were experienced at moving. As children they'd lived in several different houses, and they knew all about the work each move made for the women—stocking the kitchen, dressing the windows, planting a new vegetable garden. It helped to get the lay of the land and meet the shopkeepers early— especially, Louisa thought with dread, since they would soon be testing those shopkeepers' generosity by asking to buy things on credit.

As they descended the hill, they turned west on Middle Street and then north into Washington Square, where the town's few shops were clustered. The butcher's shop occupied the southwest corner of the square. Bronson's aversion to meat made Anna and Louisa a little skittish about the carcasses hanging in the windows, and they looked away as they passed by. The square contained two village bookstores that were local centers of political discussion. On the west side of the square, men interested in the philosophy of the waning Whig party argued over what to do about slavery and how modern technology like the railroads might change the country. Directly opposite, on the east side of the square, Democrats stood with their arms crossed, some pensively fingering their beards, as they lamented the death of the idyllic farming society President Jefferson had envisioned in their grandfathers' time. And the men who cared for neither politics nor books gathered at the tavern that sat between the stores, to imbibe and gamble until their wives prevailed upon them to return home for supper. Abba was at least lucky on one account: Bronson was a temperate man and never once set foot in *that* place of temptation.

Louisa fought back the welling irritation that made her jaw feel tight. Walpole seemed to her wholly unremarkable. Over the last few years she had felt herself growing restless, yearning for freedom from the domestic obligations that came with continuing to live at home. Though the chaos of Boston frightened her—the noise and heat of the trains, the looming shadow of steamers discharging immigrants at India Wharf, where vendors sold peppered oysters soaked in vinegar near the overcrowded tenements—she loved the excitement and freedom of the city. With her family she had bounced between Boston and Concord over the years but never had the chance to live in the city on her own, to have the space and time to think and write.

Since her father had announced the solution to their current financial woes, his plan to move the family here to Walpole, Louisa had been scheming for a way to get back to the city as soon as possible. She had promised herself she would accompany them to her uncle's house, help unload the trunks and be on the train from Bellows Falls back to Boston by the end of the first week. She still had most of the money left from the ten dollars she earned for "The Rival Prima Donnas," a story she wrote under the name Flora Fairfield, and the advance on *Flower Fables*, her collection of fairy tales published in a tiny local run the previous fall. The publisher had sent her a mere thirty-two dollars for that work, though even this small sum had astonished her at the time. She gave a portion to her father for the good of the household and squirreled the rest away, professing an oath to Anna and her mirror that she would safeguard the money for one express purpose.

"I, Louisa Alcott, do swear—"

"—do *solemnly* swear," Anna offered, her hands cradling the green leather Bible on which Louisa rested her palm.

"—do solemnly swear to resist temptations large and small, be they in the form of particularly bewitching bonnets, slippers . . ."

"Gloves?" Anna asked with her eyebrows raised.

Louisa nodded. "Gloves . . ."

Anna was quick to test her sister's conviction. "Even if they happen to be the sort that close with those tiny pearl buttons?"

"*Especially* if they have pearl buttons. As well as chocolates, pecans, new books, fine pens . . ."

"And cream laid writing paper. Don't forget that." Anna pressed her lips together to suppress a smile.

Louisa groaned and closed her eyes. "The very thought of it tests me this moment! Yes, yes—no fine writing paper. Now, where was I? Oh, yes . . . resist temptations large and small, so noted, in the service of my especial aim: to secure for myself in the city of Boston a *place apart* and a room in which I might write my stories and sell them to the highest bidder."

"Well done!" cried Anna. And the oath was sealed.

The savings was enough to pay her room and board for a few weeks until she sold a story or two, or found some other way to earn her bread. She pictured a cozy rooming house, perhaps a little dilapidated, with a long dining table full of boarders swapping tales of their travels. It wouldn't be hard to convince her father to let her go. Obtaining her mother's blessing would be the more difficult task.

But now that they had arrived in Walpole, Louisa could see the route to freedom wouldn't be smooth. Her uncle's house hadn't been lived in for some time. Linens moldered in a damp cabinet; spiders nested in the corners of the parlor; and the kitchen was in lamentable shape. How could she leave all this work for her mother and sisters while she went off on her own to spin her tales and merely hope to earn a little income? Louisa fought hard against her rising despair and tried to muster the patience that often eluded her. *I'll stay on until they get settled*, Louisa promised herself. *Until the house is fit to live in and Marmee has her kitchen up and running. It won't be so very long. And then I'll be on my way.*

They passed the Elmwood Inn and at last came to Singer Dry Goods. When the bell jingled as Louisa first stepped inside, it took her eyes a moment to adjust to the dim light after the searing July sunshine. The floor creaked under her boots as she followed her sister, who had already scurried over to the rows of dress fabrics, ribbons, and lace. Despite their father's warnings, Anna couldn't help being enamored with the beautiful dresses her wealthier cousins had. The fashions seemed to change so quickly, and she felt hopelessly left out of the running. She ran her hand along a bolt of shot silk and noticed a few magazine pages pinned on the wall featuring crinolines so wide she wondered how the wearer traversed a doorway.

Louisa rolled her eyes and found the shelf of calicos that would make a simple set of drapes. She didn't dare admit, even to herself, that she ached to touch the pale mousseline the color of an eggshell and imagine her broad shoulders slimmed by a flattering sleeve. The spirit of self-denial that colored every aspect of her family's life was strong in her, but so was a yearning to, just once, have the things others had.

"Good afternoon, Miss. Have you found something you like?"

Louisa looked up. She felt her cheeks color, as if she had been speaking her thoughts aloud. A freckled young man stood tall in brown suspenders and grinned at her. She shook her head, feeling suddenly shy, and turned quickly back to the fabric to avoid his eyes.

He shrugged and turned toward the counter, where a woman stood waiting to place an order. Louisa peered at her from behind a post. She wore a light cotton dress and a straw spoon bonnet with a cluster of daisies over her left ear.

"Good afternoon, Miss Daniels," the clerk said. "Is that a new bonnet? It's awfully becoming."

Miss Daniels tilted her head to the side and preened with a demure smile. "Why, thank you, Mr. Singer. It was a gift."

He clutched theatrically at his chest. "Not from some wealthy suitor, I hope. Don't tell me you've gone and given your heart away. After I've been waiting here pining for you all these years!"

She giggled, clearly enjoying the attention, Louisa noted, and touched the curls that hung beneath her bonnet. "You know very well Mr. Ross and I are to be married in a few months' time."

He gave a dramatic sigh, then narrowed his eyes at her. "I'd swear all you beautiful women are in on the conspiracy. The way you break hearts for sport—it's cruel and unusual!"

"Joseph Singer!" Miss Daniels pretended to be scandalized. "Does your father know what a terrible flirt you've become?"

Joseph chuckled. "He should—he taught me himself."

Miss Daniels rolled her eyes. "Well, if you are quite recovered from your broken heart, might I trouble you for six yards of that gray gabardine?"

The clerk chuckled and walked over to the bolts of fabric, glancing at Louisa as he passed. "Still deciding?"

Young men like this were the worst sort, Louisa thought. Flippant and casual, utterly amused with themselves.

"I only *just* arrived," she snapped.

His eyes widened with surprise and he pressed his lips together to conceal a grin. "Of course, take your time." He carried the gabardine back to the counter to fulfill Miss Daniels's order. A few moments later the bell on the door gave a cheerful ring as she exited the shop and Joseph took up his post near—but not too near—where Louisa browsed.

Anna appeared at her side. "Oh, Louy, you must come see this yellow silk. It's just divine." Anna noticed the young man waiting patiently and took a step toward him. "Oh, how rude of me. Good afternoon." He returned Anna's demure nod. "Is this your store?"

"My father's. But I help from time to time and . . ." He trailed off for a moment. "Well, he has been ill. So here I am."

"I'm Anna Alcott, and this is my sister Louisa. We just arrived in town." Louisa felt a sting of envy at Anna's bravery. "I'm sorry to hear about your father's health, but I'm happy to meet you," Anna said.

"Joseph Singer," he said, nodding. "Yes, it has been a difficult time for my sister and me. We want to keep the business in the family if . . . You see, I haven't any brothers. I'm doing my best for now and hope he will soon recover."

Anna nodded sympathetically. "Well, I'm glad to see that you stock grains and spices as well as the dry goods," she said, gesturing to the barrels in the corner. "That must help your business."

Joseph nodded. "We just began selling those in the spring. Used to be people ordered the spices from Boston and the deliveries came once a week. But when the Boston train started running all the way to Bellows Falls—that's just across the river there into Vermont—" he said, gesturing vaguely west, "people in town came around asking about them more often. And we like to keep our customers happy."

"Well, you've just earned some new ones. Our family has let a house down the road," Anna said, the lie tumbling easily from her lips.

"Is it Yellow Wood? That place is a beauty."

Anna smiled. "It is, though the windows seem quite bare."

"Ah, so it's drapes you'd like to make? I tried to inquire with your sister here, but she seems a bit shy." Louisa felt Joseph's eyes on her again and fixed her face into an indisputable scowl.

"Louy, shy? Wait until I tell our mother you said so—we'll all have a good laugh about that. Won't we, Lou?" Anna nudged Louisa with an elbow and she forced a smile.

Louisa tried to think of something clever to say in response, but charm had abandoned her for the moment. She kept her eyes safely trained on her sister's face. "Nan, what do you think of this one?" Louisa said, pointing out a blue floral print.

"Oh, I don't really care for cornflowers. Isn't there anything with lily of the valley? It's my favorite."

"We just got some of the new designs in this morning. They're in the back." Joseph walked around the counter and through the open door of the stockroom. Louisa watched his back arch as he tilted his head back and reached for a wooden crate on a high shelf. His face didn't have a hint of a beard, but as he eased the heavy shipment from the shelf his shirt pulled taut across the muscles in his back. He was older than she'd first suspected, but only just.

"Lou, do you think that room will have much of a draft?" Anna rubbed the fabric between her thumb and index finger. "Will we need something heavier than these cottons?"

Louisa stared out the window to Washington Street, which was empty except for a few pigeons fighting over an abandoned crust of bread. Her fingers grazed the bolts of fabric, as if they contained some message only discernable through touch.

"*Louisa*—I'm talking to you."

She looked up, blinking. "Sorry, Anna. What was that? I drifted off for a second."

"What were you thinking about just then?" Anna looked at her sister and then at the stockroom door, where Joseph crouched inside, removing brown paper wrappings from the new fabrics.

"A story I'm working on," Louisa blurted. This was her standard excuse. When her first book had been published the year before, her family was quite taken aback that all Louisa's dreamy after-noons holed up in her room with a stack of paper had actually led to something—and they'd all been a bit penitent ever since.

Anna looked her over carefully. "I thought perhaps you were think-ing that Joseph Singer is handsome. That's what *I* was thinking."

Louisa looked her dead in the eye and whispered her reply as Joseph approached them, the lily-of-the-valley print atop a pile of fabric in his arms. "No. I was thinking about people who aren't even real. As always."

"What do you think of this one?" Joseph asked, holding the sam-ple out for Louisa to touch. Before she thought to stop herself, she looked up and met his eyes. They were a pale smoke blue but seemed to change even as she looked at them.

Her eyes darted to the fabric. "It's up to my sister, really." Louisa turned to Anna.

"This is perfect," Anna said. "We'll need five yards—what's the price?"

"I'll have to check the list," Joseph said, turning back toward the counter. "If you'll just follow me over here . . ."

While Anna went to settle the payment with Joseph, Louisa hovered near the door contemplating her sudden skittishness as she pretended to assess the selection of ribbons and trim. She was simply tired, she supposed, and unaccustomed to meeting new people after many safely predictable years amongst friends in Boston and Concord. She heard Anna's footsteps on the broad plank floor and pulled open the door without turning around. The bell mounted on the frame announced their departure.

"Very pleased to meet both of you," Joseph called out as they left. Only Anna turned back to wave.

Back outside, the sun was blinding once again. Anna clutched the package of fabric to her chest.

"Well, so far this seems like a friendly town."

"Nice enough." Louisa touched one of the pins that held her raven mane in place to make sure it was secure.

"Oh, Lou, be reasonable. I think Mr. Singer was friendly, though not for any reason I can see—you were quite rude. What's come over you?"

"*I* was rude to *him*? *He* was rude to *me*. I was simply trying to browse in peace. It's startling to be spoken to by strangers. We *knew* everyone in Concord," she muttered.

Anna rolled her eyes. "Well, we aren't in Concord anymore."

"That's right—we aren't. We never would have been buying fabric for drapes in Concord, because we wouldn't have had any windows to put them in." Louisa could feel her speech taking a turn toward the dramatic. "We would have been homeless, cast out by debtors. If only Father would have tried a *little* harder to find work."

Anna stopped dead and turned to Louisa, her face a mixture of astonishment and an older sister's reproach.

Louisa put her hand on Anna's forearm. "Of course, you *know* I think Father is more brilliant than just about anyone else. But aren't you tired of worrying about money? I would say we see it differently now that we are older, but doesn't it seem like we've always worried about the debts more than he has? And, of course, Marmee has worried too. God only knows how much."

Anna nodded and took her sister's arm. "It won't always be this way. It's lucky we're girls, I guess."

Louisa furrowed her brow in confusion and Anna smiled. "What do you mean?" Louisa asked.

Anna leaned against her sister and for a moment rested her cheek on Louisa's shoulder. "Well, my dear, it's not as if we'll be living with Father and Marmee forever."

A short hard laugh escaped from Louisa's lips. "Well, I certainly don't intend to do *that*." She thought again of Boston, rolled the calendar forward in her mind to the date when she might be able to leave.

The two strolled in silence up Main Street and then east along the woods at the edge of the square, taking the long way back to

Yellow Wood. Louisa continued to brood. They were in this unfamiliar town, Louisa knew, because her father was a man of many grand ideas and little common sense. As a child, she had revered him, and never doubted that the problem lay with a world unwilling to comprehend his brilliance. But eventually she had come to see him in a different light, one that revealed his flaws. For a time, in response to Emerson's urgings, Bronson had worked at becoming a writer, but he found the public either wouldn't or couldn't accept his ideas. His affected prose had earned many polite nods and one harsh critique that his writing conjured an image of fifty boxcars rattling by containing only one passenger. After that he abandoned literary pursuits, though he continued to journal extensively and focused his efforts on teaching. A great lot of money was invested by others in his schools, which promised to transform children's minds and souls through Transcendental teachings. Each had temporary success, but ultimately Bronson would reach too far outside acceptable boundaries and offend a wealthy contributor. The Quakers had influenced his philosophy and he came to believe that no religious ritual or temple could substitute for direct communication with God. Bronson was reluctant to accept dogma of any kind and told his students that Jesus was a great teacher but was not divine. None of this sat well with the Episcopalian and Unitarian ministers who contributed to his school fund. But the theological disagreements were nothing compared to what came later on, when Bronson tried to engage his young students in a discussion of where babies came from. It was brave for Bronson to speak his mind to Boston's powerful interests, Louisa knew, but he had never learned how to choose his battles.

Of course, *he* believed the world did not understand what he was trying to tell it. His ventures would fail and the family would soon be back to living in poverty. In Bronson's estimation, his family's money troubles weren't his fault—they were the fault of a world too cowardly to consider new ways of thinking. After all, Louisa thought bitterly, what would we have him do? Put his philosophy aside and *work*?

They passed a cluster of white pines, impossibly tall and sturdy on their slender trunks. Anna pointed toward a bench nestled beneath the outermost trees. "Let's rest a moment."

Louisa looked worriedly at her. "Are you well, Nan?" All the Alcotts worried constantly about illness since Lizzie had become so frail after her bout of smallpox.

Anna rolled her eyes. "Fine, fine. I just want to sit a moment and look at these trees."

They pulled their skirts up at the knee to keep the hems out of the dirt. The pale blue of Anna's dress made Louisa think of a robin's egg in a nest of dark leaves and branches. They shared the same dark hair. All the sisters swapped clothes, particularly the older two, which contributed to Louisa's feeling that she was looking into a mirror when she looked at Anna. A prettier, sunnier mirror, she thought, but in truth while Anna was noble, measured, and plain, Louisa's deep-set eyes were magnetic, appraising the world with brazen intensity.

"Lou," Anna began in a serious tone, then laughed out loud.

"What? Why are you laughing?"

"I just realized the futility of the conversation I was about to start."

Louisa felt a burning in her chest as she strained to withhold her frustration. "Am I really so predictable?" As a young girl she'd been given to angry explosions and had to work hard to keep her sudden changes in mood concealed from the people around her. A fiery twelve-year-old was amusing, perhaps even charming, but a woman of twenty-two wasn't given nearly so much license. "Perhaps I will surprise you," Louisa said weakly.

Anna grinned. "Louy, do you ever think about getting married?"

Her eyes widened and she drew in a sharp breath. *"Married?"*

Anna laughed again. "Yes, married. Don't act as if you've never heard of it."

"Oh, I've heard all about it. I've watched it my whole life." She pictured their mother, straining over the arm of her chair toward the oil lamp as she mended the heels of their father's stockings, her shoulders tense from hours at the washtub. When Abba wasn't tending to her family's endless needs, she spent her time knitting or baking bread or collecting medicine for Boston's poor. Bronson was deeply committed to one man's charity for another, though practical implementation of the notion seemed to escape him.

"I suppose no one is lamenting our prospects just yet, but it's about time we start thinking about it—we've reached the conventional age." Anna looked down. "It wouldn't have to be like Marmee and Father, you know."

"No, I don't know." Louisa sat stiffly, her body aware of the conversation's direction before her mind could catch up. At twenty-four, Anna had so far been content to resist any attachments that might take her away from home and instead remained with the parents who adored her.

"There are choices. There are different sorts of men. Different from Father."

Louisa looked at her, surprised to hear this veiled criticism from her angelic sister, their father's favorite.

"There's love. That's something. Wouldn't you like to be in love, Lou?"

Henry Thoreau appeared in her mind, his sodden boots, his beard snagged with leaves, a notebook clutched in the black half-moons of his fingertips. He had been another of their Concord neighbors. Love was a foreign country Louisa didn't care to visit, and the only time she'd ever come close to the feeling was developing a pupil's adoration for her teacher. Henry could peel a wide strip of birch bark with one deft slice of his knife and fold it into a box to hold the leaves and flowers and stones they collected on their explorations. Once, they found a store of Indian spearheads poking out of the earth beneath a huckleberry bush. They would walk all afternoon until the sun baked them red. When she shrank from the delicate brush of a cobweb, he told her it was a handkerchief dropped by a fairy.

From the time she first walked alone with Henry as a girl, she dared to hope he saw in her a like mind, a ruminator. But Henry only loved his trees, his work, his solitude. Louisa had heard through the Concord gossip that her tutor Sophia, a young woman closer to Henry's age, confessed her love and hopes to marry him. She'd left town the following year, shattered by his rejection. Henry grew still more reclusive then, no longer inviting the children to walk with him. When Louisa's breasts began to fill out, he hardly spoke to her at all, except to wave from a distance.

"I didn't know it was as simple as deciding to do it. Why are you bringing this up now, Anna?" Louisa's voice was cross.

"Because I'm trying to tell you about me. About what I want."

"And what is that?"

"Oh, Louisa, you are so *trying* sometimes. *I* want to be in love. *I* want to get married. I want to have a different kind of life than this one. My own life."

Louisa turned to her, softening her voice with all her might. "You believe getting married is going to let you have your own life? Don't you think the way to do that is to *avoid* marriage?" For Louisa, marriage and love had almost nothing to do with each other. Love, or at least what she had been able to glean about love from books, represented a kind of sweet and everlasting acceptance, a companionship, an adoration that aimed to preserve its object, not wrestle it to the ground. Marriage was something else altogether. Once Abba had told Louisa, "Wherever I turn, I see that women are like beasts of burden, under the yoke, dragging their lengthening chain." Louisa had never forgotten that image, the hopelessness of it. Marriage was no kind of freedom.

Anna struggled to be patient with her sister, who always seemed to make the simplest things difficult. "It depends on what kind of 'own life' you mean, I suppose. I want a husband. I want children. My own home, even if it is a humble little place. And rugs and china and furniture."

Louisa was quiet a moment. "Well, I want to be a writer. I *am* a writer. Did you ever hear of a married woman writer?"

"I'm sure there are plenty," Anna sighed. "Why should you have to choose, if you find the right sort of husband? One who would indulge your interests."

"I don't want to be indulged," Louisa shot back, rankled. "I want to *work*. And besides, when, amongst all the birthing and bathing and china washing and rug sweeping and fire stoking do you think I'd have time to write? Or should I let my family go hungry and languish in frayed clothes while I place my work above their needs, as Father has done to us?"

"*Louisa!*"

Anna's scolding was more provocation than her restrained temper could resist. She flew to her feet. "Well, why shouldn't I say it? It's the truth! It's selfish and neglectful. Marmee has done her best for us, but in *spite* of him, not with his help. I could never put my children

30

through that, knowing how it felt to me as a child." She sat back down, her eyes full of tears. "Don't you see? I do have to choose. I have inherited Father's love of ideas and books but I also know how that love can separate you from the people who need you most. And yet, I can't imagine my life without books. I don't even know who I'd *be* then."

"Oh, poor Louy." Anna put her arm around her sister, pulling Louisa's head down onto her shoulder. "To me you'd still be you— exactly the same. Funny and kind and working yourself into a frenzy."

"As *soon* as I can—as *soon* as you're all settled in—I'm leaving for Boston. It's as if—" Her voice had taken on a childish whine that embarrassed her, and she stopped short.

"What?" Anna asked. "As if what?"

". . . as if my life depended on getting out on my own, away from all this. And I intend to send home my wages, but . . . well, do you think wanting to go is awfully selfish?" Louisa felt her cheeks grow hot with shame.

Anna shook her head. "No, I don't. I think it is honest. But it doesn't matter what I think."

"Of course it does!" Louisa exclaimed, looking up at her.

Anna shook her head. "No, it doesn't. Not when it comes to decid-ing how to make a happy life for yourself. And you will."

Though Louisa faced the trees, Anna knew just the look that was on her face: brows wrenched skeptically, her lips a twisted prune.

"You will," she said again.

My definition [of a philosopher] is of a man up in a balloon, with his family and friends holding the ropes which confine him to earth and trying to haul him down.

—*Louisa May Alcott: Her Life, Letters, and Journals*

Chapter Two

Leaves of Grass . . . is too frequently reckless and inde-
cent. . . . His words might have passed between Adam and
Eve in Paradise, before the want of fig-leaves brought no
shame; but they are quite out of place amid the decorum of
modern society.

—CHARLES A. DANA,
New York Daily Tribune,
July 23, 1855

Bronson balanced his weight on one knee and patted the soil
into place around the delicate sprout of a pumpkin vine, newly
emerged from the ground just that morning. It had been ten days
since he drew up his plan for the garden, and he was pleased to see the
plants taking root. He chose not to dwell on the fact that it was nearly
August; this vine would not produce fruit until at least November,
assuming there was no frost before then. No matter—he felt a pro-
vider's pride. He was making food for his family out of a few seeds
and a patch of earth.

Louisa stood nearby, hanging laundry on the line. Tuesday morn-
ings they washed the linens, and she'd volunteered for the chore of

hanging the wet laundry out of sheer self-preservation. She felt if she did not get out of the washroom, away from the bubbling vat of soap, she might pick up a chair and hurl it across the room. She didn't trust herself to keep her temper. It seemed she was getting less patient, less able to accept her duties, despite the fact that she wanted desperately to be good. All her life she had observed Anna as a scientist observes the object of his experiment; she watched for patterns that might reveal how Anna was able to move through life with ease while Louisa trailed behind her in fits and starts. But Louisa couldn't seem to discern Anna's secrets. She doubted Anna herself understood them.

And now Anna wanted to get *married*. How she could come to that conclusion after watching their mother suffer all these years was baffling to Louisa. Abba's entire adult life was one test of endurance after another. She'd birthed five children, one too early to survive, and had the misfortune of a husband who floated through the world, his feet rarely touching the ground. When she fell in love with Bronson and his ideas, she knew his philosophy and teaching would not provide the means for a life full of fine things. It mattered not to her—dresses and fine furniture were dull compared to Plato and Shakespeare. But Abba had underestimated just how little he thought of practical things, like how they might pay for a place to live, or how they would raise healthy children on a diet of vegetables and bread alone. Abba tried for her daughters' sakes to bear up, but the strain showed. Louisa had decided from an early age that she wanted her life to be nothing like her mother's.

Bronson stood up and arched his back, his eyes closed a moment to the glare of the sun. He glanced over at Louisa as she stretched to pin a sheet on the line. "You make a lovely tableau, my daughter."

Louisa noticed a bit of dirt trapped in the cloud of his wiry sideburn and smiled, feeling her heart swell in response to this rare bit of praise. No matter what she wanted to achieve, who she wanted to be, it was her father's love and approval she wanted more than anything else in the world.

"Ho, Alcott!"

Father and daughter looked up to see the familiar gait of their Concord neighbor Mr. Emerson as he moved up the path, clutching a large glass jar between his elbow and ribs.

Bronson stepped forward to shake his hand. "Hello, my friend. I knew this promised to be a pleasant day."

Emerson smiled, the deep creases in the outer corners of his eyes stretching to his temples. "I've come to see how you're settling in." He held out the jar. "Lemon preserves for your wife, with best wishes from Mrs. Emerson. Good morning, Miss Louisa," he said, tipping his hat in her direction.

"Good morning," she replied, her voice barely louder than a whisper. Mr. Emerson was sober and polite to most, but the Alcotts awakened a joviality in him. When Louisa was fourteen, he patiently read her writing and offered encouraging words. The attention astonished her and she began to wrestle with the question that would trouble her all her life: Why would God give a woman talent if he meant her to be confined to the kitchen and washtub? Though to her father he was simply Waldo, Louisa never forgot she was in the presence of a great man and couldn't help but be self-conscious around him. Bronson placed his hand on Emerson's shoulder and turned him toward the house.

"Let's go inside to talk." Bronson pulled his handkerchief from his pocket and used it to mop his face. "Perhaps Louisa will be kind enough to get us something cool to drink."

Bronson and Emerson retired to the parlor and Louisa turned toward the kitchen carrying the preserves. Abba stood at the sink, her knife poised above a half-peeled potato. A mountain of the knobby root vegetables and a large cabbage that looked to be half rotten lay heaped at her elbow. She gazed out the window toward the woods at the edge of the garden. Louisa looked out in the same direction to see what had captured her mother's attention, but nothing was there. She reached for the metal pitcher that hung on a rusty hook above where Abba worked.

Abba's knife clattered to the floor. "God in *heaven*—you startled me!"

Louisa touched her mother's arm. "I'm sorry, Marmee. You looked lost in thought—I didn't want to interrupt you."

Abba blinked at her daughter, as if she knew she should recognize her but didn't. Then the vacant expression disappeared and Abba stooped to pick up the knife. "Did you finish hanging the laundry?"

"Yes. Father was working in the garden and Mr. Emerson has come. He brought you some of Mrs. Emerson's preserves." Louisa placed the jar on the worktable. "I was going to take them something to drink in the parlor."

Abba already had turned back to the sink and was digging a black spot out of a potato with the tip of the blade. Louisa observed Abba's stooped posture and the silver streaks in her hair. Abba spoke over her shoulder. "It's nearly eleven. Perhaps they would like something to eat as well."

Louisa brought the pitcher of water into the parlor a few moments later, along with half a loaf of brown bread and some butter from the larder, and placed the tray on the low table between the sofa and armchairs that faced the hearth. Behind the sofa was a narrow shelf with two chairs and Louisa slipped into one, quietly taking up a stocking from the mending basket and hoping for a chance to listen to the men talk without being noticed by them or by Abba, who would likely find a chore for Louisa to do.

"Well, my friend, how do you find Walpole so far?" Emerson's face was dominated by his Roman nose and prominent brow. "Have you gone much into town?"

"I have stopped in at the village store but haven't spent much time there," Bronson said. "In general I find the men here have a tendency to pontificate endlessly."

Louisa bit her bottom lip and jabbed the needle into the toe seam to stifle a giggle.

She could see the irony of the comment did not escape Emerson either, but he continued kindly. "What have you been reading lately? I have something intriguing that I think you'll quite enjoy."

"All my old texts—*Pilgrim's Progress*, *Aids to Reflection*, Plato. You know how I feel that one must read the same works again and again to truly extract the meaning. But let no one say Alcott's mind is closed to the new."

Emerson grinned at the proclamation. Bronson fancied himself a grand man, and though his lofty way of speaking endeared him to Emerson, it sometimes earned him ridicule from others.

"This appeared just a few weeks ago, out of the ether." Emerson pulled a volume the size of a prayer book from his jacket pocket. The book was bound in green cloth with gold-stamped type on the front cover and spine, and Louisa strained to see the title. "The poet calls it *Leaves of Grass*. And—you will not believe this when I tell you—his name is nowhere to be found on the cover."

Bronson's eyes widened. "He doesn't identify himself?" To two men quite enamored of the sight of their own names in print, the news was shocking.

"None. Only this." Emerson opened to the frontispiece. "A daguerreotype of the poet. Dressed like a scoundrel, I might add."

He handed the book to Bronson, who flipped slowly through its pages. "And what is the nature of the verse?"

"It is the most extraordinary piece of wit and wisdom an American has ever contributed."

Bronson, who knew his friend was not prone to exaggeration, raised his eyebrows.

"His words and form are *transcendental* in every meaning of the word. There's nothing else like it I've ever seen."

Louisa realized she had been holding her breath. The hole in the much-darned stocking remained, the needle pinched between her index finger and thumb. She had never heard Mr. Emerson talk this way before. He sat on the edge of his chair, his typically sober demeanor alive with excitement.

"You will find, I think . . ." Emerson hesitated. " . . . that his subject matter is . . . peculiar. A bit shocking." He gave a quick glance in Louisa's direction. "And certainly not meant for the eyes of our counterparts." Louisa realized glumly that he'd been aware of her presence all along. "In any case, they wouldn't be able to make much sense of it, I don't think. This is the poet of the man, the American man, and the meaning and responsibilities of his radical freedom."

Bronson turned the volume in his hands. "And you know nothing of his identity?"

"Aha." Emerson raised an index finger. "I did not, until a few nights ago. I saw an advertisement with a picture of the book, and beneath that, for the first time, the poet's name. Mr. Walt Whitman, of Brooklyn, New York. You must read it as soon as you can, my friend. I am anxious to hear your thoughts on his work."

"I will begin it as soon as we part. Your recommendation is enough to convince me." Bronson smeared butter on a slice of bread he'd been eyeing throughout the conversation. "And your own work—does it go well?"

Emerson nodded. "I am finishing a volume of essays on my visits to England." He pulled his watch from his waist pocket and squinted at it. "In fact, I should be on my way now. It is nearly afternoon."

The men rose. Bronson walked his friend to the front door and shook his hand. Emerson nodded to Louisa and asked Bronson to wish Mrs. Alcott well. When Bronson turned back, his eyes registered Louisa's presence, but he took no notice of her. His mind was far away on something else. He reached for the strange volume of poetry Emerson had been so eager to show him and turned toward his study.

Louisa set down her mending and followed him. "Father?"

Bronson turned, startled. "Yes, child?"

She had to think quickly now. "Do you think . . . do you think Mr. Emerson will be thought of in the future as a philosopher? The way we think of Plato now?" She hadn't actually meant to ask that, but now that the question was out, she did want to know the answer. Just as she'd hoped, he began walking slowly toward his study. She walked alongside, her hands clasped in front of her.

He thought a moment before he spoke. "There is no question that Emerson's mind knows no equal. But he is too interested in fame and scholarship, not enough in the divine." Bronson squared his shoulders, forever at the podium. "He sees all but doesn't always feel. Do you understand my meaning? He has a capital intellect but an undeveloped soul."

Louisa nodded, surprised to hear her father speak so critically. They reached his study and he walked around to his desk, pulling out the chair and settling in to shuffle through the disorganized stacks of papers. His face glowed in the light of the green-shaded brass lamp on the corner of his desk. He laid the mysterious volume of poetry off to the side and placed his journal on top of it, then looked up, surprised to see Louisa still standing in the room.

As he opened his mouth to speak, they both turned toward soft footfalls in the hallway. Lizzie appeared at the door holding a small tray that held a tarnished coffeepot. She entered the room behind Louisa and placed the tray on a table under the window, then turned to Bronson. "Father, I'm sorry to interrupt your conversation."

"No need to apologize, little bird. What is it?"

Louisa wondered at her sister's ethereal appearance, the dove-gray cotton of her dress doing nothing to enliven her pale complexion and light hair. She seemed at times like a slender ghost who fluttered from room to room, enamored with the textures of domesticity: the smooth bone of the knitting needle, the snap and flutter of a sheet in the breeze. They called her their little bird, little housewife, though Lizzie brushed off this praise.

"Marmee says there's a family on River Road that has the scarlet fever?"

Bronson nodded. "Yes, I believe I heard something about that in town just yesterday."

Lizzie reached into the right pocket of her apron and pulled out a handful of coins. A bulge in the left pocket squirmed and two orange ears poked out.

Louisa giggled, pointing at the kitten. "I see you've already taken on a new charge," she whispered. The sisters had long joked that stray kittens throughout the northeast flocked to Lizzie, knowing she wouldn't refuse them. Once, in Concord, Bronson finally put his foot down and ordered them out of the house when he found a whole litter scattered in the spaces on his bookshelf. Louisa had helped Lizzie hide them under the bed until he forgot about his prohibition.

Lizzie smiled, putting her finger to her lips. Bronson was flipping through a hefty book and failed to notice the feline interloper. Lizzie pushed the fuzzy head back into her pocket and held out the money. "Father, I'd like to send this to them, and I have some brown bread cooling. Marmee says they have no flour."

He looked up. "This is a kind gesture, Elizabeth, and it gives me pride to see it."

She smiled. "It wouldn't be right *not* to give, when we can." Louisa felt humbled by her sister's generosity, though she wondered about whether they truly had anything to spare. Lizzie floated out into the hallway but then turned back. Bronson sighed impatiently.

"Will you be going into town today?" she asked.

"Yes," Bronson said with a little irritation. "Just as soon as I have a moment to complete this letter. I will deliver your gifts then."

Lizzie nodded. "Thank you, Father."

Bronson turned back to Louisa, who stood waiting patiently to reclaim the thread of their conversation. "And now to you. Did I answer your question about Mr. Emerson well, my child? It is time for me to work."

"Yes, Father. Very well." Louisa marked the place on the desk where Whitman's book lay concealed, already calculating the hours until her father's evening constitutional when the study would be empty and she might slip in and claim it. "Very well indeed."

That evening, Louisa climbed wearily up the steps under the strain of a feigned headache and waited until she was safely ensconced in the attic room before liberating the book from the waistband of her dress. She settled upon the sagging bed and leaned back against the wall, feeling her chignon press against the faded wallpaper.

The book felt smaller than she'd expected after dreaming about it all afternoon. She stared at the frontispiece image of the poet. He did indeed look like a scoundrel, with his hat tipped to the side and a rumpled shirt, open at the collar. He reminded her of the vagrants she'd seen lurking in Boston Common when she crossed the park on walks with her father. All the poets she'd ever seen had gray hair, wore neat, if not new, frock coats and top hats, and took their tea in parlors. Whitman looked like the sort who might tear across a parlor like a maniac, frightening the ladies and overturning all the furniture. She thought back to Mr. Emerson's warning that the book was not meant for a woman's eyes, though she didn't for a second consider retreating from her investigations.

And then she turned past the introduction to the opening verse.

> *I celebrate myself,*
> *And what I assume you shall assume,*
> *For every atom belonging to me as good belongs to you.*

She turned the pages and a glowing candle on the table beside the bed sank into its pricket. The verse was at once crude and reverent, panoramic and microscopic. With a kinetic rhythm, the poet wrote of an America Louisa scarcely knew, of bodies at work, sweating, cursing, praying; of slaves; of lovers; of buds folded in the earth. Line by line, the words lapped at her like waves crawling the shore. When she finally slept she dreamed of train whistles and the rhythmic clang of a blacksmith's hammer, her hand clutched as if it held a pen.

All I have to say is, that you men have more liberty than you know what to do with, and we women haven't enough.

—"The King of Clubs and the Queen of Hearts"

Chapter Three

Wednesday

To the Misses Alcott:

*If you find you can set your sewing aside, please join me and
the other young Walpoleans for an afternoon of picnicking and
swimming at the riverbank near the Arch Bridge, this Saturday
at one o'clock.*

Yours,

J. Singer

New Englanders spent much of the year shrouding their bodies
from winter's frigid gloom, but August, hot and fragrant, drew
them into the open. Out-of-doors became a state of mind as well as a
place. In the meadows, vanilla-scented wildflowers the locals called
"joe pye weed" broke into pink feathering blossoms and were soon
papered with monarchs. Spicy bergamot edged the woods. In the

shadow of the canopy, the crisp scent of teaberry filled the air; beneath its waxy leaves, white flowers draped like a string of pearls. A week passed in which no rain fell and the heat stretched from mid-morning until late into the evening. All that sunlight was cultivating something in Louisa as well, though she wouldn't know it for a while.

Louisa and Anna walked with Margaret Lewis along the narrow forest path that led from town to the muddy bank of the Connecticut River. Besides the relatives who had provided their accommodations, Margaret was the only other person in town the sisters had known before they arrived. Margaret's uncle lived in Concord with his wife and children, and she had visited the relatives for a fortnight each spring and fall. Unfortunately, she could scarcely bear the company of her cousins, three dreadfully dull and pious young ladies who shunned music, dancing, and parties as works of the devil they lived to thwart. Margaret often found her way across the two yards that separated the Lewis home from Hillside. She was Anna's age and found in the Alcott girls a bit more spirit of adventure.

Louisa carried a bundle that contained their lunch and clothes for swimming. She had been hunched over a meandering draft—a story about a vicious family feud that finally ends one New Year's Eve because of a child called Alice—late into the previous night, and her back ached. With her free hand she slapped away a cloud of mosquitoes that seemed to be following them all the way through the damp woods.

Anna clapped her hands. "Girls, what do you think about putting on a play?"

Margaret squealed with unencumbered delight. "That's a wonderful idea! Assuming I get to play the lead, of course."

Louisa felt a small wave of dread. A play would take months to arrange and would interfere with her Boston plans. But she tried to cover her feelings with wary enthusiasm. "It could be fun."

"Do you think anyone else would be interested?" Anna asked her.

"Oh, yes," Margaret said. The quiver in her substantial bosom threatened to settle once and for all the ongoing battle between her flesh and the seams of her dress. "There is little to interest the young people of this town in the way of entertainment." Margaret had an affected way of speaking that Louisa found irritating but tried to ignore.

"Well," Louisa said, "we will have to ask the others about it today."

They reached a bright clearing where the ground sloped toward the river. Anna and Margaret, uncertain how to appear dignified, slowly descended the steep path down to the bank where the rest of the group lounged in the sunlight mottled with shadows the shape of birch leaves. Louisa, who didn't mind her manners as well as her sister, let her momentum build untempered and nearly careened into a girl with curly red hair who sat with her back to the path, eating a handful of blueberries.

"Please excuse me," Louisa said, embarrassed.

The girl smiled. "It's all right." She offered a friendly smile. "I'm Nora. You must be one of these Alcott girls I've been hearing about."

Louisa stuck out her hand. "Louisa Alcott," she said. After a surprised look, Nora took her hand and gave it an awkward shake. In her experience, only men shook hands. Louisa resisted the urge to roll her eyes. So many girls, especially in the small towns, were still being raised in the old way—demure bows and curtsies. But why shouldn't they shake hands, the way men did, with dignity?

"And this," Louisa gestured behind her as her sister and Margaret approached, "is my sister Anna."

Anna tilted her head and smiled. "It's a pleasure to meet you, Nora."

"That's my brother over there," Nora said, pointing toward a pair of boys struggling to secure a tent between two trees. "Nicholas. The one with the dark hair. He's older than I am—closer in age to you and your sister. That is, I think so—well, how old are you?" Nicholas was a full head shorter than his friend. He sported the bushy sideburns just coming into fashion and his hair was precisely combed and greased.

"I'm twenty-two," Louisa said.

"Our little Nora's but nineteen," Margaret said, then sighed. "That's Samuel next to Nicholas. Is he not the tallest young man you've ever seen?"

The girls laughed and walked together toward the water. Margaret had confided in Anna earlier that morning that she was smitten with Samuel Parker and believed he returned her favor. Louisa could see now from his wistful gaze in Margaret's direction that he was indeed a man in love. In a rare moment of courage the previous Sunday, Samuel had suggested the swimming party when Margaret told him that the Alcotts were in Walpole for the summer. As they stood on the lawn beneath the arched windows of the Unitarian church, the pale pink and yellow panes glinting in the morning sun, he had suddenly grown shy. Margaret tried to put him at ease by suggesting whom he might invite and how they might send around the invitations. Samuel seemed only too happy to oblige her wishes. She had told Anna that though he wouldn't admit it, welcoming the Alcott sisters was for him the perfect pretense for a gathering he could be sure Margaret would attend.

She had then further divulged that at a party the previous fall, after Samuel drank three glasses of champagne punch, he'd told Margaret, haltingly, that her blond curls reminded him of corn silk at a husking bee. Or, rather, that corn silk reminded him of Margaret's curls, since he had touched the slick fibers many times but could only dream of touching her hair. Anna had giggled and rolled her eyes, but Margaret nearly went into a swoon as she relived the encounter. Louisa just shook her head, amazed at the nonsense to which young women her age seemed devoted.

Once the tent was fixed securely between the trees, Samuel and Nicholas waved the girls over. Inside, the swimmers could change from their Saturday clothes into proper swimming attire, which for the boys meant wool tunics with short sleeves and wool breeches that stopped below the knee, and for the girls a heavy flannel dress with pantalettes beneath, swimming boots, and a cap for their hair. All the girls but Louisa emerged from the tent one by one, shapeless, bobbing along like bald old men toward the water.

Louisa peeked out of the tent to see the group gathered on the water's edge, splashing in the warm current and pointing out a red deer that eyed them from the opposite bank. She crept out and folded her dress into a neat square, then rested it atop her boots, which she placed in the modest line the other girls' boots formed. Their laces were cinched into bows, as if leaving them untied signified less than total commitment to matters of propriety. She'd been unsure just what to do about her feet. She had only one pair of boots, and it had taken her all morning to help Anna fashion something *she* could wear in the water, a pair of slippers their father had abandoned, which the girls cut down with a kitchen knife and sewed into rough shape, the laces jutting in irregular zigzag down the front. Anna had refused to go to the party at all until Louisa convinced her that no one would be looking at her feet.

Since their conversation on the bench at the edge of town, Anna had grown demure, reticent. She was thinking now about impressions, taking note of the names of important families in town, particularly the ones with sons. Louisa had no choice but to leave her own feet bare. She didn't care at all whether the others thought the Alcotts were poor—they probably knew it anyway, since why else would they drag themselves to Walpole for the summer, unless it was to live as another family's charge? But Louisa knew it mattered to Anna.

Better to be called brazen than destitute, she thought, forsaking her bathing cap. She pulled the long steel comb out of her coiled hair, shaking the dark waves free until they hung to her waist, skimming the gray flannel belt of the swimming costume Margaret had lent her. At times like these, Louisa felt quite proud of her ability to rise above the frivolous material trappings of feminine existence. She did not have dresses with lace bodices or bonnets decorated with velvet ribbon; she did not own jewels or cashmere shawls. It simply was not possible in their current circumstances to attire all four girls as well as most young women would have liked. But Louisa knew she had something far more luxurious within reach: a thick stack of paper and ink in the well. In the quiet of the evening she could hold the blotched sheets in her hands and marvel that she had once again captured and set down in words the thoughts and images that careened through her mind. There was something deliciously permanent about those sentences on the page. The world could take an awful lot from her, but it couldn't take those words. As long as she had her ink, her paper, she told herself, she was content with her lot and yearned for nothing.

She stalked to the river, her shoulders back, her head held high. The other girls stood in the river, the water lapping at their waists.

The echoing chatter halted as she approached, and Nora, a few tangerine curls poking out along the edge of her swim cap, stared at first Louisa's hair and then down to her bare feet, white and cold, like two stones. Nora pointed a slender finger; the skin on her hands was nearly translucent. "Your feet—" she began.

"It's simply too warm—I just couldn't *bear* to put on my swimming boots," Louisa replied, too loudly. She forced herself to slow her pace, though she longed to rush into the water before anyone else looked too closely at her feet. Anna watched as Louisa's thick hair floated away from her torso where it met the surface of the water, then Anna closed her eyes, willing her mortification down deep in her chest, away from her face where everyone would see it.

A girl with fine black hair like moss and round toad eyes gasped. "Aren't you going to turn up your hair?" she asked in a superior tone. There was one in every group, Louisa reflected, who relished rules and the chance to police those who dare to defy them. It seemed this one had generously volunteered for that task.

Louisa shook her head and shrugged. "I don't mind if it gets wet. I'm Louisa, by the way." This time she didn't offer a handshake.

"I know. I'm Harriet Palmer," the girl said, eyeing Louisa like she might be daft. Harriet stood with her shoulders hunched severely forward, her back curved like a lady's fan. Louisa tried to conjure some compassion for the unfortunate girl but felt only irritation.

An uncomfortable silence fermented as the others looked away and tried to gather the fragments of their interrupted conversations. A sharp whistle came from the top of the hill and they all turned to look.

"Ho, swimmers!"

Joseph Singer waved his arm above his head, descending the hill on his heels, a paper sack wedged between his elbow and ribs. Louisa felt her chest tighten and was glad for the river's cold swell against her torso, glad to turn and face the opposite bank long enough to arrange her face in bemused calm. Turning back she saw Anna's eyebrows climb and a social smile unfold.

Margaret's cheeks were full of color. She whispered to Anna and Louisa as Joseph made his way to the water. "That's Joseph Singer. His father owns the dry goods store on Washington—"

"Yes," Anna cut her off. "He is very charming. We met him last week on our errands. Remember, Louisa?"

"Of course I remember," Louisa replied. "He seemed like quite the dullard to me." She felt instinctive dislike for Joseph as she heard her sister praise him, but she hadn't intended to speak quite so loudly. Joseph stood shaking hands with Nicholas, but his face whipped in the direction of her voice. When he saw Louisa, he broke into a wide grin and waved.

Anna and Margaret whispered in unison: "Louisa!" Nora and Harriet moved closer and the five girls stood in a cluster, their hands undulating in the river's miniature whirlpools.

Margaret rolled her eyes and continued softly. "The Singers are one of the oldest families in this town. But people are saying the father—"

Splash. Louisa tucked her feet beneath her and plunged her head into the river's murky surface, feeling her scalp tingle as the water spread through her hair. She didn't want to hear Margaret's gossip, didn't want to watch her sister prudently cataloging details about Joseph's suitability as a prospective match. Louisa's own impressions were enough for her. He was skinny and smug, and anyone who married him would have to suffer his company for years to come.

"Good afternoon, ladies," Joseph called to them with a wave. "What a lovely painting you'd make, perched there in the sunshine."

Margaret stopped talking immediately and preened while the other girls giggled, then Nora began chattering about a harvest party her parents were planning. Louisa, standing apart from them, ignored Joseph's attempts at charm and watched a turtle climbing onto the opposite bank.

Joseph joined the other boys a little way down the bank. Louisa peered furtively at him as he walked slowly into the current, his eyes closed against the bright light reflecting off the water. He stopped when the water reached his waist and spread his palms across its surface. Nicholas and Sam stood behind him setting up their fishing poles. Much as Joseph irritated her, Louisa perceived that something made him different from his friends, who fumbled with their tackle boxes and argued the merits of earthworms over grubs. Joseph seemed to be somewhere apart, absorbing the river's stillness, taking it inside himself.

It was rude and strange to stare and Louisa looked away. She decided it was an opportune moment to exit the water without attracting too much attention and climbed to the bank, sheets of water cascading off the layers of fabric in her swimming costume. She gathered her long hair out to the side of her body, twisting it like a rope to wring out the water, and walked over to where her dry clothes lay folded next to her sister's to fish her comb out of her boot and refasten her chignon. But her hair was too heavy to arrange now, wet up to her ears—if she tried it would give her a headache. She decided to let it dry a little in the sun. She chose a flat rock and sank wearily onto it, her body becoming aware of the fatigue that comes from fighting to stand still in a swift current. She closed her eyes, the late summer heat on her cheeks, and nosed the scent of syrupy mud lumpy with buried frogs, the verdant, mossy side of tree trunks untouched by the sun. This was the smell of *outside*, the smell of endless re-creation, the only place, her father and Mr. Emerson would say, where man can seek to transcend the confines of body and rational mind.

"Hungry?" A cheerful voice pried its way into her reverie.

Louisa opened one eye and squinted. Joseph stood barefoot in the grass, a fragrant pear proffered in his hand. She blinked at him a few times and glanced over at the bank. His fishing rod was lodged between two rocks, bobbing gently with the current.

"Oh," she blurted, struggling to steer her focus back into the present. Seeing him took her by surprise and her thoughts scattered. "Thank you, but that's all right. We brought our own lunch." She gestured to the basket containing hard rolls, deviled eggs, and cake made with the preserves Mr. Emerson had brought for Abba. Louisa noticed the icing had melted and smeared against the newsprint wrapping, and she fumbled with it, trying to tuck the cake under the rolls and out of the sun. Her hands felt clumsy—she realized she was nervous.

"Well, would you like to join me? I'm famished."

She grimaced—imperceptibly, she hoped—and nodded. "Just let me call my sister."

He nodded. "Of course. The more the merrier."

"Nan!" Louisa called out to the covey of girls now perched on the bank, their hems still floating in the water. Nicholas had gone over to them and sat on the bank with his legs outstretched, leaning back on his palms. When Anna saw Louisa and Joseph waving her over, she moved toward the bank. Nicholas offered her his hand and helped pull her to her feet. Louisa felt the ache of conflicting emotions. Once Anna became enmeshed in the world of courting, dances, dressing the part, Louisa felt she'd lose her sister forever. But she knew Anna wasn't happy in the family home, waiting for her life to begin, dreaming of what it was to be in love.

Anna joined them on the rocks, her dress now dry from the waist up, and tucked her strangely fashioned slippers beneath her heavy skirt.

"Mr. Singer has invited us to eat with him." Louisa affected a strained smile. She wondered whether Anna fancied Joseph, whether she should try to prod the two of them toward conversation.

Joseph chortled at her formal tone. "Please," he said. "Call me Joseph. Mr. Singer is my father."

"And how is he, your father?" Anna practiced compassion like an art form. She knew how to apply it with a delicate hand, knew its gradations and nuances, could distinguish its authentic form from imposters like sympathy and voyeurism. It came naturally to her, almost a physical impulse. Louisa had always admired this ability. She felt in comparison like some kind of lumbering boar, unwieldy, slow, low to the ground. She wasn't any better with others' emotions than she was with her own and often felt a thrashing within her she struggled to contain. But Anna was serene.

Joseph smiled gratefully. "How kind of you to ask. He has recovered a great deal in the last few days, is up out of bed, and came to the table for dinner yesterday noon." His lips tightened slightly, a somber quality deepening his voice. "We fear, though, that he'll never fully recover. His lungs were quite weakened with last year's bout of pneumonia. He seems to get ill more frequently. I've taken over most of the work at the store."

"I'm sure he is grateful to have such a dutiful son," Anna said, breaking her square of lemon cake in two and handing him a piece. "Did you tell us that you don't have any brothers?"

Joseph shook his head, fixing a steady gaze on Anna's eyes, her lashes turned down as she brushed crumbs from her lap. Louisa took note of it and felt the twin pangs of vicarious excitement and jealousy, to her dismay.

"I have one sister, Catherine. She is not yet fifteen and most of the time seems even younger than that. I wonder why it is that the expectations are so different for the youngest child in the family." He was thinking aloud and, once he realized what he had said, looked embarrassed at his frankness.

Louisa and Anna grinned at each other. They knew something about this phenomenon. "Your sister Catherine must meet our youngest sister May," Anna said. "I believe they will find they have some things in common."

A breeze rustled the umber fringe of Joseph's hair. He waved his hand as if to brush away his frustration. "Why should I begrudge her her childhood? She could be as serious and straight as an arrow, and it wouldn't change the fact that our father is going to die."

They sat silently for a long moment. Joseph's embarrassment was palpable—he seemed to be wishing for a way to withdraw his words. Up on the road at the top of the hill they heard a carriage pass, the hooves of the horses pounding the dusty path. Louisa was grateful when Anna spoke.

"It must feel at times like a great burden, but it snaps life into focus, does it not? We know we must appreciate all that we have been given. It isn't ours to keep." Even the tone of Anna's voice was a balm.

He nodded in agreement, gazing at a squirrel, its cheeks loaded with food, frozen halfway down the trunk of a nearby tree. "Thank you for your kind words." Joseph noticed the cake, his voice bright once again. "This looks delicious."

Anna seemed amused by how quickly he flitted from the weighty topic of his father's illness to the frivolity of dessert. He was indeed scarcely more than a boy.

"And how are you liking Walpole so far?" he asked. "Are you happy with your new drapes?"

"They aren't finished yet." Anna tucked a now-dry and unruly curl behind her ear. "It seems we've had too many distractions the last few days."

"Is that so? What have you been up to?"

"Well, Margaret has been so nice to take me along when she calls on friends, and Louisa too, *when* she'll agree to come." Anna elbowed Louisa teasingly. "It has been hard to tear her away."

"And what is it that has such a hold on your attention, Miss Louisa?" Joseph inquired, affecting his own formal mode of address, to her chagrin.

Off at the edge of the clearing, where the changing tent stood, Nora and Margaret were wringing out their swimming costumes and refastening their hair, preparing to head home for supper. "Please— call me Louisa. It's probably nothing you'd be interested in," she replied curtly, eager to turn the focus away from herself. *Blast Anna and her loose lips!* she thought.

"Don't be so sure," Joseph replied with a grin. "We dullards can surprise you."

Louisa colored, her pulse beating like a hummingbird in her throat. She couldn't decide if she should apologize for the rude comment he'd overheard, or if that would only draw more attention to it. After a few perilous seconds she managed to croak out, "I've been reading a new collection of poetry. It only just appeared last month."

Joseph swallowed the last bite of the cake, licking the icing from his fingers. "Would this be the work of the indecorous Mr. Whitman?"

Louisa's jaw fell. "How do *you* know about that?"

"Miss Alcott, as I get the distinct impression that you dislike being proven wrong, you'll be disappointed to know that your initial judgment of my character is turning out to be incorrect. I am a ravenous reader and have a cousin in New York who sends me all the new volumes. But how did *you* come by yours?"

"Mr. Emerson is our neighbor—well, *was* our neighbor, when we lived in Concord. He is a close friend of my father's and . . . has taken an interest in my literary education." It wasn't really a lie. Mr. Emerson *had* given her books in the past. Just not this one.

Joseph's eyebrows leapt. "Emerson was your neighbor? How fortunate you are!"

"Louisa is a published author herself," Anna said, reliably eager to bolster her sister. "Perhaps you have heard of *Flower Fables*?"

Joseph shook his head. "I can't say that I have, but nonetheless, how intriguing. Perhaps you will be so kind as to lend me a copy."

"I'm sure I don't have the book here in Walpole," said Louisa, her chin raised. "But perhaps you could secure one at the bookshop in town."

Joseph chuckled. "Protecting your sales numbers, I see. Well, I can hardly blame you for that. Authorship is not a lucrative career. You must make the most of it."

"On the contrary." The late afternoon sun cast long shadows behind them and Louisa paused to check her defensive tone. "My work is going quite well, and I have a few more irons in the fire. I'll be off to Boston soon to get some real writing done." Anna smiled, amused as usual by her sister's stubbornness.

Louisa tried once again to redirect the conversation. "Anna is an avid reader as well. And she also loves the theater."

"Really?" Joseph turned toward Anna and Louisa breathed a silent sigh of relief. "Do you put on plays yourself?"

Anna nodded. "I *adore* the theater. If it weren't for my bad ear, I would have tried to make it on the stage in New York. There's just nothing like it. As a substitute we do like to put on plays for fun. In fact, we were just discussing on the way here that we might like to stage something in Walpole. Do you think the others would be interested?"

"Certainly. You could call it the 'Amateur Dramatic Company of Walpole.' Which play were you thinking of taking on?"

Louisa piped up then, as she hoped to have her say before Margaret tried to take over and boss them into some unbearably frivolous charade. "What about *The Jacobite* by J. R. Planché? That's an old favorite." As she said it she wondered why she should even bother pressing for a particular play. She didn't plan to be around by the time it was performed. "Have you read it?"

Joseph nodded and gave an indifferent shrug.

"You don't share my sister's good opinion of it, I see," Anna said with a grin.

"It's fine. Probably just right for this group. Anyway, you shouldn't consult me. I probably will not be able to participate. The store takes up all of my time these days." He crumpled up the empty newsprint. "Have you ever staged *Hamlet*? It's my favorite play."

"Why, that's Louy's favorite as well. Isn't it, Lou?" Anna and Joseph turned back to her once again. Louisa felt exasperated that the focus of the conversation kept returning to her, and for some reason it rankled her to know Joseph had read all the same books she had.

Joseph surveyed her face and broke into the infuriating grin Louisa was beginning to realize he wielded like a weapon. "I think I've got you figured out, Miss Louisa: the more I impress you, the angrier you get," he said. Anna suppressed a giggle with her slender fingers.

Louisa's jaw ached from clenching it against one of a few biting replies careening through her mind. She summoned a benevolent smile and a calm tone, reminding herself that the only thing that could trump her pride was her desire to keep from embarrassing her sister in front of this young man she obviously favored.

"Anna, Marmee will be wondering where we are. We should be getting home."

The three of them stood, brushing crumbs from their laps and shaking hands good-bye. Louisa and Anna began up the steep hill, still wearing their mostly dry swimming costumes, as the other boys had folded up the changing tent and taken it with them. Joseph lingered a moment, inspecting the clearing to ensure that nothing had been left behind. He glanced up at the girls, happily chatting with their backs to him, then to the rock where they'd sat to eat their lunches. As Louisa would discover many years later, her comb, adorned with a steel chrysanthemum, lay forgotten by her in the grass. Joseph crouched down and slipped it in his pocket.

"I am angry nearly every day of my life, Jo;

but I have learned not to show it."

—*Little Women*

Chapter Four

When Louisa and Anna arrived back at Yellow Wood, they found Abba in a distressed state. Bronson had spent the day in his study sketching elaborate plans for the garden he'd begun planting. He whistled and plotted space on the paper for corn, asparagus, and beets, with sweet william for decoration. Louisa and Anna exchanged a glance, wondering when he would realize it was too late in the season for planting the vegetables.

Meanwhile, Abba continued the overwhelming task of scrubbing the floors, beating the dust out of the furniture, and airing the rooms. No one could settle in comfortably until these tasks were completed. May, full of resentment that she was too young to have been invited to the swimming party, reluctantly joined Anna and Louisa in coming to Abba's aid. Lizzie was feeling the early signs of a cold and had retired to her room to rest.

As the evening breeze dried the floors, Abba and May hung the woolen carpets out on the line to be beaten, though Louisa suspected it was Abba who did most of the work. May had been blessed with a slender physique and petite shoulders. Anna and Abba would say that her features were simply God's design, but Louisa sometimes wondered if they resulted from a lack of hard work. No matter who did the chores, once the carpets were sufficiently free of dust, someone would have to roll them to be stored in the attic and lay the simple painted oilcloth across the boards until the weather cooled again.

Anna and Louisa began the particularly smelly task of dipping candles. The family's present budgetary constraints put whale oil for lamps out of reach, and candles were the next best thing. Anna heated a kettle of sheep tallow on the stove until the acrid smell of burning fat engulfed the kitchen.

"Did you know," Anna began, stirring the burping sludge with a flat piece of wood reserved for the task, "that the brick house at the corner of River Road and Westminster Street belongs to the Sutton family? The house with the two chimneys?"

Louisa worked a dull knife through the cotton cord, cutting equal lengths for the wicks. "Oh, that house is lovely."

"As a boy, Nicholas's grandfather built it with his father."

"Is that so? How lucky to be a Sutton!"

"Indeed."

Louisa counted the pieces of cord. "Does Marmee want us to make the extra this time, for the charity collection?"

"I think Mrs. Parker organizes it here. I wonder whether Marmee has met her." The last solid hunks of fat had dissolved in the pot.

"I'd better go ask her before we begin." Louisa looked into the parlor but Abba wasn't there. She passed back through the kitchen and down the hall. The door to Bronson's study was open, and she heard the voices of her parents within. Abba's grew sharp and Louisa froze, a few steps away and out of sight.

"I do not see how working for *bread* implies unworthy gains."

Louisa heard the familiar sound of her father absently shuffling through his papers. He did not like any of them to come into his study when he was working, certainly not to question or criticize him. "Wife, I must be true to this philosophy, no matter what the cost."

Abba responded with an irritated sigh. "Give me one day of practical philosophy. It is worth a century of speculation and discussion."

Bronson's voice was measured. He rarely lost his temper. "I know this is the righteous path."

"What could be righteous about taking food out of the mouths of your own children?"

"I am teaching them that acts of commerce divide man from man, lead to greed and selfishness," he explained, as if he were speaking to a small child. "I am teaching them not to let their bellies lead them through life. When we abstain from physical comforts, inside we are made whole. If I work for pay, I violate my conscience."

"If you don't work, you violate mine."

"And God in his wisdom made the *husband* the head of the household."

It was silent a long moment. Louisa bit her lip in anticipation of her mother's reply. She had heard her father talk at length on the "woman question," advocating for the rights to vote and be educated the same as men. She had never heard him evoke his supremacy in this way. Perhaps he had shocked Abba into silence.

"It's August," she said. "We always manage in the summer with vegetables and fruit. People here have been very generous indeed. But it is a sin to rely on charity when you can do for yourself—that is *my* philosophy. When winter comes, we will not have enough wood to keep that fire going." Louisa thought of the cherished little coin purse concealed in the lining of her trunk and felt a wave of guilt. How could she let her mother suffer under the burden of this worry when that money from her advance could help the family, at least for a little while? But behind the guilt was despair—how could she let the money go when the dream of her freedom in Boston meant everything in the world?

Louisa heard Bronson clear his throat. "You would have me write to Emerson again, I suppose . . ."

"No—I would have you work enough to feed our family."

"God will provide, if we trust . . ."

Louisa backed quietly down the hall away from Bronson's study. In the past her mother had always deferred to his wisdom on matters of housing and provision. Louisa had never heard her speak so bluntly before, but she was glad Abba was questioning his decisions. After all, it was easy for Bronson to claim allegiance to his philosophy when it was Abba who suffered, Abba who had to quietly ask the neighbor to spare a few eggs, Abba who arranged free housing from a sympathetic relation. Why should they eat potatoes for every meal when they had a healthy father who *could* work but instead sat reading in his study all day?

And yet Louisa knew better than most that it wasn't so simple. She couldn't bear to give up the money that would buy her the freedom to write, just as her father would not consent to set aside his philosophy to work as a clerk in a stifling office. Men in Boston respected her father not only because of his ideas but because of the ways in which he challenged himself and others to go beyond the talking and *live* them. She had heard the story from Mr. Emerson of the previous May, when Bronson proved his allegiance to ideas of equality and compassion. Anthony Burns, a twenty-year-old runaway slave from Virginia, was arrested in Boston and taken to jail. President Pierce was hell-bent on enforcing his pet law, the Fugitive Slave Act, which dictated that northern states must return runaway slaves to the southern states from which they'd escaped, or face federal sanction. Despite the protests of Massachusetts officials, Pierce sent a federal marshal to Boston to retrieve Burns.

Bronson heard of the case and immediately began to organize a group of abolitionists to free Anthony Burns. Bronson led the mob to the jailhouse steps. They broke down the door and forced their way in, but the sheriff and his men fought them back out into the street.

Bronson looked at the defeated crowd and said, "Why are we not within?"

He then ascended another staircase alone, unarmed. Even when pistol shots could be heard within, he stood firm before the massive oak doors. Though there was nothing the men could do to stop the captured slave's prosecution, Bronson proved that night that he was a man of more than just words. When the case was lost, the president sent two thousand troops to ensure that Burns was returned to slavery in Virginia. They lined the path to the courthouse with their bayonets drawn. Louisa would never forget the scene—the windows of Boston draped with black crepe in silent protest, as she stood in the early summer heat holding her mother's hand. Burns was led to his ship in shackles. It surprised her to see that Burns was just a boy, his eyes wide with fear, his cheeks smooth, save for the deep scar of his master's branding. Bronson watched the scene with his jaw clenched tight, his anger barely contained. For the next twenty-four hours he did not speak, except when the family gathered for a solemn supper of cold vegetables and hard rolls.

"Lord, bless this food to our use and us to Thy service," Bronson murmured, his voice near breaking. "And make us ever mindful to the needs of others. Amen."

.   .   .

Anna looked up, annoyed, when Louisa came back to the kitchen. "Well, that took long enough. What does she say?"

Louisa knew her mother would tell them to make the extra candles—she always gave to charity, even when they had nothing to spare. But they would need every penny this winter, and someone— Louisa perhaps—had to be the voice of reason. "She says we do not need to make the extras. Mrs. Parker received a large donation just last month."

"Well, that's a blessing," Anna said. "I can scarcely stand this smelly job long enough to make the candles *we* need." She turned back to the stove and began stirring again. "So, as I was going to say before, despite having this wonderful house of his grandfather's, Nicholas is building his own."

"Ah, to be a man," Louisa said wistfully. "To be able to say, 'I would like a house,' and simply begin to build it."

"Well, he won't be able to do it *all* on his own. Samuel and Joseph are helping him with the construction."

Joseph sprang into her mind like a bird roused from a bush. She remembered how he had stalked to the river's edge but entered the water almost reverently, walking in up to his waist, smoothing his palms in two arcs over its surface. She recalled a line of Mr. Whitman's. *As he swims through the salt transparent greenshine . . .*

"It is just down the lane from the first. They started on it back in the spring. It sounds like they're a little crowded over at the elder Mr. Sutton's, now that Nora is back home for good, probably. That poor girl." Anna held the center of the length of wick and dipped the two ends into the tallow, pausing a moment and pulling them back out. She waited for the tallow to harden, then plunged them back into the kettle. "Did you know she was meant to be married to a man from New York City?"

Louisa shook her head absently.

"Anyway, Nicholas told me about the house today at the party. Don't you think that's interesting?"

Anna draped the finished candle over the wooden rack to dry and put out her hand to take the next wick. Louisa stared out the window over the sink, thinking of the saturated folds of Joseph's shirt . . . *lies on his back and rolls silently with the heave of the water.*

"Louy?" Anna touched her arm. "Did you hear me?"

Louisa shook off the reverie. Why on earth was her mind floating off this way? Perhaps there was such a thing as too much poetry. It was making a mess of her thoughts. "I'm sorry, Anna. Yes, I did hear you. Building his own house. Joseph must be so pleased."

"Joseph? Louisa, I don't think you *are* listening to me. I was talking about Nicholas Sutton, not Joseph."

"Of course—Nicholas. That's what I meant to say. I'm sorry, Nan. I think I had too much sun today."

Anna looked curiously at her. "I think it's *who* was sitting near you in the sun that's got you out of sorts," she simpered. "Miss Lou, I think you have a little crush."

Louisa gave her a scandalized stare. "I don't know to *what* or *whom* you are referring, but if it has anything to do with Joseph Singer, you can leave off right there. Even if we were the last two left on earth, I'd still remain a happy spinster."

Anna rolled her eyes. "This is all part of it, you know—the defensiveness, insulting him, telling me how he is the *last* man on earth you'd consider. Come now—I know you have read more romances than I."

Louisa shook her head. "Anna, I assure you that Joseph Singer is too much in love with himself to begin to dream of loving any-one else. And if he ever did, I should take pity on the object of his affections. This short life would be unendurably long with him by your side."

Anna gave her a skeptical glance, then turned her attention back to the bubbling tallow. She wiped a film of sweat from her forehead. Both of them had grown pale from the smell of the burning fat. "You may be in for trouble, then. He seemed quite taken with you."

"Nonsense—have you not noticed that he talks that way to every young lady who crosses his path? Don't put any stock in it—your sis-ter is safe with you at home, and at home I will *stay*."

"Love will change you," Anna said.

Louisa shook her head. "Perhaps you, my dear. But not me. For me it is a disease I am lucky not to catch."

She believed what she said, but Anna's comment needled its way into her mind. Louisa felt a fluttering in her ribs like the pages of a book fanning out in a breeze, a sensation that something was beginning that she wouldn't be able to stop. She rushed to divert the conversation.

"And now to more important matters. When shall we begin rehearsing the play?"

When the candles hung drying and the supper dishes were washed, Louisa and Anna joined Bronson, Abba, Lizzie, and May in the small parlor off the kitchen. Bronson held his Bible open on his lap—he often read passages to them in the evening and asked for his daughters' thoughts on the quandaries of Christian theology. Louisa plucked at the front of her dress a few times to cool her damp underarms. The heat from the kitchen had been stifling, and the small parlor window let in only a hint of a breeze.

"My daughters," Bronson began, his high forehead gleaming in the light of a candle, "what have you written today about our journey?" Abba turned expectantly to them, her face revealing a bit of sympathy. When would they have had time to write on this of all days? But Bronson believed in the importance of self-discipline above everything else, and he often asked to read his daughters' reflections to ensure they were adhering to the routine of writing each day.

And in truth, this chore seemed small in comparison to what he had asked them to do in the past in the service of his philosophical searching. Years back, Bronson had dragged his wife and daughters into an experiment in communal living. He envisioned building a new Eden, where his natural family and new chosen family, Abba and the girls as well as other like-minded people, could live according to Transcendental ideals. As pioneers, they would abstain from commerce of any kind and spare animals the enslavement he believed they suffered. This meant no meat or milk or eggs, no leather, wax, or manure. No ox would work the plow, and Bronson forbade the planting of root vegetables for fear they would upset the worms in the soil. Though he spent a great deal of time searching for just the right site and participants, Bronson failed to plan for the practical aspects of such a harsh life. When the group was established at Fruitlands, a rocky farm fifteen miles from Concord, it became clear that keeping the children warm and free from hunger would be Abba's burden. Several months into the experiment, as the winter descended, Bronson had to accept that the experiment had failed. Around Christmas, the Alcotts moved back to Concord.

Devastated, Bronson began to contemplate the idea of setting himself free from his family obligations. He was interested in the ideas of free love, a philosophy that cast doubt on whether traditional marriage could or should be sustained. True to form, rather than leave in the night or hold a private conversation with his wife on the matter, Bronson called a family meeting to discuss whether the family should split up. Anna was only thirteen, Louisa twelve, Lizzie only eight, and May just a toddler. In the end he hadn't left, though the knowledge that he had even considered it was a betrayal from which the Alcott women never quite recovered.

After surviving this difficult chapter, keeping a journal now hardly seemed like something to complain about. Bronson began with May, whom they all freely admitted was already more beautiful than her three older sisters combined. Unlike the others', her tawny hair held a natural curl, and she tied it back from her face with a ribbon.

"May writes about a woman in our train car on the journey here," he said, skimming over the pages. "She wore fine lace that 'must have been from France' and carried a basket covered with a cloth. May wondered what delicious treasures might have been inside."

Bronson smiled tolerantly at his youngest daughter. His full gray hair and wiry brows gave him a stern appearance, but his blue eyes softened his face. "You have an artist's eye for detail, my dear, but your words reveal a covetous nature. Remember that fine things make us their prisoner. It is in having nothing that true freedom can be found, freedom as *we* are blessed to experience it."

May nodded, her blue eyes far away and a sweet smile on her lips that Louisa knew meant his warnings passed out of her head the moment they were issued. Louisa herself felt amused by her father's claim that the hunger they had experienced on the train, the hunger that still rumbled unsated in their bellies, represented freedom.

Bronson turned his attention to Lizzie, who rested her cheek on

Abba's shoulder. She stifled a small yawn as she sat upright and tucked a wisp of her fine hair back into its plain bun. Lizzie moved to retrieve her journal from the table but Abba clutched at her elbow.

"Rest, child. You've had plenty of exertion for today."

"But Marmee, I've written something as well. Shouldn't I read along with my sisters?" Louisa often had to remind herself that her younger sister was a woman of twenty. Lizzie still had the voice and mien of a much younger girl.

Bronson hesitated a moment as if he were weighing the risk of taxing his soft-spoken daughter against enabling any self-indulgence. Abba spoke before his mind was settled.

"No, little bird. Your sisters are strong and healthy, but your burden is a weaker constitution. We must at all times be cautious."

"But Marmee," Lizzie said, touching her forehead to prove she did not have a fever. "I'm well."

"It may seem so, but you've only just recovered from that dreadful spring cough. Please—rest."

Lizzie looked at Bronson and he nodded, giving her a gentle smile Louisa rarely saw. Lizzie seemed to think it over a moment longer and relented. "Perhaps tomorrow, then," she said.

"You can read mine now, Father." Anna handed over her journal and sat back with her hands folded on her lap. They were white and fine like two little doves.

Bronson glanced over her pages, his eyes full of pride. "Anna writes that she was sad to leave Pinckney Street but eager for the challenge of a new town. 'Hard work,' she says, 'is God's design for our bodies and minds, and we must not question His will.' She is grateful for the new embroidery needles from Mrs. Emerson and longs to put them to use in readying the new home."

Anna beamed as she saw she had won his coveted approval once more. It was among these sisters nearly as important as water or oxygen.

Bronson looked in turn at each of his daughters. "I wish we were all as diffident and unpretending as this sister of yours."

Louisa nodded with a clenched jaw and thought about how her father had approached child-rearing like a scientific study. He collected evidence, keeping written observations of his subjects and, as the girls grew, reviewing their own journals. And like any scientist worth his salt, Bronson formed theories and then constructed experiments to test their veracity. One of Louisa's earliest memories was of such a test, designed to assess his young daughters' moral fortitude.

Bronson sat five-year-old Anna and four-year-old Louisa in two chairs in his study that faced his desk, on which he placed a polished apple. He glanced deliberately at the fruit to ensure the girls had noticed it, then addressed Anna. "Anna, should little girls take things that do not belong to them, things they might like to eat or drink?"

Anna's face grew solemn. "No, Father, they should not."

He nodded and turned to Louisa. "And you, little one—would you do such a thing?" Louisa shook her head.

"Very good," Bronson said, then crossed the room toward the door. "Now I must go fetch some wood for the fire. I shall return in a moment. Please keep your seats—and remember what you said."

"Yes, Father," the girls replied in unison. Bronson closed the door softly behind him and Anna and Louisa were alone with the beguiling fruit. When he returned with an armload of cedar the girls remained in their places, but the apple had been reduced to a spindly core.

Bronson pressed his lips into a line, more intellectually intrigued than angry. He pointed at the apple core. "What is this?"

Louisa's legs were too short to reach the floor and they swung beneath the seat of her chair. "Apple," she said.

"Well," Anna added, her linguistic abilities slightly more developed, "it *was* an apple."

Bronson nodded. "And what happened to it?"

Louisa looked blankly at her father. Anna spoke up. "Louisa took it. I told her she must not, but she did. And then I took a little bite but I knew I was naughty. So I threw it on the floor, but *Louisa*," she said, pointing her finger at her sister, "*Louisa* picked it up and ate the rest."

"Is this true?" Bronson questioned his younger child. Louisa nodded. The notion of telling a lie to cover her misdeeds had not occurred to her.

"I was naughty, wasn't I, Father?" Anna asked, twisting her fingers together. "I *stole*, didn't I? Will you punish me for it?"

Bronson thought a moment. "I will answer your question with a question of my own, something I am anxious to know. Did you think you were doing right when you took a bite?"

Anna shook her head. "No, my conscience told me I was not."

"And next time you will obey that precious voice inside, instead of ignoring it?"

"Yes, Father. I think I shall."

"Then I shall not punish you." He sat down in the wide armchair behind his desk and motioned with his index finger for Louisa to approach. She hopped down and toddled around to him, the back of her dress caught up in her lace-edged pantalettes. Bronson pulled Louisa onto his lap. "And what about you, my little hoyden? Why did you take the apple before Father said you could?"

Louisa looked up at her father, surprised by his question. "Because I wanted it."

Bronson had learned much from his experiment that held true as his daughters grew, and he never declined an opportunity to remind

Louisa of how she differed from her older sister. And he was right—Anna was skilled in the womanly art of self-sacrifice. For as long as she could remember, Louisa had prayed for God to change her into someone more like Anna: a reasonable girl ruled by her intellect and sentiment rather than her passion. Anna had never despaired that she had been born a girl. Perhaps it helped that she was beautiful. Louisa wanted with all her heart to be good like Anna, but she knew she wasn't.

Bronson turned to Louisa. "And last, my little hoyden. What have you written today, Louisa?"

Louisa felt a grim smile stretch across her face. Indeed, how little had changed! She handed over the journal, its pages mashed together with the haste that indicates a disorganized mind. A disintegrating black-eyed Susan, pressed between the pages since the previous summer, fell out on the floor. Bronson took no notice—he had scolded her on her untidy habits many times. He opened to the place she had marked with her thumb, then turned the page forward and back again, drawing his eyebrows together like two dark curtains. "Louisa has written only two sentences: complaints about doing her share of the work and the size of this home we're lucky to have at all."

Bronson pressed his lips into a taut line. "While the rest of us feel gratitude for our good fortune, Louisa finds fault in her new surroundings." He turned to her. "Do you agree that you have indulged in self-pity?"

Louisa looked down at her lap and nodded, shame burning along the edges of her ears.

"Father," Anna said. "I think what Louisa was *trying* to say is that though she will have to adjust to a new place, she intends to hold herself to a high standard and keep accomplishing her work, even if it is difficult." She glanced at Louisa, tilting her head tenderly.

"Loyalty is a lovely trait in a sister, but it will not help her improve." He turned to Louisa once more. "Do you know why I ask the four of you to write?" He waited until their eyes all blinked expectantly at him, save Lizzie's, which were now drawn in sleep. "The evils of life are not so much social and political as personal, and so we must work toward personal reform. Through writing we reveal what is in our minds. If goodness and selflessness be there, the words will show it. If evil lurks, the words reveal it, and all the better, for we must root it out and improve. Always, always work to improve, my girls." He closed his Bible and rose, indicating that the evening was ending and in a moment all would go to bed. "It is the very reason we're alive."

He shuffled toward his study to begin the work that would keep him awake long into the night while the women slept. Abba kissed each of her girls good night. She was a plump woman with a round face, and her daughters resembled her. When she embraced Louisa, she held her an extra moment and whispered, "You are full of promise and vitality, my darling. Do not let his words discourage you. Bear up under them and resolve to be the best of who you are." She kissed her daughter's temple and sent her off toward bed.

"Is this the stage? How dusty and dull it is by daylight!" said Christie next day, as she stood by Lucy on the very spot where she had seen Hamlet die in great anguish two nights before.

—*Work: A Story of Experience*

Chapter Five

Despite Louisa's reluctance to commit to another project that would keep her away from Boston, Anna's enthusiasm prevailed and the Walpole Amateur Dramatic Company assembled a few days later for its first rehearsal. Mrs. Ferguson, keeper of the Elmwood Inn on Washington Square, offered her attic to the company in exchange for free tickets, acknowledgment in the program, and a promise that her son Paul could have a role in the performance.

The Elmwood was a Georgian beauty built in 1762, and the grand old home towered above the neighboring buildings with three full stories and two massive chimneys. The attic proved to be the perfect spot for rehearsals. It formed one open room, spanning the length of the house, and was sparsely furnished with a few chairs, a long table, and decaying velvet drapery. The six dormers, three on either side, let in plenty of light, and there was no chance of anyone peeping in at the clumsy first steps the actors would take as they worked to refine their performances.

Nora had refused to come, saying she couldn't shake the feeling that they would be laughed at. The others waved off this assertion with slight nervousness. Nicholas and Samuel extracted a commitment from Joseph on the grounds that if they had to be there, he did too. That first day, Louisa, Anna, May, along with Margaret, Harriet, the boys, and Paul Ferguson, climbed the creaking stairs to the attic.

Though Louisa dreaded getting caught up in a lengthy project, she also couldn't bear to take direction from a Walpolean who couldn't possibly know as much as she did about the theater. So as she usually did, she took charge and appointed herself director. She brought the group to order with a few claps of her hands. "Thank you for coming. I know with hard work and dedication we will put on an excellent performance. I thought we could try *The Jacobite*. How many have read it?"

A few hands went up, including Joseph's. Margaret pursed her lips. "I thought we might do something Greek."

Louisa groaned. She supposed no one could mount a successful argument against the classics, but she felt Planché's light comedy would have a wider appeal. "My sisters and I have done those tragedies dozens of times. They're so *sober*. I thought it might be a lark to do something new. Something modern and comical." Louisa handed her the play. "Just read it over—you'll see."

They waited while Margaret scanned the first scene. Samuel shifted his weight from one foot to another. May patted the curls along her forehead to ensure they were in place. Harriet scoffed, annoyed at the delay, and sat down in a chair that scarcely creaked under her paltry weight.

Margaret giggled over a line, then flipped the page closed. "You're right, Louisa. This *is* quite amusing. Let's try it." She stepped toward the center of the room. "So, who will assign the parts?"

Joseph could see vexation rising in Louisa's face and broke in to stop Margaret from running roughshod over the enterprise. "Louisa knows the story better than anyone else," Joseph said.

"Well, I suppose that's true," said Margaret, unconvinced. She stepped back. Louisa reclaimed the reins.

She flipped to the first page. "There are three male and three female parts," Louisa said. "Let's see . . . Lady Somerford. She is the gentlewoman caught up in an affair."

"Louy, please don't give me a part. I want to be the prompter," May said.

Louisa and Anna turned to their youngest sister in surprise.

May giggled, embarrassed. "I know your thoughts—it's rare indeed that I would pass up the chance to be the center of attention. But this way if Lizzie feels well enough to come, we can work together."

Anna kissed May on the cheek. "What a kind little sister I have."

Louisa nodded her approval. "Speaking of roles offstage, we're going to need someone to work on the sets." She looked over at Paul Ferguson, who hovered at the back of the group. He looked mortified when all the eyes in the room turned in his direction. "Paul, I happen to know that you are quite the artist yourself. Your mother told me those paintings in the parlor are yours."

Paul looked down at his shoes and nodded.

"Would you be willing to design and build some sets for us?"

"It would be my pleasure," he mumbled, his voice scarcely above a whisper. "But perhaps—d-do you know Alfie Howland?"

May's eyebrows went up. "The painter? Yes! I *worship* his work."

"He was born in Wa . . . Walpole. Comes here for the summers, though he lives in Boston now." He took a long breath, as if getting through the last sentence without his stutter had winded him. "Maybe we could ask him to help."

"Oh, that would be a dream," said May with her hands clutched at her breast.

Paul gave her a shy smile. "I'll see what I can do."

"Thank you, Paul," said Louisa. "Now, then—back to Lady Somerford . . ."

"I'll take that part," Harriet said. "I don't really *want* to be in the play at all. But I suppose I could play a noblewoman. Provided the costume is something rather fine."

Louisa blinked at Harriet and contemplated spontaneously adding a new role to the play: irritating girl who looks like a toad. Instead she decided to ignore Harriet for the moment. "Lady Somerford is engaged to be married to Sir Richard. Samuel, perhaps you could play that role?"

"My pleasure, Miss Louisa," he said, anxious to be agreeable.

"Samuel, please call me Louisa." He nodded.

"I wonder," Margaret piped up, "if it might not be better that *I* play Lady Somerford." Harriet began to pout. Her hunched shoulders and sallow complexion made her seem like a deflated example of womanhood next to Margaret, who was pure fleshy vivacity. Margaret turned to her with mock solicitude. "Harriet, dear, it's *only* that, as you know, I have *been* to London—my grandmother was British—and, well, perhaps I can render the upper-class accent a bit more . . . authentically. It's not *your* fault that you haven't traveled."

Harriet pursed her lips and thought a moment. She knew better than to challenge Margaret. "Well, what other female parts are left?"

Louisa glanced at the list. "The Widow Pottle. She owns the tavern. And her daughter Patty."

"No. I don't like the sound of either of those," Harriet said.

"Harriet," May said. "Why don't you help with the prompting? We have to copy out the parts for all the characters and whisper their lines to them if they forget." Harriet nodded reluctantly and went to stand by May.

"Very well," Louisa said. "Margaret will play Lady Somerford. As I said, she is engaged to be married to Sir Richard—that's Samuel," Louisa said, caught up in making her notes on the page, unaware that this statement caused both Samuel and Margaret to blush. "But Sir Richard is cruel to her and she doesn't love him. Secretly, Major Murray is the *true* object of her affections."

Margaret's face fell—she wanted *Samuel* to play the true object of her affections. Louisa looked up at the remaining young men. "Nicholas," she said, "perhaps you could play the Major?"

Margaret broke in. "Louisa, I don't mean to *insert* myself where I'm not needed . . ."

"Certainly not," Louisa said with a sarcasm Margaret ignored.

". . . but doesn't it say here that the Major is a 'tall, fair man'?"

Louisa looked back at the description, exasperated. "Yes. Indeed, it does."

"Well," Margaret said. "Perhaps, then, would it not be better if Samuel played the role of the Major? After all, he is a head taller than both Nicholas and Joseph."

Louisa looked at Samuel. He nodded, smirking at Joseph and Nicholas. "It is true that I am *far* taller than either of my friends."

"Not very bright, though," Joseph shot back with a grin. "Without a doubt, you have the feeblest intellect of the three of us."

"Why don't *you* take Sir Richard, you lout?" Samuel said, chuckling. "Miss Louisa, didn't you say he is the villain?"

Louisa nodded, ignoring the formal mode of address he seemed unable to abandon. She turned to Joseph. "You don't mind?"

He shook his head. "Mind a role that asks me to thwart the intentions of Mr. Parker? I believe I was born to play it!"

Louisa rolled her eyes. "Well, now that we finally have *that* settled . . . Anna, will you play Patty Pottle?" Anna nodded. "Oh, thank goodness. And I will take the role of the foulmouthed widow—I suppose no one will argue with me about that." Joseph smiled. "And that just leaves . . . John Duck. Nicholas, you're left. Would you mind?"

"Not at all, Louisa."

"Right then. Let's read through the first scene. I have only two copies here. So until May and Harriet finish the rest, we'll have to pass it back and forth. Will you set up the scene for us, May?" Louisa asked, handing her the play.

May nodded. "This scene takes place in the parlor of a public house or roadside inn called the Crooked Billet. Patty and Lady Somerford enter first." May handed the script to Anna. She and Margaret stepped forward. Margaret assumed the posture she imagined to be a staple of the genteel class, though Louisa observed that she looked rather like she'd injured her neck.

Patty Pottle spoke first. *"It's all safe, my lady. There's nobody down here, and mother and John are down in the cellar bottling cider."* Anna passed the script to Margaret.

"Then tell me quickly. Did you put the note where I told you?"

"No, my lady."

"No!"

"Pray forgive me, my lady; but I couldn't help it. It was all along of John Duck."

"John Duck?"

"Yes, my lady, our man—he—he—would try to . . ." Anna stared at the page, blinking furiously. Nicholas examined the skin around his thumb. Anna rushed quietly through the remainder of the line. *". . . kiss me, my lady . . . and I ran away and he ran after me, and somehow or another, I lost it, my lady."*

"Anna—" Louisa broke in, oblivious, as usual, to subtexts of any sort, particularly those of the romantic variety. She took her role as director very seriously. "You must speak up."

Anna nodded, her cheeks flushed. Louisa noticed their color, and, as she glanced at Nicholas, it dawned on her why her sister was losing her nerve. "Cast, let me explain a little more about what is happening in this scene," she said, turning the attention away from the skittish pair for a moment. "Lady Somerford is fretting over this lost note. Sir Richard is a possessive and powerful man"—Joseph straightened his shoulders and tipped his chin in the air—"and he already suspects the Lady's love is not true. The lost note was meant to reach Major Murray and urge him come to the Crooked Billet at eight o'clock so the lovers might safely meet. But Lady Somerford fears that if Sir Richard happens upon the note, it will confirm his suspicions."

"And he intends to challenge the Major to a duel if he finds out about the affair?" Margaret asked.

Louisa shook her head. "It's not only her secret affair that she means to protect. The Major is an accused Jacobite. Only Sir Richard can pardon him and spare his life, but he'd speed the Major to the executioner if he had an atom of proof that the Lady loves him."

May shimmied with excitement. "This sounds *very* romantic!"

Nicholas cleared his throat, summoning his nerve. "May I ask you to summarize the plot surrounding John Duck and Patty?" Anna appeared to chomp down on the insides of her cheeks.

"Well, John works for Patty's mother, helping out around the inn since her husband died. John is in love with Patty"—Margaret gave Anna's forearm a furtive pat—"but because he hasn't any money, her mother won't let her marry him. So Patty won't own that she loves him and he makes a fool of himself again and again to win her affections. Soon, the widow—that's me—agrees to consider the marriage *if* John can come up with a sum of one hundred pounds. The widow believes, of course, that it will be an impossible task and Patty will be rid of him forever."

May gave a little gasp. "Does he get the money? Does he win her in the end?"

"We shall see," said Louisa, who was fond of a little suspense. As she was drawn in to rehearsing the first scene, long moments passed in which she could scarcely hear the incessant voice in her head urging her toward Boston and freedom.

There is no fairy-book half so wonderful as the lovely

world all about us, if we only know how to read it.

—"Morning-Glories"

Chapter Six

The following Saturday afternoon, Louisa sat at a narrow table in the sweltering attic room she shared with Anna. Bronson had gone to the village store, apparently poised to withstand the endless pontification of the locals if they would let him sit all day without buying anything. The Alcott women had been invited to lunch with Eliza Wells, Abba's niece, who was the object of much sympathy amongst the town's women. It was well known that Eliza's father was partial to drink, and between his episodes and her husband's ragged temper, she was rarely able to leave the house. Abba urged the girls to come along and try to cheer her, but Louisa was always keen to get an afternoon to herself—no interruptions, no guilt for reading while the others dutifully washed and sewed and baked—and so she asked to stay behind. They didn't mind granting her request. It was a relief sometimes to leave their moody, pensive sister behind with her thoughts and conduct their social lives in peace.

Once a week the stores in town stocked the newspapers from New York, and occasionally Bronson brought them home. Louisa had the previous week's edition of the *New York Daily-Times* spread open on the tabletop. She skimmed the page for notices about *Leaves of Grass,* but this edition carried no news of the book. Despite herself, she loved to read about the outrageous crimes of passion sometimes reported—a woman in a jealous rage confronts her husband's mistress and they both end up dead; a man kidnaps his child to save her from spending her childhood with a heartless mother. As she searched for the scandalous details, an article caught her eye.

Mrs. Butler, or Miss Fanny Kemble, as she prefers to be known since her much-publicized divorce, gave three of her lauded readings of *Othello* this week at the Stuyvesant Institution on Broadway to a room of six or seven hundred persons. The audience members flocked to the space two or three hours before the time of the lady's appearance to procure seats and sat in tedious anticipation, the delicate women displaying their rich taffeta or shot silk dresses and intricate lace gloves while their grave gentlemen companions filled their pipes and reclined in the hard wooden chairs as they waited. They were compensated for this long wait by the performance Miss Kemble calls a "labor of love." And she is well-compensated for her efforts. Shakespeare never earned as much for writing his plays as Miss Kemble does for reading them.

Louisa leaned back in her chair and closed her eyes, imagining herself sitting in the front row of that crowded room on Broadway. Like everyone else in America—and England, for that matter—the Alcotts had followed the story of Fanny Kemble's divorce and emancipation, which unfolded throughout Louisa's teenage years.

The Kemble family had dominated the British stage for generations. Fanny's mother, father, aunt, and uncle built livelihoods and fame on Shakespeare's plays, and when her father's share in the Royal Opera House at Covent Garden looked like it might be in danger, he thrust his twenty-year-old daughter onto the stage. From then on she bounced back and forth between London and New York, living in a hotel with her parents while she was performing away from home. It was well known that Fanny found America to be a little less refined than her native country, though she loved to ride her horse along the Hudson River north out of New York City. An incident at the Park Theater amused her American fans, who liked to see British visitors' delicate sensibilities challenged by what the Brits still thought of as the frontier. During a quiet soliloquy, a rat emerged from a hole in the stage floor and scampered through the orchestra pit, eliciting quite a scream from poor Fanny.

Fanny's romantic life caused great speculation amongst Louisa and her sisters. She had many admirers, but one in particular finally convinced her that becoming his wife offered more happiness than a life on the stage. Pierce Butler was the son of wealthy landowners who lived in Philadelphia, and the grandson of one of the founding fathers, his namesake. After they married, Pierce inherited his family's sea-island cotton and rice plantations in Georgia, and he took Fanny there to live. To the satisfaction of New England abolitionists like Bronson, Fanny was appalled when she saw firsthand the conditions under which the slaves lived and suffered. She found in her conscience that she was opposed to slavery and began to write about her beliefs.

The drama continued to fill the papers when she publicly implored her husband to consider the morality of enslaving fellow human beings, but he refused to be swayed and began to regret having married a woman with so fiery a personality. She agitated the situation further by writing an anti-slavery treatise with descriptions of what she had witnessed on the plantation. Pierce resented her insolence and forbade her to publish it. Eventually, she left the plantation for England to return to the stage, leaving her daughters behind with their father. It was this final act of independence that prompted Pierce to file for divorce. Louisa never forgot the press statement Pierce made, in which he explained that the relationship had failed because of Fanny's peculiar view that marriage should be "companionship on equal terms."

What Louisa really admired was Fanny's determination to go on after the marriage dissolved. She worked and traveled, she made her own money, and she lived her life independently, on her own terms. To Louisa, Fanny's view of marriage was not brazen and shocking but simply logical—not to mention the only guiding philosophy under which both parties could expect to find happiness. But rather than encourage Louisa to look for a husband with enlightened views, Fanny's experience seemed to prove the impossibility of equality in marriage.

A sweating glass of cold tea sat beside the newspaper and Louisa's open journal on the table. She always kept a stack of paper and an inkwell nearby just in case a lightning bolt of a thought struck. It was known to happen, and then she'd be off again into her vortex, where she could work without stopping for days on end, to the point of total exhaustion. The fantasy of imagined characters and events gave her a kind of temporary euphoria. She couldn't choose when to enter that furious state, so she had to be ready to seize it when it flashed by, like a runaway carriage headed for the Commons.

She took up *Leaves of Grass* once again, though she knew soon she would have to slip it back onto her father's desk or risk being caught with it and having to explain. The room was sweltering and the pages clung to her damp fingertips. She had read the volume straight through once and had begun again that morning. Now she reached the end of the first poem: *Failing to fetch me at first keep encouraged, / Missing me one place search another, / I stop somewhere waiting for you.*

Suddenly she heard a soft tapping on the first-floor window. She had every intention of pretending not to hear, so she rose and moved carefully toward the window, shifting the new drapery to the side ever so slightly. It was Joseph Singer.

Louisa froze, her hand still on the fabric. Should she answer the door? No one else was home, and surely he wanted to see Anna. Just as she'd resolved to slink back to her desk and wait for him to go away, he looked up and grinned at her figure in the window.

She reluctantly descended the stairs, drawing her sleeve across her damp forehead before opening the door.

"Good afternoon, Miss Louisa."

"Hello, Joseph. We weren't expecting you."

"I hope you don't mind."

She clutched the door with both hands, willing her nerves away from her tongue and into her fingers. "Oh, of course not. But everyone is out. Anna is with my mother and sisters at our cousin's for lunch. I know she will be disappointed that she missed your visit."

Joseph smiled, amused by how flustered she was. "It's always a pleasure to see your sister, and I hope you'll tell her I said so. But I didn't come to see Anna. I came to see you."

Louisa processed this information through her sluggish brain. Perhaps he was coming to inquire after her sister's feelings. Should she tell him that Anna seemed to favor Nicholas Sutton, at least for the moment?

"Would it be all right if I came inside? I'm likely to melt out here."

"Of course! Oh, forgive me," she said, throwing open the door. "Please, come in."

The skin of his temples was pink and his eyes were bright. The heat from outside wafted in after him. Louisa tried to think of what she was supposed to do next.

"If you don't mind," Joseph began, "I would love something cold to drink."

"Of course!" Louisa knew she was going to have to calm down if she had any hope of carrying on a conversation with him. She felt at any moment she might take wing and crash right through the glass of the front window. *What has come over me?* she thought, angry at herself. Over the years she'd received plenty of her father's friends, and Abba had trained her well on the duties of a hostess. Perhaps she had felt shy in the presence of some of these men, like Mr. Emerson, who seemed to her like royalty. But never before had she found herself so . . . *flustered* by anyone.

She handed him the cold tea and they sat down on opposite ends of the horsehair sofa. His cheeky self-assurance seemed to have dissolved. He drank a few nervous sips and they sat in silence.

Joseph cleared his throat. "Do I remember your saying you will be leaving for Boston soon? We'll all be awfully sorry to see you go."

Louisa sat up straighter, folding her hands in her lap. "Yes, that's right. Probably just another few weeks and I'll be on my way."

"And you'll go . . . all on your own?"

She disliked his tone; it seemed to question her willingness or determination to follow through with her plan. "Yes, alone. Freedom and independence—that is my aim. Nothing else means anything to me."

He clamped his lips closed and nodded, chastened. She checked the pride in her voice and decided to change the subject. Louisa had watched Anna fill awkward social pauses with tidbits of gossip. "My mother told me this morning that Samuel Parker has proposed to our friend Margaret and she has accepted," she said.

Joseph brightened. "Ah, that's wonderful news! You know that whole swimming party was an elaborate ruse designed to give him an afternoon with her. I don't mind admitting I was a co-conspirator. All for a good cause, I can now say."

Louisa grinned. She loved a good conspiracy. "Samuel's parents must be happy about the match?"

Joseph hesitated. "Yes, I believe they are. Mr. Parker is, anyway. Mrs. Parker—well, she can be a tough one to please, especially when it comes to convincing her a young lady is good enough for her son. But I won't say a thing against her—she has been like a mother to me since my own died."

Louisa pressed her lips together. "Well, that is wonderful to hear, though I'm sorry to know about your mother." Her curiosity prompted her to ask more, but she refrained.

Joseph shrugged. "Thank you—it was a long time ago. But my father and sister and I were blessed to have Mrs. Parker. When Mother died, we moved to the apartment above the store so Father could keep an eye on us while he was working. We were quite small then. And Samuel's mother brought us our dinner each afternoon. I don't know how she did it, but my father was grateful. And Mother too, I'm sure." He trailed off. "But happy news should be our focus. And Samuel is the happiest of all today, I think."

"I'm sure he will make a devoted husband. Our friend deserves only the best." Something gave a quarter turn in Louisa's belly as she thought of Anna and their talk on the walk home from the store. "But it's all so soon, don't you think? It seems only last summer we were all romping around together and having larks," she thought, but found she had said out loud.

"I don't know. I don't think age has anything to do with it. Of course, it is a serious endeavor, and one must treat it as such. But more years don't necessarily better prepare one, I imagine."

"I suppose we never know what life is going to send our way."

Joseph considered her remark. "Some people just seem to know what they want and go after it full steam ahead."

She nodded, thinking that not every woman was so free to pursue what she wanted, if her object went against convention. An awkward moment passed.

Joseph reached for his pocket and pulled out the thin volume. "Since we talked about these poems the other day at the party, I cannot stop rereading them. They really are remarkable."

Louisa cheered a bit. Here was something she could speak freely about; here was a subject that had nothing to do with her.

"I wonder, what do you think of his punctuation?" Joseph flipped forward a few pages with his index finger and pointed to several ellipses that dotted the page like a strange kind of Morse code. "I've never seen poetry set on the page this way."

"Neither have I. It is odd—as if the poem is one long sentence. You can scarcely stop for breath as you read it. Perhaps he wanted the appearance of the page to match the content of its message. His philosophy is unorthodox, so why shouldn't his grammar be as well?"

Joseph nodded. "He certainly has a way of shocking his reader, does he not?" Louisa looked at her knees. The poetry was full of talk of the body. The first time she read some of the passages, she had blushed to the ends of her hair. "In fact, I wasn't sure I should bring it with me today. I don't wish to make you uncomfortable."

Louisa felt her temper rear like a colt. "Because I am a woman, you mean?" She snatched his copy of the book from his hand, flipped to the page she'd reread ten times to imprint it on her brain, and recited: "*I am the poet of the woman the same as the man, / And I say it is as great to be a woman as to be a man.* What do you say to that? Is he wrong?"

Joseph tried to hide his amused smile and gazed admiringly at her. "No, Miss Louisa, I do not think he is wrong," he replied softly. "If anything, I think he may be underestimating *you.*"

Her eyes darted around his face, trying to discern whether he spoke sincerely or was teasing her. She sighed, exhausted by her own defensiveness. She knew her temper made her silly and childish. But it was as easily triggered as ever.

The coy demeanor dropped from his face. "Miss Louisa—"

"Just Louisa, please," she interrupted.

"—I don't believe I ever have encountered a woman quite like you."

Louisa's eyes darted back to that safe place on her knees. It was a wonder she had not stared a hole straight through them.

"I feel I could talk to you about anything and you would understand. Do you feel the same?"

She did not nod or shake her head or move her lips. She felt she heard the top and bottom rows of her eyelashes crashing together, so silent was the air in the room as he spoke.

"And a writer yourself, with success at so young an age. Think what a long career you have to look forward to, all the stories you will bring to the world."

Louisa grimaced. "Nothing is guaranteed. Some interests are more easily carried over into adulthood than others. Women have many responsibilities that fill their time—they cannot depend on the luxury of hours on end to write."

"But what a *shame* it would be to let your talents languish."

Louisa gave a short, sad-sounding laugh. "You haven't read a word I've written and yet you fret over the loss of my talent. Take care not to heap on too much praise until you are familiar with its object."

"I'll soon change that. I wrote to my cousin Edward asking him to send me a copy of your *Flower Fables*."

"Oh, dear," Louisa said, her face full of dread. "Please remember— I wrote most of those tales when I was just a girl. I like to think, to hope, that my writing has improved *somewhat* since then."

"I know I will enjoy your work. I can hear it in our conversations. You have a gift."

"I fear some people believe it should be a youthful amusement and nothing more. Perhaps you have heard that the singular preoccupation of a young woman's life is to find a husband." Louisa gave him a wry smile.

A strain passed across Joseph's pale eyebrows a moment, as if her comment called forth an unpleasant thought, but as soon as the troubled look appeared it vanished. His freckles dotted the apples of his cheeks like spilled wheat. "Yes, I believe I am acquainted with the idea," he said, grinning.

Louisa sighed. "And when he is found, the work has only begun. Take Margaret, for example. Soon she will be a wife, keeping a home for her husband, nursing his relatives and her own, preparing for children, God willing. She won't have time for anything else."

Joseph scoffed. "Hardly! Margaret lives for parties and gossip—two things she'll be able to pursue just as well, if not better, in marriage."

"I beg your pardon—I don't like your tone." Louisa's voice surprised her by sounding sharp. She softened it. "Please don't speak about her that way. Margaret is my friend."

"And mine. I only meant that she is very different from you, is interested in different things."

"We may be unlike each other, but the duties of a wife are the same for each."

"I disagree. Husbands vary just as wives do. The possibility of a happy marriage hinges on the choosing, though most girls are so eager to make the pact, they do not take the time for careful consideration."

His smug tone needled her. "Is that so? You seem to have thought an awful lot about this matter."

"Not at all—it's just that the facts of it are very clear. You, for example. It will be very important that you marry the right sort of man—"

"And I suppose *you* think you know what sort of man that is." Louisa felt her cheeks get hot.

He nodded and broke into that infuriating grin, his playfulness returning. "I do. Primarily, he will have to be the sort of man who does not mind being interrupted. You know—the sort who would rather *listen* than talk. With you, one is apt to do a lot of listening."

Louisa felt her temper swing inside her head like the tongue of a bell. "When someone has graciously accepted your visit—an unannounced visit, I might add—do you always put such *effort* into insulting her?"

Her anger only compounded his amusement. "On the contrary—finding things to say that you will interpret as insults takes very little effort at all."

Before she could stop herself, Louisa was on her feet. "Aren't you clever? Well, here is something that will surprise you: 'Conventionality is not morality.' Miss Charlotte Brontë wrote that, and it is as true for me as it was for her. To do things just because others do is cowardly. Not that it is any business of yours, but I have *no* intention of marrying."

He watched her, his lips pressed into a line. "You are wrong. *That* doesn't surprise me at all."

Louisa ignored his quip. "I could never love anyone better than I love my independence."

"And you shouldn't. Your independence suits you." Joseph's face grew serious. "You know, Louisa, there are some men out there who are *charmed* by an independent woman, who feel that marriage can be an equal partnership of head and heart. Who would love you just as you are—fiery, overwrought, as passionate as any man."

Louisa felt something snatch her breath down deep into her lungs. She'd never met a person who spoke so bluntly, even to people he barely knew. She couldn't think of a thing to say.

"And to those men," Joseph said as he clapped his hands together and broke into a grin, "I say, God be with you, friends!"

The blood drained from Louisa's face and was replaced by hot mortification. Louisa took a slow breath.

"All this," she said, recovering as she gestured from his head to his feet, "*and* a sense of humor. How fortunate for the young ladies of this town."

Joseph grimaced at her bitter tone. "Miss Louisa, I have taken up too much of your lovely afternoon. I should leave you to your books."

She stood up and walked with him to the door, afraid to speak for fear of betraying how much he'd rankled her.

"Well, then . . ." He tucked *Leaves of Grass* into the crook of his elbow. "Thank you for the . . . *lively* discussion."

She nodded. He stepped across the threshold into the blinding sun.

"And I . . ." he continued as he placed his hat on his head and wiggled it into place by the brim. "Well, I'm . . . perhaps we could meet to talk again sometime."

"Perhaps," she said in a tone assuring him they would *not*, and closed the door. She started toward the stairs, eager to take advantage of the last quiet moments the afternoon promised, but she turned first down the narrow hall leading away from the parlor. The door to Bronson's study stood open an inch, and as Louisa pushed, its hinges creaked. Lizzie had been in to tidy the room earlier that morning. Books Louisa had seen stacked in piles of various sizes across the floor like buildings in a cityscape had been returned to their place on the shelf between the room's two windows. The surface of the desk was clean, save for two piles of paper.

Louisa shook her head as she touched the cream-colored stock. One stack was blank and the other contained Bronson's writing, a scant four or five sentences scrawled across the center of each page, leaving inches of unused space. Her father insisted on the most expensive paper and was determined to use it as wastefully as he could, she thought bitterly. Up in the attic room her own journals were bursting at the seams, each page full to the corners, front and back, until the ink bled through and rendered the text unreadable. The green-shaded lamp sat in the center of the desk next to a vase of pale purple verbena, the tart perfume of the flowers filling the space. Another of Lizzie's silent gestures.

Her father hadn't discovered that the book was missing, and Louisa wanted to keep it that way. The top shelf held books he rarely read but liked to keep at hand, and there was a space at the end of the row for one more slim volume. If he did notice it, perhaps he would conclude that Lizzie had moved it there. She pressed the book into place with her index finger. With its spine facing out it looked just like any other of the black, gray, and green books in the shadowed rectangle of the shelf. How strange, she thought, as she scanned the titles of his library. That paper and board and ink could work such alchemy.

She shut the door to the study and turned toward the stairs, passing the front door on her way. Something on the floor caught her eye. The white corner of a folded piece of paper was wedged under the door. Louisa crouched down and pulled gently to avoid tearing it. She unfolded the paper as she stood.

Dear Louisa,

Lest you persist in your belief that I am a dim-witted country boy, here is a letter to prove that I can write as well as read. I know these rare talents will astonish you.

Perhaps I only wanted an excuse to thank you for receiving me this afternoon. The cold tea was welcome comfort from the heat, but the conversation scarcely allowed my mind a moment of leisure. There isn't another person in this town, perhaps in the whole of New Hampshire, with whom I could discuss the work of Mr. Whitman.

You have the spirit of one who will let nothing separate her from her object. Do not let your visitors, eager as they are to share your company, get in the way of your work.

Yours,
Joseph

Money is the root of all evil, and yet it is such

a useful root that we cannot get on without it

any more than we can without potatoes.

—*Little Men*

Chapter Seven

Singer Dry Goods

WALPOLE, NEW HAMPSHIRE

ITEM	
Miss Louisa Alcott, credit for flour, ten pounds	*$1.75 (of which 50 cents has been paid)*
Balance Owed	*$1.25*

Louisa, did you set aside the candles for the collection?" Abba's voice startled Louisa, and the steel brush she was using to scour the soot from the stove door clattered to the floor.

"I'm sorry, Marmee. What did you say?"

"The charity candles—I can't seem to find them." Anna glanced up from the peas she was shelling into a bowl, her fingers glistening wet and green at the tips. She gave Louisa a confused look.

"No, Marmee. It's my fault—I think I forgot to make them."

Abba pulled a week's worth of the slender brown sticks from the bin under the sink, wrapped them in a stiff rag, and tied them with twine. Louisa felt a disappointed pang in her stomach as she tried to calculate just how many late-night writing hours she would lose without those candles.

"Take these to Mrs. Parker," Abba said, handing the parcel to Anna. She pried the lid off a tin box and shook a few coins into her hand. "And here's the rag money. We have only a dusting of flour left, so you'll have to see how far you can make this stretch."

Louisa felt a vibration whisk through her veins. They would buy the flour at the dry goods store. "Please, Marmee—can't May go? I find that Joseph Singer *intolerable*."

Anna looked at Louisa and rolled her eyes. "Don't mind her, Marmee. We'll go."

Abba nodded. "Wipe your face, my dear—you've soot on your chin."

Louisa nodded, putting the money in the pocket of her dress and dabbing at her chin with a rag from the sink.

"I'll finish the peas, Anna." As they turned to go, Abba took note of the creases in Louisa's forehead and her voice turned sharp. "I will not abide self-pity, Louisa."

Louisa cast her eyes down to the floor. "Yes, Marmee."

"I know we do without—I know better than any of you just how much we do without. But I hope I never live to see the day when we have too little to share with those who are worse off than we are. God has blessed us in so many ways, and in return we must give with an open heart. And we don't do it for a reward, even though the Bible says we *will* be rewarded, tenfold."

Louisa nodded at the toe of her boot. The floor was bare and clean. She had swept it that morning.

Abba smiled faintly, finally letting her stern façade retreat just a little. "All right, off with you. When you return we will make the stew."

Outside, Louisa inhaled a giant gulp of air and imagined it could cleanse away all her selfish feelings.

Anna cinched the string on her bonnet. "What was that all about? I thought you said Marmee told you *not* to make the extra candles." They moved along the dusty path in the late morning sun. Lizzie's marmalade kitten poked its nose out of a shrub and watched them, slipping silently out after they had passed and following behind their footsteps.

"When I went to ask Marmee the other day I overheard a . . . tense discussion she was having with Father. It certainly wasn't meant for our ears."

"What did they say?"

"Some of it was muffled—listen to me, speaking so easily about eavesdropping on our parents!"

"Well, if they won't tell us the truth, what choice do we have?"

Louisa eyed Anna carefully. In recent days something had changed in her. The slightest whiff of haughtiness put an edge on her comments. It was so unlike the Anna she had always known. "Yes, perhaps that is true. Marmee questioned Father's choice to refuse work and accept charity from Mr. Emerson instead. He explained that his philosophy and beliefs were the very foundation of his character—that violating them was . . . well, out of the question."

Anna said nothing but exhaled sharply as they approached the lane where the Parkers lived.

"So, as I was not going to interrupt the discussion, I crept back down the hallway the way I came. Certainly we can*not* afford to give candles away, and I thought I would try to be the voice of reason on Marmee's behalf."

"No chance of reason when it comes to money in this family," Anna said, exasperated. "Father doesn't think of it at all, and Marmee gives it away as fast as we can get it."

"One thing's certain," Louisa said, pointing to Anna's pocket. "That rag money won't get us more than a half-pound of flour."

Anna sighed. "I know."

Louisa couldn't bear the guilt that weighed on her heart. She stopped in the road and turned to her sister. "You know, Anna, there is that money I've been saving back for Boston. It just doesn't seem right—"

"Louisa Alcott, don't you say it." Anna's voice was fierce as she fixed her eyes on her sister. "That is *your* money, and I won't let you chip away at it. You'll never get to Boston without it. I won't even discuss it."

Louisa opened her mouth to protest as they approached the Parkers' house. Anna shut her up by raising her palm to their friends. "Hello, Mrs. Parker! Hello, Margaret!"

The women, future mother and daughter-in-law, sat on the porch sipping cold tea. The humidity was already thick in the air—anyone could see it would be a sweltering day. Anna and Louisa lingered a moment to join their conversation about the details of Margaret's trousseau. Both she and Mrs. Parker looked uneasy. They were just beginning the process of forming a friendship based on mutual adoration of the same man—for very different reasons. They seemed relieved to be interrupted.

"Miss Louisa, you're of at least reasonable intelligence," Mrs. Parker said, turning to her. She was a birdlike woman with a pointed nose and fragile-looking wrists. "I heard about your book—well done. Tell me, what do you think of this crinoline business? I myself think they are outrageous."

Louisa smiled at what Mrs. Parker clearly believed to be her neutral presentation of the topic. "I must agree that they certainly aren't practical. I've heard appalling stories about the largest ones overturning in a brisk breeze, exposing the lady's petticoats. Why do you ask, Mrs. Parker?"

"My future daughter-in-law was just telling me how much she admired the fashion. Taste is a curious thing, I suppose."

Margaret's eyes flashed with anger and she opened her mouth to respond.

Anna, always aware, always nimble, spoke just in time to smooth Margaret's quills. "Crinolines are very dignified, though—you must admit. Of course, I wouldn't want to wear one to weed the garden, but I can't imagine wearing anything else to the theater or a dance." She laughed. "That is, if I ever went to a dance, a crinoline is what I would want to wear. Wouldn't you agree, Margaret?"

Margaret looked up at Anna, the flush subsiding from her cheeks. "Yes. That is what I meant, of course. You see these things in the ladies' books, but we know they aren't meant to be worn all the time. Only for special occasions."

Mrs. Parker nodded. "I see. Well, that seems reasonable enough. I suppose you feel one of these special occasions might arise in association with the wedding?"

Margaret nodded, the blond coils of her hair trembling from her exertion at keeping her temper. Louisa watched in awe. Once again Anna was three steps ahead of her. Louisa hadn't picked up on the subterranean tension between the two until it nearly exploded. Her mind had been on other things.

"I suppose that is acceptable. I will speak to your mother about it. Heaven knows your parents won't be able to afford it." Anna put her hand inconspicuously on Margaret's back, willing her not to take the bait. "But with Mr. Parker's assistance, we should be able to make it so."

Louisa observed that the women's appearances had little in common. Mrs. Parker was stern and almost disturbingly thin, as if she believed any additional tissue to be a frivolity. Margaret was plump and fleshy, and her faded dress stretched to contain her curves. Louisa wondered if Mrs. Parker was offended that her son had chosen someone so unlike herself as his wife. Or perhaps it was that one could not look at Margaret without the mind drifting, however briefly, to the more carnal aspects of marriage. Louisa thought of the skin of Joseph's neck that sloped along the top of his collar, brown from the sun with a narrow white strip along his hairline. As soon as the image appeared, she banished it, recoiling. Perhaps it was all the heat that was making her behave so queerly.

The sisters said their good-byes to Mrs. Parker and Margaret, and turned down Washington Street toward the shops. When they entered Singer Dry Goods, the bell above the door jangled, summoning Joseph from the back room. Louisa couldn't help but be buoyed by the smell of cinnamon and nutmeg that permeated the shop.

"Well, it's the Misses Alcott. Good morning." He wore a half-apron around his waist, and a pair of dusty boots. His face was pink and the tips of his ears looked tender. "What brings you here today?"

Louisa felt her voice wither in her throat like a cluster of drying leaves and it filled her with frustration. She had been around plenty of young men as a girl and thought nothing of it. In fact, she'd always *preferred* the company of boys over other girls—boys loved to run and shout; they carried pocketknives and knew how to coax shad and speckled trout out of the river. What could girls do that compared with that? So what was it about *this* young man that made her so nervous?

Anna squared her shoulders and placed the rag money on the counter with all the dignity she could muster.

"We'll be needing some flour, if it's not too much trouble."

"No trouble at all." He wiped his hands on a cloth. "How much would you like?"

"Well, you see," she began, clearing her throat to eke out the lie. "We'd already walked halfway here when I realized I forgot my purse. This is just what I had in my pocket." She slid the coins toward him. "Will it stretch to cover a few pounds?"

"Well," Joseph stalled. "Ah . . . let me see what I can do." He disappeared behind the canvas curtain between the front of the store and the back room. Anna grimaced, and Louisa gave her a weak smile.

A moment later Joseph reappeared, ten pounds of flour in a cloth sack cinched closed with twine. "Here we are. Is there anything else I can get you today?"

Anna's mouth made a small red circle. "Surely ten pounds of flour costs more than what is here on the counter."

"Well, it's your lucky day. We are having a sale." He winked at the sisters, his hands on his hips.

Louisa twisted her mouth to the side. To stand in the shadow of his pity, to see his self-satisfied ease, transformed her shame into fury. Stepping up to the counter, she asked, "How much is the discount?"

"What's that?" Joseph asked, busying himself with sliding the coins into his palm and dropping them into the sections of the drawer.

"The sale. What percentage have you deducted from the total cost?"

He looked uneasily between the two of them and rubbed his palms together. "Ah, I've never been one for math. It all works out in the end—that's what my father always says."

"Well," Anna said, shoving in front of Louisa to take the flour. "I'm glad we didn't wait until tomorrow to come."

Louisa pushed her sister's hand away from the bag. "Anna, we can't take this." She turned back to Joseph. "You are generous, but we cannot accept charity."

"Please don't think of it as charity. Anna forgot her purse—she said so herself. You can make up for it next time."

Louisa sighed. "Anna doesn't even own a purse." In her peripheral vision she saw Anna close her eyes, radiating embarrassment. "I suppose it's all over town that we can't pay for things. Well, I won't be pitied." Her voice had grown louder and two elderly women examining folded cotton scraps stopped and looked in their direction.

"Louisa, please," Anna hissed into Louisa's ear. "You are making a scene." She composed her face and turned back to the counter. "Thank you, Joseph. We will, of course, pay the balance next week." She clamped her hand on Louisa's forearm and wrenched her toward the door, the sack of flour perched on her hip like a baby.

They were a hundred yards down the lane when he came running up behind them. He put his hand on Louisa's shoulder and turned her to face him.

"Here." He held up a yellow paper and then pressed it into her hand. "This is what you owe. You can pay it next time you come in. Do you understand? It's not charity." Eagerness raised the pitch of his voice and his eyes searched her face for pardon.

Louisa stared at him a moment, and when no words would come she nodded. She tried to call up the righteousness that had propelled her to anger a moment before, but the weight of his palm on her shoulder had caused it to evaporate.

"Agreed?" he asked, his forehead still creased with concern.

"Yes."

"All right." He nodded as if that settled the matter and turned back toward the store. "Good afternoon, ladies."

"Good afternoon," Anna called. Louisa felt the oxygen coming back into her brain. Anna twisted her lips into a coy smile. "Well, he was certainly worried about upsetting *you*."

Louisa gave her a blank look.

"My brilliant sister, the idiot. *He likes you.*"

In the evening the family sat in the parlor. A book lay facedown and open over Bronson's knee like a tent. He stared into the fire. The expression on his face had in Louisa's mind always been associated with *silence*, from the first time the word's sibilant pronunciation skated across her tongue. As a little girl she had asked him about it.

"Father," she whispered, appearing at the side of his chair, twisting the end of her braid between her fingers. "Why do you stare so?"

He had turned to her with a startled look on his face, his eyes softening into his temples as his mind returned to the present and he recognized this sprite as his daughter. "My child, I am thinking about grand ideas, enormous ideas with a collection of smaller ideas inside them. And so I must be still to allow my mind to work."

"But you are so quiet."

"My body and voice are silent. But the noise inside my head is like a carnival. A cacophony."

Louisa had nodded, solemn. "What is *cacophony*?"

"Tomorrow, my dear. I will tell you all about it tomorrow." He had taken her on his knee and she watched him fade back into his faraway place. She stared at the fire then and yearned for some grand ideas of her own, but all she could think of was a hand mirror she'd seen that day at school. Rebecca Carson, a clerk's daughter, held it in her palm as the other girls crowded around her to look, the silver flowers etched along its handle glinting in the sun. Louisa had wanted to touch it but stayed behind the other girls, her hands pressed to her sides. Knowing the pretty little mirror existed filled her with a kind of grief she had never known before. Something so exquisite was in the world, and she would never, ever be able to have it. Sitting on Bronson's knee, she held fast to her whimper until it died in her throat.

And now here she was so many years later, and she understood little more about the workings of her father's mind. She turned her needlework on her lap and smoothed the stitches of the nosegay she was embroidering on a handkerchief. A lady in Boston who knew Mrs. Emerson bought them by the dozen. Anna and Abba sat beside her knitting caps for the newborn babies in town. Lizzie sat near the fire at Abba's insistence to avoid a chill, though the balmy August night held little chance of that.

Suddenly May galloped into the room, her voice bursting through the peaceful parlor.

"Catherine Singer is having her birthday! She is turning fifteen, and guess where her father gave her permission to go?"

"May," Abba scolded. "Please don't shout."

"It's the circus, Marmee. She is going to the circus in Keene, and she has invited me and Anna and Louisa—I mean, Anna and Louisa and me—along. And Lizzie too, if she is well enough. May we go? Please, Marmee?"

Lizzie snapped her book closed and pressed it to her chest. "The circus?" She exhaled a plaintive sigh that tugged at Louisa's heart. "I have always wanted to see the circus."

Abba looked at Lizzie in surprise and then turned to May. "My dear, you know how I feel about those dreadful displays. The people and animals are filthy, they travel from place to place doing so many . . . unnatural things."

"But . . . everyone from town will be there."

"Everyone? Is that so."

"Well, everyone who is anyone, of course. I simply *must* go."

An amused smile flashed across Abba's face. "I see. Well, only if your sisters go with you."

"Does that mean," Lizzie ventured tentatively, "that *I* may go along?" She reached into a basket on the hearth and removed a pair of tattered slippers, edging on her knees to the foot of Bronson's chair, and placed them gently on his feet. His gaze never wavered from the fire.

Abba grimaced. "Oh, my darling, I didn't mean . . . Well, I was thinking of Anna and Louisa. I fear you aren't well enough for a long journey in an open carriage."

Lizzie's face fell, her eyes filling as she looked away. "Of course. I suppose I would ruin everyone's fun if I were to have a spell."

Louisa watched her carefully, then looked at Anna. She could see from her older sister's expression that they shared a common thought.

"That's nonsense, Lizzie," Louisa said. "I think you're well enough for an afternoon—and whose health can't be improved by fresh air and a day out with friends? Please, Marmee—reconsider. Lizzie can accompany May."

Abba clutched her hands together in her lap. "I don't know. . . . Let me think about it."

Lizzie gave Abba a pleading look and Louisa felt a surge of compassion. It was true that as a girl Lizzie hadn't loved to run and play like her sisters, but when had she ever been given the chance? Abba held on to her so tightly, protecting her, limiting her exposure to the world. It was important to Abba to be needed.

"Marmee, you are too protective. Lizzie is not a child!"

"Louisa, that's enough. I said I will consider it."

"What is there to consider? As an adult she should not *need* your permission."

"*Louisa.*" Anna's mouth was agape. "Do not be insolent. You've made your view clear. Now, leave off. Marmee, forgive her. You know how her mouth can run away from her." Louisa glared at Anna.

Abba looked silently between her two older daughters and then over at Lizzie, whose eyes were trained on her lap. "I hope I never see the day when my protection and care are unwelcome."

Louisa's righteousness subsided and remorse took its place. "Oh, Marmee, I'm sorry. It is only my passion getting in the way of my mind again. You know we would be lost without you."

Abba gave her a steely expression and sighed. She turned to May. "As to the general outing, I could not consent unless your older sisters accompanied you."

"Oh," Anna broke in. "Please don't ask it. I have so little freedom as it is, and Saturdays are my only day . . ." May turned to her, her hands clasped beatifically.

"When is the party, May?" Louisa bristled. May often asked for, and got, all the things she wanted.

"Next Saturday."

Anna relaxed. "Then I cannot go. I've promised Margaret I will help her shop for fabric."

"Louy, then," May said, turning to her. "My dear, dear, lovely older sister."

Louisa rolled her eyes. "May, I do not wish to spend my Saturday with a bunch of children and smelly elephants."

"*Marmee*," May squealed in desperation. She made her final desperate appeal. "Last year, Rose Wilson had the tiniest of fevers and her mother made her stay home from the school picnic. She missed out on everything, and all the other girls stopped talking to her. She told me later she would rather have gone to the picnic and died the next day than suffer the ostrich-iza . . . ostrich-era . . ."

A grin burst through Louisa's worried expression. "May, do you mean to say *ostracism*?"

She looked puzzled. "You mean it has nothing at all to do with the bird?"

Anna giggled beside her and placed her arm across May's shoulders. "No, nothing at all."

"Well, anyway, they did give her an os-tra-cism, and—"

Louisa broke in. "Oh, for *heaven's* sake!" She looked at Abba, whose dour demeanor had been washed away by May's charm. Perhaps because she was younger, perhaps because she was the prettiest, the one who demanded that the world take notice of her, May seemed to represent for Abba the possibility that the family might one day transcend its humble circumstances. Louisa knew her mother had come from a family of Sewalls and Quincys—good New England stock with a history and station. Abba's own marriage had been an imprudent match in the eyes of her family, and she liked to boast of this fact, as proof, Louisa supposed, that the things of the world meant nothing to her. Yet it was plain to see that she had ambitions for her youngest daughter.

Louisa ventured tentatively back to the subject she'd left off, as if it were a scab she couldn't help but pick. "Abba, if I agree, then Lizzie may come along as well?" Lizzie sat forward, clutching at the book in her lap, the ends of her fingers gone white with the pressure.

"That I cannot promise. We must wait until next Saturday morning to see that she is feeling strong and the weather is fair."

Lizzie turned to Louisa. "I am feeling quite strong now—I'm *sure* I will be well."

Abba rubbed her arm. "We will see, my darling."

Louisa gave her youngest sister a weary look. "Very well, May. You have won your prize. I'll go with you to Keene."

May squealed and clapped her hands, then danced around the room to kiss her mother and each of her sisters on the cheek.

"May, how will you girls travel to Keene?" Abba asked.

"Ah, I can't believe I forgot to tell you the *best* part," she said, placing her palm on her chest for dramatic effect. "We will travel in Catherine's father's new carriage. Her brother will drive us."

"Joseph?" Anna said with eyebrows raised. She looked coyly at Louisa.

Louisa dropped her eyes to the fabric pinched between her fingers.

Abba's eyes darted from Anna to Louisa, instantly sensing what passed between them. "Has this information helped ease your reluctance to spend an afternoon with—what was it you said? 'Children and smelly elephants'?"

Anna nodded. "Yes, I believe that *is* what she said."

Louisa tipped her nose toward the ceiling. "Not in the slightest. If anything, I have something else to dread."

Lizzie looked worriedly at Louisa.

"Oh, don't worry, Lizzie. Joseph Singer may be the most presumptuous, disagreeable—"

Anna cut her off, laughing. "Take care not to say anything you'll regret, Louisa."

"—insufferable young man," she continued, "but I wouldn't let *that* stand in the way of making sure you get to see the circus."

Lizzie beamed.

"Provided you are well," Abba cautioned, as she placed her hand on Lizzie's. "Provided the day is warm and dry."

May pirouetted around the parlor. Passing the table next to Bronson's chair, her knee upset his saucer, and the lukewarm tea splashed across his lap. He jumped to his feet and, for the first time since they'd settled in the parlor two hours before, acknowledged the existence of his family.

"What the *devil* is going on?" he barked.

"May has prevailed upon Louisa to perform the chore of chaperoning her to the circus with her friends," Abba said, accustomed to Bronson's tendency to arrive late to conversations taking place right in front of him. She looked knowingly at Anna, all the while maintaining the rhythm of her knitting needles. "But we do not believe Louisa will suffer *over*much."

The acre on which Nicholas Sutton's partially constructed house stood had a rocky western edge and sloped away from the river, cresting in a broad hill. The site was a quarter mile up River Road from the much larger property where Nicholas had grown up, the home where his parents and sister still lived, shaded by a stand of beech trees edging the meadow where their horses nosed the grass in fair weather.

June had been a productive month, as Nicholas had explained to Anna at the swimming party. With his father's help, as well as Joseph and Samuel's, Nicholas had drawn up plans for the house, a two-story Italianate like the ones springing up all over Boston. By the first day of summer they'd raised the frame and amassed all the materials needed to complete the job—shingles for the roof, glass for the windows, and wood for the trim. If the weather cooperated, Nicholas said he thought he'd be finished by summer's end.

Anna and Louisa decided to walk the long way to the Elmwood Inn for rehearsal on Friday morning, heading west toward the river instead of northwest toward Washington Square, so they might walk by and see the project for themselves.

They heard hammering and the wheezing rasp of a saw before the house came into view. Then they passed a stand of trees and it appeared. The sun shining between the ribs of the frame made a shadow like a railroad track across the ground. Samuel noticed the girls first. He stood at the base of a tall ladder leaned against the side of the house, holding it steady for Nicholas, who was perched on the top rung hammering a board into place.

"Good morning," Samuel said with a friendly nod meant to substitute for a wave. He didn't take his hands from the ladder.

"Isn't it?" Anna said. "I try to imprint this sunshine in my mind and save it for January. It never does seem to work, though." Samuel smiled.

"Ho, there!" Nicholas called from above, waving his hammer. "Where are the pretty ladies off to today?"

Louisa cupped her hands around her mouth and shouted, "To the same place you should be going. Rehearsal."

"Rehearsal! Of course!" Nicholas called down. "We were just about to finish up here and head over."

Louisa laughed, shielding her eyes from the sun. "Yes, I've no doubt of that. All the same, perhaps it *is* fortunate we happened to pass by."

Nicholas affected the mien of the wrongly accused. "I hope you don't mean to imply we *forgot* about rehearsal."

"Oh, never." Louisa and Anna giggled.

Nicholas held his hammer to his breast. "And disobey our commanding officer? We wouldn't think of it."

"I should hope not," Anna said. "Louisa does not look kindly on dissent in the ranks."

They heard a rhythmic thudding above as Joseph made his way across the open slats in the roof to their side of the house. He scuttled on all fours like a crab, his boots on one slat and his palms on another, moving two boards at a time. Louisa felt her body tense up when he came into view. It was thrilling to see him in the yellow morning light, his shirt cuffs rolled up to the elbows, his skin brown. But just behind the excitement was her dread of what it all could mean.

He peered down at them. "What's all this racket over here?"

"Joe, I was just explaining to the young ladies that we fully intended to repair to rehearsal at the designated time."

"Oh, yes," said Joseph, catching on. "We planned to arrive just when we were told."

"And what time was that?" Louisa asked, willing confidence into her voice.

"Why," Joseph replied, "the very time you instructed and not a second later. You are the director after all, Miss Louisa. Your word is law."

Louisa relished the praise a moment, then rolled her eyes. "Yes, but *what* time was it?"

Joseph looked at his friend. "Well, that would be Nick's department. I believe we put *you* in charge of the schedule."

"No, sir. It was Mr. Parker," Nicholas replied, then shouted down, solemnly shaking his head. "Samuel is in charge of all appointments."

Samuel chuckled, looking first at Louisa and Anna and then tipping his head up toward his accuser. "It seems unwise to sell a man down the river when he is holding your ladder, friend."

Nicholas pressed his lips into a line. "That's a good point, lad. Ladies, it was Joseph. He has a corrupting influence on us all, and I hope you'll forgive our weak wills."

Joseph shifted his weight onto his heels to free his hands, one of which held a hammer. He smiled, a half-dozen nails glinting between his teeth. "Look—no hands."

Louisa gasped. "Are you soft in the head, Joseph Singer?"

He thought for a moment. "Yes, that is quite likely. But what does that have to do with the matter at hand?"

"You are two stories up, teetering like an inebriate. One gust of wind and you'd be finished. Will you please be careful?"

"For you, Miss Louisa? Anything. We'll even come down right now and walk with you the rest of the way to the inn."

"Splendid," Anna said, and they waited as the boys made their way down the creaking ladder.

I don't waste ink in poetry and pages of rubbish now. I've begun to live, and have no time for sentimental musing.

—*Louisa May Alcott: Her Life, Letters, and Journals*

Chapter Eight

Louisa woke in the early morning to a pale sky and the whisper of raindrops. In the half-light, her mind cluttered with the images of a retreating dream, she felt a pang of disappointment. Surely Abba would now insist on Lizzie staying home. She sat up and swung her feet to the floor, pulling the drape aside to assess the weather. The rain was steady, gaining strength. Perhaps none of them would go to the circus. Anna slept soundly in the bed next to her, her hair fanned across her face and the cotton blanket. Louisa rose and descended to the kitchen to put on the water for tea.

As it boiled, the others rose. Bronson went into his study. Anna scoured the floor, then dressed and left to meet Margaret in town. Abba entered the kitchen and put on a pot to cook down plums for jam.

Louisa dreaded asking the question she felt she already knew the answer to. "Marmee, where is Lizzie?"

Abba clucked sympathetically as she sliced the plums and pried out the stones. "Still in bed, I fear. She was restless in the night—perhaps she was overwrought with the possibility of coming with you girls—and did not sleep well. We shouldn't have gotten her hopes up. By the looks of that rain, none of you may be going."

Poor Lizzie, Louisa thought.

By noon the rain had subsided but Lizzie remained in bed in the room she shared with May. Louisa knocked softly on the door and stuck her head inside. Lizzie wore a nightgown cinched around her collarbone with a blue ribbon and sat in bed reading a book, a stack of pillows propping her up.

"How is my little patient?" Louisa asked, crossing the room to sit on the edge of the bed.

Lizzie sighed and closed the book over her finger to hold her place. "Sleepy. And more than a little disappointed. I'm sorry to have caused all this trouble."

Louisa put her hand on Lizzie's. "I only wish you could come. Are you sure Marmee isn't being a little too cautious?"

Lizzie shrugged. "I feel fine, but I know she is right that I tire easily. Keene *is* a long carriage ride away. I think it is best that I stay home." Lizzie reached toward the floor and pulled her orange kitten into her lap. "Say you will wave hello to the tigers for Ginger and me. I promised her I'd tell her all about her wild ancestors." Since Louisa had first seen Ginger poking her head out of Lizzie's apron, the kitten had grown lanky, her fine puff of fur now sleek.

"I promise, my dear, if you're sure you won't try to come? Wouldn't you like to have just a *little* adventure?"

Lizzie looked at Louisa a moment, as if mulling this over. Finally, she shook her head, though her eyes were a little sad. "There is nothing I love better than home, wherever home happens to be."

Louisa nodded. "Then I will leave you to it. Good-bye, Ginger." Louisa rubbed the kitten's ears. "I'll bring you both a souvenir."

. . .

Louisa and May sat down to eat a light luncheon before walking into town to join Joseph and Catherine. May flitted about the room, scarcely ingesting a bite.

Exasperated, Abba took her by the waist and guided her into a chair. "Abigail May, you *must* eat something, or you will pass out from hunger somewhere along the road."

Afterward, they set out for the Singers' store. The sky remained gloomy but the rain held off, and Louisa couldn't help feeling cheerful on her sister's behalf, though at the same time her heart pounded in her ears. What would she and Joseph say to each other?

They were a few minutes early coming up the road. Catherine sat on a bench in front of the store in a new dress, her hair pulled tightly away from her face. Her brow was just like Joseph's—fair and freckled—but her hair was darker, arranged for this special occasion in intricate coils just behind her ears. May sighed reflexively when she saw the ribbon edging on Catherine's dress. It was a blinding white, the way only new clothes can be. The girls began a vigorous conversation about the other young people from town they expected to see at the circus. Louisa decided to go inside the store to find Joseph. She expected to hear the jangle of the bell when she entered, but the door slipped open silently. She looked up to see the bell bent off its bracket, as if it had been broken when someone slammed the door. No one was behind the counter. She walked toward the curtained doorway that led to the back room but stopped short when she heard Joseph's voice take on a sharp tone.

"Isn't there any other way?"

"I don't see one. There just isn't time."

"So that is how it will be? 'The sins of the father are to be laid upon the children'?"

"You've let your anger bring you so low you'd use the Bible—"

"I was thinking of Shakespeare, Father. *The Merchant of Venice.*"

It was silent for a moment then. Louisa heard a rustling, the scrape of a stool across the worn planks of the floor.

"Sit down, Father. Rest a moment. I'm sorry for what I said."

"You think I don't know God will judge me for my sins? Why don't you leave it to Him and let it be? Think of your sister, Joseph. If she had inherited her mother's measured temperament, I would not worry. But I'm afraid she is just like her father—frivolous, impulsive. Easily led astray. We have the chance to protect her. We must take it."

"We? You mean *I* must take it—"

"I cannot stop death from coming for me, boy. I can do many things, but I cannot do that."

Louisa backed quietly toward the door, opened it, and shook it on its hinges so the bell, mangled as it was, produced a small sound. The voices in the back room stopped. She heard a shuffling of feet and Joseph emerged.

"Well, then. Are we all set to go?" Joseph's jaw moved slightly under his skin as he worked deliberately to relax his expression.

Louisa smiled at him with bare kindness for the first time. There was no pride in it, no defensive edge like before, when she'd felt overwhelmed by the competing desires to be near him and not to let him know that she thought of him at all. Hearing his conversation with his father broke through all that. He looked calm enough now, but instinctively she knew he was writhing inside, like a butterfly on a pin before the life goes out of it.

"Yes, before our sisters start walking to Keene on their own." She watched him gathering his things—two blankets for their feet in case of a chill, umbrellas, a bag of lemon candies from one of the glass jars behind the counter. She wondered if he thought of her as his friend. She wanted very much to be his friend just then.

Out behind the store, Mr. Singer's new phaeton rocked back and forth on its wheels as its two harnessed horses shifted in place, anxious to move. Joseph stretched open the extension-top and secured it in place. It was covered in fine leather dyed the blue of a church hymnal.

He felt along the harness, making sure it was secure, then smoothed his hand over the blond mane of one of the horses. "This here's Juliet, and that one's Romeo. But we call the back half of Romeo 'President Pierce.'"

Louisa laughed and the girls rolled their eyes. To them, nothing was duller than politics, and they were bored to death by the recent griping about how the first president to hail from New Hampshire seemed to be protecting the interests of slave owners over the good people of New England.

Joseph swung the half-moon–shaped door open and gestured for the Alcott sisters to climb into the more comfortable and well-covered seats in the rear. May grinned and nearly bounced inside. Louisa realized May probably had not ever been in a carriage this nice, then admitted to herself she hadn't either. Louisa moved to climb in after May but paused when Catherine conspicuously cleared her throat.

"I believe since it is *my* birthday, I should sit in the rear. This *is* a new dress, after all, and if it rains again, there will be mud." She gestured toward Louisa's dress, which she and Anna had worked on into the early morning hours, sewing on a new flounce cut from some leftover cloth, scrubbing stains along the hem out with a worn wire brush. "You dress is so old, you won't mind, will you?"

Before she could stop herself, she turned to look at Joseph, her eyebrows arched. He closed his eyes and shook his head. "Forgive my sister. Catherine, these are our *guests*."

May sat in the shadow of the carriage with her hands clasped, silently pleading with Louisa not to make a scene.

"Of course I don't mind," Louisa replied, plastering a smile on her face and moving out of the way. Her nerves were returning and she was uncertain again. Catherine climbed in next to May and settled her skirts around her knees. Joseph offered Louisa his hand to help her climb over the wheel into the front seat. She felt a fluttering in her chest as their hands touched, and tried to avoid his eyes. He seemed unfazed, reminding her to tuck her hem behind her boots so that it did not get caught in the spokes of the wheel. Louisa watched him climb in after her and take up the reins. Her eye followed the line of his coat, where it was faded and frayed along the collar.

They started off, lurching and chugging down Main Street. This was the long way around to the road that led out of town, but Catherine and May begged Joseph to take it so that any of their friends who happened to pass by would see the manner in which they were traveling.

"This is a lovely carriage," May said, her breath in her voice. She ran her hand along the buff-colored seat, touched the gold ties that held the drapes up.

"It is, isn't it?" Joseph said. And then he half muttered, "It's a shame we'll have to give it back soon."

Catherine whipped her head in his direction. "Give it *back*? What do you mean?"

"Carriages aren't free, my sister. One must pay for them."

"But can't Father pay—"

"I shouldn't have said a thing. Let's not talk of family matters now. Besides, it's your birthday! This is a celebration!"

Louisa sat turned sideways. She could see Catherine's face in profile and recognized the familiar pouted lips made by one who still had the emotions of a girl, despite looking very much the part of a young lady. May had made the very same expression days before when begging to come on this trip.

"Must we walk everywhere from now on?" Catherine whined.

Joseph slowed the horses to a stop so that he could turn and look her square in the eyes. Louisa and May shifted uncomfortably. "I asked you not to talk of family matters now. I will ask you once more, and then I will turn us around and take our friends home. You are too old now to behave in this way. Do you understand me?"

Catherine looked down at her lap and nodded.

"Right then. Let's go." Joseph started off again and they rode along in silence. Louisa could tell by the look of the sky that the weather would taunt them all day. A placid blue seemed now to be breaking through the clouds, but a slate-colored cloud loomed on the horizon like a steamship chugging slowly across the ocean. It was lovely to ride along in silence, though this moment of silence felt charged with anticipation. She realized she spent much of her life searching for quiet, trying to determine when she would next have the chance to sink into its intoxicating comfort. Even when she was with other people—especially when she was with other people.

May, on the other hand, could not abide silence. It was true she loved to talk, but she was also sensitive to tension. She needed constant reassurance that the people in her vicinity were enjoying themselves so that she felt she had permission to enjoy herself too.

"How many elephants do you think they'll have?" May asked.

Catherine turned to May and watched her brother from the corner of her eye to discern when his anger had subsided. "Three or four at least. Have you ever seen one before?"

May shook her head.

"As big as you expect them to be, they'll be bigger. *I've* been to the circus lots of times, so I won't be surprised. But—"

Joseph smiled, in spite of himself. "'Lots of times' is an exaggeration, don't you think?"

She looked at him, a haughty expression turning down the corners of her mouth. "I'd rather walk the rest of the way than have you interrupting me every time I try to speak and ruining our good time. It is my *birthday,* after all."

Joseph held up a hand. "Fine, fine. Never mind." Louisa smiled. Catherine and May certainly seemed to have a few things in common.

They could smell the animals before they crossed into Keene, the acrid aroma of manure mixed with the smell of wet fur closed into train cars. The road into town sloped up and then down again, and when they crested the hill Catherine spotted the yellow flags on top of the circus tent. "There it is!" she cried, forgetting for a moment she meant to display a veteran's disinterest in the novelty of the day.

They descended into town and pulled the carriage into line behind the dozens of others parked outside an old barn. Joseph hopped down and circled around to Louisa, offering his hand to help her descend. Her stomach leapt when she allowed her eyes to meet his. His gaze was unflinching and he seemed to be searching her face, though she wondered at what he hoped to find there. She reached for his arm, her hands feeling constricted in their borrowed gloves.

They made their way across the field. To the left of the main tent stood an elephant, tied to an iron spike driven into the dirt. The beast siphoned water up his trunk, then extended it into the air and sprayed it across the bony ridge of his back. A cloud of flies circled the elephant's head and it flapped its ears like giant paper fans to shoo them away.

"What a beast," Joseph said, his eyes wide in admiration as they approached the animal. "Magnificent."

Louisa assessed the stake: a piece of iron six inches thick was all that stood between a jolly afternoon and a stampede. But the elephant didn't appear to be struggling against its constraints. "Look at his eyes," Louisa said. The lashes were long and pale. "They look like an old man's. Sad." She wanted to reach up and touch the leathery skin, but she was afraid.

Joseph pulled the gold chain connected to the watch in his vest pocket. "If we hurry we can catch the show starting in a few minutes. Or we can go see the rest of the animals and the marvels tent first, and see the later show."

"Now, now. Let's go now!" Catherine said, tugging his arm toward the main tent.

He grinned and turned to Louisa and May. "What do you say?"

May nodded vigorously.

"I am happy to oblige the birthday girl," Louisa said.

"All right. Let's find our seats." May took Louisa's arm and they followed Joseph and Catherine. A crowd amassed at the wide entrance as a few hundred people streamed up the hill from Keene's train station and the muddy lot where rows of carriages rocked slightly in the breeze. Catherine's father had purchased four tickets for the fifty-cent seats, which offered a better view than the spots in the pit that went for a quarter. They climbed the creaking steps of the hastily constructed stands to a bench about halfway up.

"Not too much higher," Joseph said, glancing toward the rail-less end of the row, which dropped off into the dark. "This is high enough."

Catherine scoffed but didn't argue. Joseph went in first, followed by his sister and May, with Louisa settling near the middle of the bench. She turned her attention to the bright center of the tent, where two men on stilts bobbed unsteadily in opposite directions around a circle that had been formed by plowing the earth up two feet high all around. One by one they lit tall torches that marked the perimeter of the ring. In the far corner, half in shadow, a steam trumpet blared out a hypnotic song.

The fidgeting in the audience subsided, and they began to clap as they heard the music. Stagehands closed the flaps at the entrance of the tent, blocking out the last of the natural light. The torches burned a bright amber. Suddenly, off to the left, Louisa saw a flash of white. A small man, dressed in a white tunic and close-fitting trousers covered all over with large red dots, ran toward a springboard that catapulted him, tumbling through the air, into the ring. His head was covered with a cap made of the same dotted white fabric and he had a large black mustache and exaggerated eyebrows painted above his eyes.

The clown stood with his arms outstretched and the quiet audience broke into applause.

"Good afternoon, ladies and gentlemen and members of the colored population." Louisa glanced toward the pit, where a small cluster of black audience members stood. She noted that none of them sat in the stands. "I am Billy, but you can call me your fool for the afternoon."

The audience laughed. Billy turned toward the dark corner from which he had emerged and whistled. After a slight delay, a small pony cantered toward the ring and jumped over the earthen divider. The pony's mane was long and pale, like straw.

"Folks, this is Blind Jim, my trusty steed. He is mighty faithful, but he can't see his hoof in front of his face, if you see what I mean."

Blind Jim pranced in a circle around the clown, then stretched out his front hooves on the ground and lowered his head in a kind of bow. The audience clapped.

"How are you today, Blind Jim?" Billy asked. The pony nickered. "Is that so?"

The audience laughed.

"You know, Jim, I'm awful tired. What do you say we lie down a moment and have a little rest?"

Blind Jim didn't take a moment to think it over. He lowered his weight down onto his hindquarters and then rolled onto his side. He rested his cheek in the dirt and swished his tail a few times. "That's a good friend, Jim," Billy said. He lay down beside the horse, snuggling against its ribs so that the horse's left front leg draped across his shoulder in a kind of embrace. Catherine and May giggled, their hands over their mouths. A man sitting a few rows below them cupped his hands around his mouth and shouted, "Why don't you give him a kiss, Billy?"

Billy lifted himself up on his elbow and looked up at the dark stands, in the general direction of the voice. "What's that, sir?"

"I said, why don't you give your pony a kiss?"

"Is your wife there with you, sir?"

"Yes," the man shouted. "She's a fine woman too."

"Ma'am," said Billy, addressing the shrouded man's wife, "you have my sympathies."

The crowd guffawed. "I'm embarrassed to have to tell you this, sir," Billy said as he scooched back into Blind Jim's arms. "But the idea of a man kissing a pony is *ridiculous*." The laughter roared out again and then subsided.

After the clowns succeeded in warming up the audience, a woman rode into the ring bareback, her blond hair trailing loose behind her. She waved her arms and a team of horses loped into view. They pranced according to her demands and leapt through a ring of fire one by one. Next came the jugglers and a team of acrobats who swung and tumbled from lines erected in the peak of the tent. Finally a mournful song played on the steam trumpet, signaling the start of the main event. A small man in formal dress appeared followed by his assistants, two small boys, who pulled a wheeled platform supporting a shrouded box. The boys maneuvered the platform through the opening in the ring and pulled it to the center. Each took a corner of the black cloth that covered the box and pulled as they backed away, revealing an iron cage that contained a massive tiger. The animal blinked as its eyes adjusted to the light. It stood up on four paws the size of platters and began to pace the small confines of its cage.

Louisa felt her chest tighten. May clutched Louisa's hand and Louisa gave her sister's arm a reassuring pat. "It's all part of the show, May," she said, though she didn't sound convinced. She shot a furtive glance over at Joseph. His eyes were wide, but when he turned to look at her, he smiled. "It's all right," he mouthed.

They watched, thunderstruck, as the man opened the door to the cage and ushered the beast out. For the next ten minutes not one breath could be heard in the tent as the audience watched the tamer crack his whip, moving in circles around the tiger. At first the animal reared up on its hind legs, growling, but soon the tamer lulled it back onto all fours, then into a seated position. The tiger lay down, resting its massive head on its front paws. At last it rolled onto its back, exposing its white belly, and purred like a barn cat in a patch of sun. The tamer took a bow and the people leapt to their feet, cheering.

After the tiger was locked safely back in its cage, the assistants wheeled it away and opened the flaps at the entrance of the tent, revealing a triangle of daylight. The show was over. The party made its way down the steps along with the rest of the crowd. Exiting was a slow process, and Catherine and May grew impatient to see the remainder of the attractions. They obtained reluctant permission from Joseph to go off on their own and flitted away as Louisa and Joseph moved through the excited crowd.

Outside they traversed the perimeter of the tent to the back side, where a smaller tent stood, the sailcloth flaps that flanked its entrance undulating in the breeze. A sign on an easel read *Martin's Marvels*. Louisa looked up and saw that the dark cloud that had seemed so far away was now overtaking the sky. "Shall we go inside?"

A man with hair that sprung from his head in all directions like a mane greeted them and gestured to a semicircle of tables and a crowd of people moving slowly from one to the next. "Welcome, folks. Welcome to Martin's Marvels, where you will see things that will shock your mind and disturb your sense of the natural order. Be the first of your friends to see the pig-faced lady in her prettiest dress, the world's smallest man and his giantess wife, the 'two-headed nightingale' singing slave songs from her plantation in North Carolina. Ten cents, folks."

Joseph and Louisa looked at each other and raised their eyebrows. Finally she shrugged and Joseph fished two dimes from his pocket. As they passed, the man turned his attention to a group of boys filing in at the entrance. "One at a time, now, boys, one at a time. The half-woman isn't going anywhere—she can't move very fast without any legs." He chuckled. "Get out your dimes now, please."

First they passed a table with a basket of eggs. A man held one out to Louisa. "Miss, could you tell me what this is, please?"

She looked at him, uncertain. "An egg?"

"And, if you don't mind, where do eggs come from?"

"From chickens, sir."

"Since the egg came from a chicken, would you not expect to find a little yellow chick inside it?"

"Yes, sir, I would."

"Would you crack the egg open, please?"

Louisa shook her head. "The chick will die if you crack it open before it's ready."

"That so?" He looked steadily at her, then at Joseph, as if to challenge him to question the next bit. He slammed the egg too hard against the tabletop. Louisa winced, then reeled as a full-grown pigeon careened toward her face. Several ladies cried out as it swerved, teetering around the tent, then circled back and landed on the table, folding its wings and pecking at the seed the man sprinkled at its feet.

"Well, that's a dirty trick," Joseph said. "You should be more careful."

"I had no idea that was in there," the man said. He winked at them and grinned. Three of his front teeth were missing, and he stuck his tongue out at them through the gap.

Louisa moved closer to Joseph and he pulled her away to the next exhibit. A perfectly demure woman sat on a throne raised above the floor on a platform. She wore a vaguely rococo dress from the previous century, made of gold and burgundy brocade, and her waist was tightly corseted so that her bosom nearly spilled out at the top in a way that seemed obscene to the ladies in the tent, though they knew from paintings in museums and their grandmothers' stories that this had once been the fashion. Members of the crowd stood gaping at her, not because of her décolletage, but because every inch of the woman's skin was covered in silky black hair. It sprouted from the bridge of her nose, grew in tendrils from her ears, bristled along her shoulders. When she spoke, the people standing on either side of Joseph and Louisa reeled back.

"I am Madame Clofullia. Gaze upon me," she said, looking around. "I do not mind. I am a real woman, flesh and blood. I have a son. He is like me." She lifted the edge of her heavy skirt on one side and a small boy emerged from its dome. He wore a dusty black suit and his face was covered with hair the color of corn silk. He removed his hat and took a bow, then stood at his mother's side, clutching her downy hand.

"Sometimes I feel like life is one long string of exploitations," Louisa said. "Use or be used." Joseph had sensed that Louisa wanted to escape the disturbing sights of the marvels tent and suggested a walk. They headed out across the open field, their steps rustling crickets out of the grass and up into the air.

"I know what you mean."

"I listen to my father's friends talk about their ideas of what we *could* be, how we *could* live, and I feel hopeful. But then I go out into the world. I see a man putting these poor people on display for money. I hear that our own president agrees to let new states decide for themselves the question of slavery, when he should make their entrance into the Union contingent on an outright ban. It just doesn't end. So much needs to change."

"I think *we* will change it," Joseph said. "The men in your father's parlor—and don't misunderstand me, because I admire some of them more than anyone in the world—but all those men have done is talk and write, talk and write. Now it's time to act. It's going to be up to our generation to act."

"But how? So much of it seems to be human nature. Inevitable." Louisa was surprised to hear such a pessimistic statement come out of her mouth. Sometimes she felt so overwhelmed by managing her own existence, there wasn't anything left for other matters.

"That is why we have laws. Without them, the country becomes the sum of its citizens' impulses. We must make sure the laws represent the best of us, what we should always strive to be." The tall weeds and scrub of the field brushed his shins and fanned away.

"But in Georgia, the law says one man can own another."

"Then we must change the laws. Or break them. 'An unjust law is no law at all.'"

"Saint Augustine?" Louisa asked, smiling to herself that once again she had underestimated Joseph's knowledge of letters and ideas. "Do you mean you believe we will go to war?" She thought about that a moment. "I think I would like to fight. Do you think they would let me?"

Joseph smiled. "Those rednecks wouldn't stand a chance against you. But perhaps it won't come to that. There are other ways to take action. Do you know about what some folks have been doing over in Ohio? And right here in New Hampshire and Massachusetts? A secret transport operation. Helping slaves get to Canada." The expression on his face looked strangely familiar: eyebrows pulled high, mouth taut with the passion of his argument. It took her a moment to realize why she recognized it—it was just like an expression she'd seen in the mirror many times.

Louisa nodded. Everyone in Concord knew that Henry Thoreau was involved, though they never spoke of it. At night he guided the runaways through the dense woods, giving them food and finding them a place to hide when the daylight came. Most thought what he was doing was courageous but dangerous. He *was* breaking the law, after all, even if the law was wrong. Once, when she was about twelve, he took her out walking near his cabin to find where the scarlet tanagers were keeping their nest. The sun shining through the trees made a mottled pattern on the pine needle floor. Henry placed her palm on the cool, mossy side of a dead tree trunk.

"This is how they *know*," he'd said.

She'd lost her last baby molar the night before and the tip of her tongue rooted around in the empty space. "Know what?"

"Which way is north."

Joseph put his hand on her elbow and it wrenched her back to the present. "The most dangerous thing we can believe is that we are not the authors of our fate. God gave us reason, conscience. We must use it. To say that our life, our world, just *is* the way that it is, that we do not play a part—I think it is the worst kind of cowardice."

Dark circles began to appear along Joseph's shoulders. The light shifted like a lamp turning down and the sky opened. They turned around to see how far they had walked. The tent was a hundred yards away, and they saw the man at the entrance pull the flaps closed and cinch the rope to keep the wind and water out. The crowd that hadn't made it inside in time huddled just inside the entrance to the tent of marvels. Louisa felt goose bumps crawl across the back of her neck as the wind whipped over it. Joseph looked east. A gray barn slumped against a hill, its roof sinking in the middle from neglect. He motioned to her and they ran toward it. She felt the heels of her boots sinking into the mud and arched her feet as high as she could to run on her toes.

The wet hay in the doorway was slick beneath her feet, but a few steps inside, it was dry and rustled as they walked over it. Her hair was soaked through under her flimsy bonnet and she felt droplets crawling along her scalp. She longed to unfasten her chignon and shake the water out but she was self-conscious.

"Where do you suppose our sisters are?" Louisa asked, looking out across the field to the circus tent.

"Somewhere where their curls will stay dry." Joseph sat on an over-turned crate and pulled an apple from his pocket. Louisa realized she was ravenous. He plucked his knife from his other pocket and unfolded it, pressing the blade into the fruit's russet skin. "Would you like some?"

She felt suddenly alarmed by how comfortable she felt around him and busied herself with untying her bonnet. Throughout the day they had become increasingly easy around each other. Louisa had forgotten to monitor her words and expressions. She wondered if she had grown too familiar with him. "No, thank you."

He grinned. "Yes, you would. I *saw* you looking at it."

Louisa felt her cheeks flush and turned away. "You must be mistaken."

"You are a puzzle to me, Miss Louisa. It seems we circle each other, become friends, speak openly . . ." He carved the core out of each of the four quarters. The rain droned on outside, forcing him to raise his voice to be heard. "But then—suddenly, it seems to me—you pull away. And it's as if we are strangers again."

He was exactly right, of course. She didn't know what to say and didn't dare look back at him.

"There's only one thing for me to do, and that's to stop paying any attention to the things you say." He pulled another crate from the stack and set it on the floor next to his, then pointed at it. "Sit," he ordered, an amused smile on his face.

Louisa smiled in spite of herself and relented. When she lowered herself onto the crate, she felt the small of her back press into the damp fabric of her dress. She suppressed a shiver. "It's only that . . ." She scanned his face and noticed a bump on the bridge of his nose where he must have broken it as a child. She longed to touch it. "I believe you are a puzzle to me as well."

He handed her a piece of the apple. "What do you want to know?"

She chewed a fragrant bite. "What were you like as a boy?"

"Just about the same, I suppose. Only shorter." He grinned.

"I think that grin comes from the devil himself."

"My mother used to say that to me. She never could stay mad if I was smiling at her. Even the time I stomped out all the beets in her garden. I disliked beets more than any other food. Still do."

Louisa hesitated. "What happened to her? Your mother."

"I was to have another sister. When Catherine was just three. But our mother died giving birth to her and the baby died a few days later. Her name was Elizabeth." He examined his palms. "Like my mother."

She felt something open in her chest and her eyes grew damp. "Forgive me—I shouldn't have intruded. . . ."

He shook his head. "It was a long time ago."

Louisa didn't know what to say. She put her hands on her knees, then clasped them together, worrying the skin around her thumb-nails.

He touched her hand. "Anything else you'd like to know?" She looked up into his eyes. They seemed almost to be challenging her.

"I think I know it all now."

Joseph hesitated, his forehead creased. "You nearly do, though there *is* something else. . . ."

"Nearly is just fine, I think," Louisa said, dropping her gaze back to her lap, hoping to ease his worries.

The rain pummeled the side of the barn; the noise was deafening. They sat so close together their shoulders nearly touched. Joseph leaned toward her and she felt the fabric of his shirt make contact with her sleeve. He turned to face her, then reached up and swept his index finger across her cheek, along her earlobe, down her hairline to the nape of her neck. The toes of his shoes touched the outside edge of her left boot. She kept her eyes on the dark shape they made in the hay.

"Are you cold, Louisa?"

She tried to breathe. "No," she whispered, just as a chilly shiver cascaded down her back. She thought of the poem: *This is the touch of my lips to yours . . . this is the murmur of yearning.*

Joseph grinned again, amused by her stubbornness, and she looked up at him. A moment of delicious tension passed and she thought of the circus tumblers suspended in midair, their bodies arched, coiled like springs.

Joseph took a breath and spoke. "I wonder, do you think . . ." He looked away, raked his fingers through his hair, then looked back at Louisa. "Do you think I might kiss you?"

Her eyes widened and she felt her body arch away from him before her mind had time to catch up. "This is . . . I . . ." she fumbled, trying to regain her footing.

Joseph's face fell and contrition came over it like a cloud. "I'm so sorry—please, Louisa, forgive me for overstepping . . ."

Louisa shook her head quickly, the way one might to scatter the remnants of a dream. Her face was hot with mortification. She didn't want him to apologize. She wanted to retreat in time, wanted the chance to react some other way, but she knew she couldn't. Her mind raced in search of a diversion. "Don't you think we should check on Catherine and May? This is a terrible storm."

The rain pounded the saturated ground outside and the barn seemed to sway in the wind. Joseph joined Louisa in the doorway and looked out to see the darkest part of the sky receding to reveal a pale blue patch.

"I believe the storm has nearly wrung itself out, and I'm sure the girls are safe inside the tent." He folded his hands in a gesture of prayer. "If I promise to be very, very good, will you stay just a little while longer?"

Louisa examined Joseph's face—the arched brows, the beguiling grin. The awkwardness that had passed between them a moment before was melting away. In spite of herself Louisa smiled, then nodded. She turned back into the dim interior of the barn, where the air was sweet with the scent of hay, and Joseph followed.

To live for one's principles, at all costs,

is a dangerous speculation.

—"Transcendental Wild Oats:
A Chapter from an Unwritten Romance"

Chapter Nine

When Mr. and Mrs. Alcott and their two older daughters were invited to dine at the Suttons' to celebrate the harvest, Louisa faced her scant dress options with a slightly heavy heart but dignified resolve. She'd simply make the best of what she had, borrowing an expensive shawl sent to May by an aunt. For Anna, on the other hand, the situation was grave. Louisa could see that she felt this was her chance to make a good impression on the Sutton family, and particularly to sustain the impression she hoped she'd made on Nicholas. Louisa reassured her sister that it was her pink cheeks and dark eyes he was after, not the quality of her dress fabric. Those were the sorts of details noticed only by other women, Louisa told her. And *they* would be jealous of Anna, no matter what she wore, since she was so kindhearted and wise that no man could help falling in love with her.

"If only my sister's good opinion could act as decree!" Anna proclaimed as the four of them set out, finally, for the Sutton house.

This time of year the imposing trees on Washington Square blocked a pedestrian's view of many of its buildings. Some of the trees were hundreds of years old, with foliage so thick, hardly any light came through. Consequently, the Alcotts did not see the façade of the Sutton home until they were nearly upon it. It sat on the corner of Westminster and River Road, set apart from its neighbors by a regal white fence and gate that now hung invitingly open.

They were received by an efficient, unsmiling servant, who ushered them through the entryway, which faced the back side of the ascending staircase, rising from the rear toward the front of the first floor. Louisa tried not to gawk at the elaborate carving work around the ceiling, up the banister, and along the arches between one room and the next. The entryway and first parlor walls were covered in a pale blue paper featuring majestic-looking pheasants. She could sense her sister's surprise at just how well off Nicholas Sutton might be.

Charles Sutton stood in the center of the parlor with his thumbs hooked on his suspenders, a corpulent figure with scarlet cheeks and a bellowing laugh. Margaret had told Louisa and Anna that Mr. Sutton was born in Boston to a well-known family who built ships for the navy. The War of 1812 had the Suttons building ships faster than the British could fill them with cannonballs. By the time Charles's father passed away, he had amassed quite a fortune. Though Charles knew he was fortunate to have been born into such wealth, he had always felt his father pressured him into taking over the family business, when in truth Charles had little interest in matters of money and commerce. As an act of somewhat cowardly rebellion, considering the man it intended to irk was dead, Charles took the money with him and left Boston for the New Hampshire countryside. No one was quite sure what he did with his time now. He was said, depending on whom you asked, to be alternately writing poetry, tinkering in his workshop with a machine that boiled water without fire, or chronicling the migration patterns of New England bird species. Perhaps it was all three. People only knew that there must have been quite a bit of money to sustain his family on no income.

He had caused quite a scandal soon after his arrival in Walpole in 1830 by falling feverishly in love with the governess of his neighbors' children, a working-class girl from Dublin named Clara McCarron, who, shrewdly, did not waste time marveling at her good fortune and agreed immediately to be his wife. Hence, their children, Nicholas and Nora, who came along in quick succession, had a most unusual New England upbringing of sensitivity to all economic classes and watered-down Catholicism, though Mrs. Sutton did not hold fast to it. She was a practical sort of person, and she reasoned that if the Divine Father had cast this loving and quite wealthy man in her path, He *must* have wanted her to marry him. The small matter of his being a Protestant could be overlooked.

Nicholas wore a butternut frock coat over a silk waistcoat secured with steel buttons. An Albert chain looped around one of the buttons and connected to the watch in his pocket. He stood off to the side with the newly engaged Samuel and Margaret. They seemed to be floating just a bit above the ground, glancing every few moments at each other with a look of pure pleasure. A similar expression crossed Nicholas's face when he saw Anna enter the room. He had the features some described as "black Irish"—dark hair and countenance with clear blue eyes—but Anna's appearance lightened his features. He glided over toward the Alcotts, taking her hand.

"Mr. Sutton, this is my father and mother, Mr. and Mrs. Alcott. And of course, you know my sister Louisa."

Nicholas nodded, smiling as he took each of their hands. Louisa felt a rush of pride that her father had dressed so carefully for the evening. His coat was a little faded and his cravat not starched quite as stiffly as it could have been, but his attire was entirely appropriate for the occasion. No one in the room would have guessed that Bronson's ideas about clothing had once been a source of mortification for his daughters. Not so many years ago he had insisted on strict adherence to his philosophies in even the mundane arena of dress. He rejected anything made from an animal's hide, including leather for shoes and belts, and eschewed cotton because of its connection to the slave trade. Fleece belonged to the sheep, and man had no right to take it. Linen was nearly the only material that did not carry with it the burden of some sort of oppression, and his daughters spent many New England winters chilled to the bone in the name of his peculiar morality. Fortunately, in recent years Bronson had relaxed on matters of dress, compelled to accept gifts and hand-me-downs of all kinds. But Louisa would take this rather dusty and rumpled father over his more severe former self any day, especially because tonight he appeared so jolly. As much as he claimed to loathe the trappings of society, Bronson loved a good party.

Anna had refused to tell her mother and father much about Nicholas and her feelings for him. She told Louisa she felt it was premature, since he had not yet pledged himself to her or come to speak to Bronson. Louisa could see, though, watching them talk together, that there was no question of what was to come. She felt her heart give way, a wilted flower finally dropping from its stem. Nicholas's affections were wonderful news for Anna. She would be able to leave home and have a secure future. She would be a mother and have a garden and nice dresses—all the things she wanted.

Louisa knew that her own anguish on the matter was pure selfishness at best. Perhaps it even revealed slight jealousy. It wasn't that she was jealous of Anna's prospects; in fact, Louisa's chest tightened at the very thought of spending her days as mistress of an enormous house like this one. Rather, she envied the way Anna so effortlessly complied with others' expectations of how she should live, what she should dream about. Anna yearned for things, but they were all within the boundaries of acceptability. What Louisa wanted—to have freedom and money of her own, lots of it, so that she could control her fate and take care of her parents, to come and go as she pleased, to have an apartment of her own, with big bright windows and a desk so wide she could curl up to sleep on top of it when the words wouldn't come— these weren't the sorts of yearnings one discussed at parties. Anna was a blade of grass, swaying in the wind in concert with all the other blades. Louisa was a rare bird poking its head above them, a thing with purple feathers and a strangely hooked beak. She just could not, would not, adhere to convention when it went against her own heart.

Becoming a spinster didn't bother her. In fact, it appealed to the part of her that ached to go against the grain. Spinsterhood seemed a powerful position. At Louisa's age of twenty-two, people still asked questions, still hoped that she would find a husband. But in a few more years, certainly by her thirtieth birthday, the clamor would die down and her position would set, like the hardening of sculptor's clay. After all, *someone* has to be the governess; *someone* has to teach school and nurse the sick. No, Louisa didn't mind being a spinster, but the prospect of being completely alone troubled her. In her mind, marriage and love had little to do with one another, and she wished there could be some kind of middle ground. A few lucky people saw the two states coincide, but when they did, it was a complete accident, for it seemed marriage by its very design was meant to seek out love and destroy it. Seen with a cold, practical eye, the state of marriage was nothing more than indentured servitude, legal dependence, a claiming of property. One surrendered her mind and her autonomy when she pledged her fidelity. It was as simple as that.

. . .

Louisa's thoughts were interrupted as the party guests were called to take their seats. She felt the scuffed toes of her boots sink into the red carpet of the octagonal dining room. The table stretched toward the fireplace, recently stoked, with flames leaping up the chimney. A servant showed the Alcotts to their places and Louisa eased into her chair, her eyes roving the collage of ivory china, silver, and glass that adorned the table.

Mr. Charles Sutton stood at the head of the table, a forearm resting on his great shelf of a belly. He waited patiently for the rest of the guests to take their seats, then raised his glass in the air. The loud talking subsided, though a few of the women could be heard expressing a last giggle before he had the room's attention. He appeared to be poised to make an announcement or propose a toast. Louisa looked over at Samuel and Margaret. It seemed odd that Mr. Sutton should be the one to offer public congratulations, since Margaret's parents hadn't yet had time to organize a gathering of their own, and it was only proper that *they* should announce their own daughter's engagement.

"My friends," Mr. Sutton began, his baritone a viscous liquid oozing into every corner of the room, "as you well know, the book of Genesis, that splendid chronicle of beginnings large and small, beginnings of man, yes, but also the sun and planets, our oceans and rivers, from the thundering Nile to our stately Connecticut to the stream that bisects this very property, it is from that book of Genesis that we learn the story of Adam and Eve, the first example of that holy companionship . . ."

Louisa and the other guests continued to hold their glasses suspended above the table, though it seemed Mr. Sutton was only beginning a somewhat lengthy speech. She cut her eyes at Anna, seated beside her, and Anna raised an eyebrow, a substitute for a shrug, as if to say, *oh dear*.

". . . that we call marriage. Adam, you see, was lonely. Despite the paradise that surrounded him, which we only can imagine and will not know until we enter that heavenly place when our last breaths leave us, despite the beauty and tranquillity—no money, no death or sin or shame—he was lonely. That is how elemental our need for companionship can be. And God made the animals, all the beasts of the world, 'all things bright and beautiful, all creatures great and small,' but it was not enough for Adam . . ."

Louisa wondered wryly whether she had accidentally stumbled upon a Sunday service. She glanced around the long table, which held at least twenty guests. Mrs. Sutton and Nora looked more like sisters than mother and daughter. Each had a porcelain face framed by orange hair and they had the same delicate hands. Mrs. Sutton clasped hers in the pose of prayer and tilted her chin up toward her husband, her face full of adoring dotage. It appeared she was the only one enthralled with his speech. Next to Mrs. Sutton, Nora and Nicholas fingered their cutlery, a little embarrassed of their loquacious father. Next was Margaret with her mother and father, then Samuel Parker with his parents. Louisa continued around to a family she did not recognize, which exhausted the list of guests sitting opposite her. Those on the same side of the table, down at the other end from her sister and parents, were too hard to see without the kind of stretching and straining that would appear rude.

". . . and so God created woman. Beautiful, mild, steadfast, gentle . . ."

Margaret bugged her eyes and Louisa suppressed a giggle. She nodded her head in the direction of her father, whose eyelids fluttered on the verge of sleep, his cup of wine tilting dangerously sideways as he faded from consciousness.

". . . and it has always been thus, two people bound together by God to stand against the tyrannies, disappointments, illnesses of mind and body that are the signatures of this world. And the joys too. We can only hope and pray for many of those . . ."

Louisa's wrist ached from holding her glass aloft. She considered setting it down when she heard the familiar sound of tapping fingertips, this time on the underside of the dining chair a few guests down from her. Before she could think what to do she leaned back in her chair slightly, looking in the direction of the sound. Joseph was looking back at her, a beguiling grin on his face. Louisa would always think back on his expression, the look of a boy, really, just a boy, unaware that in a moment his life would change forever.

Mr. Sutton had gone on, though Louisa's heart seemed to fill her mouth and plug up her ears. She couldn't get her brain to focus on what he was saying. Suddenly, Mr. Singer was standing, looking quite ill, his face grave.

"And so it is with hearts full of joy"—apparently not in Mr. Singer's case, Louisa noted—"that we announce the engagement of my Nora to Mr. Joseph Singer. We wish them all the happiness God can bestow."

Louisa sat frozen in place, her eyes tracing the outline of a flower embroidered on the tablecloth. A great cry of surprise and relief disguised as good cheer went up among the guests and they drank, finally, a sip from the heavy glasses they were so glad to place back on the table. Louisa turned to see Joseph standing slowly, the color gone from his face, as Mr. Sutton pressed Joseph's hand to Nora's. She was stunning in an emerald-green dress—the perfect complement to her hair—with a white lace overskirt. The wide neckline wreathed her delicate shoulders, and a tiny locket hung over her collarbone. She is in every way, Louisa reflected, my complete opposite—petite, fair, delicate, soft-spoken. Joseph looked stricken and glanced to his father with wide eyes. The infirm man shook his head slightly, some kind of inadequate apology perhaps, and sat back down, looking away. Mr. Sutton pounded Joseph heartily on the back a few times, and Nora beamed at her father and then her intended, nearly bursting with pride at her luck in men.

And Joseph looked at Louisa. But she turned and kept her eyes on the table and clutched her napkin as if it were the rope that kept the sea from washing her away.

When women set their hearts on anything it is a known fact that they seldom fail to accomplish it.

—"Mrs. Podgers' Teapot"

Chapter Ten

The meal passed quickly in celebratory spirit. Two engaged couples in one week was big news in such a small town. The talk was boisterous and ongoing, despite mouths full of food, and guests gulped their wine mid-sentence and prattled on. They were clearly enjoying themselves, but there was also a kind of urgency to their conversation, as if they felt compelled to fill every lull in the talking, in case Charles Sutton attempted another lengthy speech.

Louisa felt she was playing her most difficult role yet—Lighthearted Acquaintance to the Newly Engaged Couple. It was a minor part, which didn't have many lines and kept her standing upstage for most of the scene. When she'd acted in *The Captive of Castile* and *The Greek Slave*, plays she'd written as a girl to perform with her sisters, she'd found it useful to think about a particular adjective and hold it in her mind as she was speaking her lines. Words were more powerful to her than images, more precise and layered. When she played Mrs. Malaprop she thought of the word *befuddled*. Now she held the word *beatific* in her mind and tried to project its essence in her face. Pleased but distant. Out of reach of more base emotions like jealousy and betrayal. She seemed to be convincing her audience. After all, none of them had reason to suspect she would care one way or the other about whom Joseph Singer planned to marry. She'd met him only a few times and had proclaimed him insufferable within earshot of her mother and sisters. Only Anna eyed Louisa carefully, searching for signs of distress. But Anna couldn't be sure. Louisa was, after all, a very good actress.

Finally the meal was ended. The Alcotts bade good evening to the other guests and congratulations to their hosts, though Louisa abruptly volunteered to see about her mother and sister's bonnets when she saw Joseph heading across the parlor toward them. The fresh night air was sweet with summer flowers as they made their way along Westminster Street. They had talked themselves out at the party, and now they walked quietly together, noticing the sound of crickets and an obsidian sky flecked with stars. Louisa was grateful not to have to talk. It was one thing to keep up the appearance of her good mood when she was with a group of near strangers, but with her family it was a different matter. She'd never been the kind of child who kept her emotions to herself. Always wanting, yearning, for something, some intangible thing that she could not identify or understand, let alone attain.

Fast on the heels of the memory of these fits was the memory of the shame that went along with them. Self-restraint, mastery of impulse—these were the qualities her father held in the highest regard, the qualities he tried to instill in his daughters from an early age. As he chronicled their early childhood in his journals, he detailed their attempts at identity, their achievements, their sins, and the corrections he made in the hopes of raising them into the best sort of women he could imagine. He was trying to prove his theory that a child came into the world blank, a sponge ready to absorb its surroundings. With

Anna the theory held; she behaved just as he instructed her to, never straying or giving in to temptation. But Louisa was different, all fierceness and petulance, poised for combat, then instantly full of regret. Furthermore, he conceded that some traits probably were inherited, particularly the bad ones. He was convinced Louisa had inherited her temper from her mother. He saw in her dark features the mark of the devil and told her often that she was "not a child of light."

Abba could plainly see that Louisa was troubled but mercifully let her be. Louisa went straight up to bed. It wasn't until she pulled the light cotton summer blanket up over her head that she finally let the tears flow. She drew a mournful breath, taking care that Anna should not hear her. Images of the last few weeks thronged her mind. How, she wanted to know, could Joseph have sat with her at the picnic as he did; how could he have come to call on her to talk about Whitman, speak to her as a close friend in the barn during the rainstorm—ask to kiss her!—and not *once* mention that he was to become engaged, soon, to a girl she knew. To the sister, Louisa realized with horror, of the man Anna might very well marry. Louisa wiped angrily at her eyes. Would she spend the rest of her life watching the man she thought she might—she hesitated even to use the word, it sounded so foolish—*love*, live as husband to a sister-in-law?

But after a few minutes more of the crying, she was through. She had been raised to believe that being denied the thing we think we want the most can make us strong and wise in ways we cannot imagine. If Louisa had anything, it was a will of iron. Once she made up her mind to do something, it was as good as done, and nothing could dissuade her. And so she made up her mind then to slough away these feelings, for as quickly as they had emerged, they could be discarded, she reasoned, and she could be free of sadness. *I cannot wish him ill,* she thought. *If he is happy, then all the better for it, and I shall be happy too, in my own way, in my own time.* But even as she told herself this, the sentiment rang hollow.

Louisa didn't fall asleep until the early morning hours, and soon the harsh light of dawn was slicing into her dream. Before she was even conscious she felt her whole body resist waking. The events of the previous night appeared in her mind like a trout surfacing in a stream. But the awareness came before she could stop it. She sat up when she heard a soft clink of something striking the window next to her bed. She looked over at Anna, who lay curled in the sheets. Louisa heard the sound again and this time saw a small stone make contact with the glass.

She slipped out of her faded nightgown and into a work dress that was in need of laundering. She pinned up her hair as she descended the steps to the front hall, smoothing the curls around her forehead flat. The bright sun stung her eyes as she pulled open the heavy door wide enough to peer out. Joseph stood with his hat in his hand. He wore the wilted white shirt from the night before, his cravat hanging untied around his neck.

It took a moment for her to summon a voice from her throat. "Why are you here?"

Joseph's eyes were red. Sandy whiskers colored the skin around his mouth. "I needed to speak with you."

"Have you been up all night?" She eyed his face carefully, wondered if he had been drinking.

"Yes. I was waiting until morning so I could come to see you. I would have come last night, but I didn't want to wake you."

"I'm sorry you came all the way here," Louisa said as she began to close the door. "But I can't talk now."

He stuck his hand through the narrow opening and grabbed her arm. "Wait."

She opened the door a few inches and sighed. She noticed he wasn't as tall as she had thought. In fact, he was about her height. She stood level with his mournful eyes.

"Please, Louisa." Desperation flashed in his eyes. "Give me a chance to explain."

"Joseph, you owe me no explanation. This is happy news for you and your family. You have my congratulations." All around them birds chirped an irritating chorus.

Exhaustion showed on Joseph's face. "But you don't *understand*," he snapped.

Louisa felt her humiliation harden into an anger that raced up the back of her neck. "I understand *perfectly*," she said, pointing her index finger at his chest. "I understand you had your fun with me while you could. I understand that you aren't who I thought you were, and now you want me to tell you it's all right. Well, I won't."

"But it's not—"

"—and if you do not leave the property this instant, I am going to scream for my father."

Joseph opened his mouth to speak but hesitated. Louisa's eyes shone, daring him to test her. She pinned her lips into a slim line. He tipped his head down and pressed his hat slowly back on, his palm lingering on its crown a moment, as if he had to muster the energy to lift his head. Louisa watched him walk slowly down the path, then pressed the door closed and secured the latch.

He came back in the afternoon, when Bronson was tucked away in his study and Abba had gone to the orchard to trade her plum jam for summer apples. Louisa was sitting in the dormer near her bed reading and looked up from the page when a movement on the front path caught her eye. Joseph wore a clean shirt, white linen, with the sleeves rolled up to the elbows. A book was tucked between his brown fore-arm and his ribs. She ducked out of the window and backed onto her bed. Anna sat in her rocker by the other window, plucking at a square of embroidery.

"Anna," Louisa said as the knock sounded below. "Joseph's at the door."

Anna looked up, surprised. "Do you want to see him?"

"No. Tell him . . . tell him I'm ill. Or that I've gone out. Yes, tell him I've gone out."

Anna appraised her sister with a sympathetic frown. "Oh, Lou, what he did to you is . . ."

Joseph knocked again.

"Hush about that. Go—before Father hears him and comes out of his study." Anna hesitated a moment before she draped the embroidery over the arm of the chair and hurried toward the steps. Louisa closed her eyes and listened to Anna's dress swish across the floorboards.

She heard voices drifting up through the open windows below but couldn't make out what they said. Soon the heavy door closed. Louisa lowered herself to her knees and peered over the bottom of the window just in time to see Joseph traverse the last few feet of the path and exit the front gate. He looked back at the house and Louisa dropped her head out of sight. She climbed back onto the bed and took up her book.

It took all her strength not to look up when Anna came in.

"Well," Anna said, standing in the center of the room. "Don't you want to know what he said?"

"Not particularly," Louisa said.

Anna rolled her eyes. "I tried to give him a piece of my mind, Louisa." Anna sat back in her rocker. "But he looked so . . . bereft.

I tried to ask him why, why he didn't tell us about . . . Nora, his plans. But he just shook his head. Said he had to talk to you."

Louisa finally raised her eyes from the paragraph she'd been scanning for a full minute without comprehension. "We have nothing to say to each other."

"I know. He wanted me to give you this." She extended her arm toward Louisa, offering a book with a letter tucked in its front pages.

Louisa didn't put out her hand. "Burn it."

"But don't you at least want to see what it says? Perhaps there is *some* explanation for what happened."

"I can imagine no satisfactory explanation for lying. Can you?"

Anna shook her head. "No."

Louisa crossed her arms. "I think we must see people for who they are, not who we wish they might be. It is hard now, but it will be for the best in the end. You know I'm not one for a fairy story."

"You used to be," Anna reminded her.

"As the verse says, 'When I was a child I spake as a child'—but the time comes to put away childish things. Some people disappoint. But not my sisters," Louisa said, taking Anna's empty hand. "Never my sisters. And for that I am grateful."

Anna bit her bottom lip. "What if *I* were to read it, and then, if it contained anything other than what we already know, I could tell you about it?" she ventured.

"You wouldn't dare. Give it to me." Louisa slid the square of paper out of the book, then lit the candle at her bedside and held the corner in its flame. She tilted the paper until two sides were engulfed, then laid it in a tin tray she sometimes used to bring tea up to their room in the afternoons. The flame flared as it consumed the fibers, then subsided into the orange perimeter of the ashes. "There," Louisa said. "Has Father made the fire in the parlor yet?"

Anna shook her head. "Not the book. Louisa Alcott—how can *you* burn a book?"

Louisa sighed. "All right, I won't burn the book." She reached for it but Anna hugged it to her breast.

"I don't believe you."

"No—I promise. I won't do anything to it. You can have it if you want. I just want to look at it for a moment."

Anna handed it to her. Louisa traced the small cover, then opened it and drew her finger across Mr. Whitman's portrait on the frontispiece. The copy was identical to Mr. Emerson's—same green cloth binding, same stamped letters of the title depicted as if they sprouted roots and leaves. The only difference in Joseph's copy was an inscription on the flyleaf:

From J.S. to L.M.A. He is "the poet of the woman the same as of the man."

Over the ensuing weeks, the letters continued to come every few days. After Louisa insisted on burning the first few, Anna made sure to intercept the mail and tuck the letters into her sewing basket, safe from her sister's wrath. She didn't open them, for they weren't hers to read, but something tugged at her, convinced her to save them in case Louisa had a change of heart.

As she made her way each day through the work that kept her hands busy but left her mind free to roam, Louisa tried hard not to let it drift back to that morning when Joseph stood on the front steps, tried not to remember his lips forming the word *please* as he begged her to listen to his explanation. But many times she could not resist and then the pictures flooded the space behind her eyes and she heard the word repeating in quick succession until it sounded like the call of a weary warbler beseeching his mate.

But Alcotts did not succumb, no matter the burden. There might not be a thing to do except struggle to wobbly feet and stand in the torrent, but sometimes that was enough to wear the torrent down, to coax out its final pathetic gust. In the end, an Alcott, though raw, bruised, and worn, was still standing. Louisa was determined that this would be so. She threw herself into the activities of daily life, hoping somehow *motion* could erase the blackboard of her memory in long quick strokes. But in her secret heart she despaired: why did anyone want to love anyone, if this was what came of it?

To keep from brooding, Louisa began work on a new volume of stories, a follow-up to *Flower Fables*, imagining she would finish it and be off to Boston at last. She cringed at her juvenile subject— Christmas elves—but it seemed prudent to stick with the formula that had worked before. She dutifully locked herself in her room for hours at a time, a basket of apples by her side, to work on it. The stories were slow going and she had no guarantee they would bring income, but when she sat by the fire in the evening in her ink-stained apron, her hand aching from clutching the pen all afternoon, Louisa felt rich in other ways. May had offered to do the illustrations and she worked at rough sketches in the evenings after dinner while Anna and Louisa scrubbed and shined in the kitchen. Louisa thought the drawings lovely, though she felt exasperated that once again her youngest sister had found a way to avoid helping with the chores.

Louisa knew that it was Anna, steady and reliable as always, who continued to do the lion's share of housework, despite her preoccupation with Nicholas Sutton. He continued to work on his house with the help of his father, Samuel Parker, a couple of uncles from Boston, and, Louisa realized, his brother-in-law-to-be, Joseph Singer.

Together they measured, sawed, and hammered boards into place in the late summer heat. Though Nicholas had yet to speak to Bronson, he had pledged to Anna that he would do so soon. He wanted to wait until the house was finished, so they could marry promptly and take residence. As usual, Bronson had his head in the clouds and did not in the least suspect he would soon be asked for his eldest daughter's hand. Anna felt she could scarcely contain her excitement, but she didn't express it. She thought of all the sorts of faces that existed in the world—fat, thin, round, dark, white, or freckled—and guessed that heartbreak looked the same on every one of them. One could spot it from a mile away. The last thing Louisa needed to hear about was Anna's expectation that she would soon become engaged.

The opening night of the play approached, but the cast had not rehearsed nearly as much as Louisa knew they needed to. One week Walpole saw the worst thunderstorm anyone in town could remember, and all the young people were needed at home to help clear downed tree limbs and sweep up broken glass. Then the boys called off a rehearsal to spend time on the construction project. Fall was on its way, and Nicholas wanted to be sure the house was ready for the winter well before it came. Just as it seemed they would get back on schedule, May came down with a terrible cold and said she couldn't bear to know they were all together having fun without her. So Louisa called off rehearsal once again.

Finally, just days before opening night, the cast gathered at the Elmwood to devote themselves to their roles in *The Jacobite*.

"I'm so pleased we're all finally here," Louisa said as the group filed into the attic. The anticipation of seeing Joseph had rattled her nerves, and she resisted the impulse to scan the room for him, dreaded the possibility of awkward conversation. "We have a lot of work ahead of us, but I know if we can just buckle down and really *work* today and tomorrow, we'll be ready for Tuesday's performance."

May and Harriet passed around copies of the play and the paper rustled as the cast flipped through the pages to their various parts.

"Wait a minute," Louisa said. "Where are Paul and Alfie?"

"Over at the Academy, in the great hall," Margaret said. "They've painted all the pieces of the set, and it didn't make sense to put them together up here, only to have to take them down again."

Louisa nodded. "Of course. Good—so there's some progress, then. Now, let's see . . ." She starting making arbitrary checkmarks on her notes so as to appear engrossed in her thoughts. In truth she had just realized the scene that needed work included Joseph. There would be no putting off facing him. Best to get it out of the way. "I was thinking perhaps we should run through the final scene, where the Major's secret identity is revealed to Sir Richard, and John Duck jumps down from the chimney just in time to save the pardon."

"But we don't have a Sir Richard today," Anna said, giving Louisa a curious look. "Hadn't you noticed that Joseph's not here?"

Louisa looked up in surprise, relief washing over her, then tried to cover it with irritation. "Nicholas," she demanded. "Where's Joseph?"

Nicholas cleared his throat and shifted his weight from one foot to the other. "Right. Well, it seems he's not going to be able to be in the play after all. You know, his father hasn't been well."

Louisa nodded. "Is he worse off than before?"

Nicholas shrugged his shoulders. "It's hard to say. But either way, there's too much work at the store for one man to do, especially one who's ill every other day. So Joseph is needed there."

Louisa held his gaze a moment, trying to assess the veracity of this explanation. Nicholas looked down at his shoes.

"He hasn't time for a few more days until the play is over?" Margaret chimed in. "He's already learned all his lines." Louisa wouldn't have asked a question that seemed so rude, but she was eager to hear Nicholas's response.

He hesitated. "My sister—she's asked him not to attend. She feels this is . . ."

"Is what?" Margaret challenged.

"Is . . . frivolous. Considering his father's illness and their upcoming wedding."

Margaret rolled her eyes. "She behaves as if she's the first girl on earth to get married. Nora never did have a whole lot of sense."

"I'll ask you to hold your tongue on that account," Nicholas said, his dark brows lowering into a V. Anna looked nervously between him and Margaret.

Louisa held up her hand. "This will get us nowhere. We have two days left and no Sir Richard." She rubbed circles into her forehead, struggling to concentrate. "Paul will have to play the role."

Margaret looked skeptical. "Paul can scarcely speak a sentence to four people, much less an entire crowd."

"Well," Louisa said, "he will have to overcome his fear. We've no other choice. But let's not ask him now—let him finish the sets first. May or Harriet, would either of you be willing to stand in, just for today?"

Harriet looked incredulous. "Play a man's role? Hardly."

Though Louisa usually found Harriet's whining amusing, today it needled her. "Not onstage—just for today's rehearsal."

"I'll do it, Lou," May said.

Louisa sighed. "Thank you, May—it's nice to see someone is still interested in ensuring the quality of this performance. Now stand up very straight and do your best to act like a mustached nobleman."

There are many Beths in the world, shy and quiet,

sitting in corners till needed, and living for others

so cheerfully that no one sees the sacrifices.

—*Little Women*

Chapter Eleven

Louisa rose before the others and pulled on her boots. This was what she loved: quiet solitude, the restful few hours when the frenetic pace of her mind subsided and she could embrace the blank rhythm of walking. Outside, the morning was golden. The angle of the light portended the coming autumn, though the trees were verdant still and full of songbirds. Louisa watched the intermittent bursts of feathers as the birds moved about, launching themselves to higher branches.

The path snaked away from the house and down a steep hill, where the trees were denser near the ravine and the morning light scarcely penetrated. The earth felt soft under her soles. Though the hoyden within her longed to run, she settled now for swift walking, as if her stride could outpace the thoughts trying to worm their way into her mind. Sometimes life seemed to her one long assault she was never quite prepared to defend herself against. If only she could slow it down, take each strange development one at a time, examine it, find some way to control it. She approached the edge of the ravine. The water slid over the limestone without making a sound.

Her father would say that the chaos of life, its unpredictability, existed to challenge one's commitment to improvement, that one must extract himself piece by piece out of the wildness and assemble a spirit that transcends the sum of mere body parts. Mr. Whitman seemed to say, rather, that the wildness *itself* was the thing to cultivate. For him, the spirit and the flesh were one, the physical experience of the world *was* divinity. Louisa supposed they both were right. Of one thing she felt certain: men would go on arguing about these matters as long as there were people on the earth. The women, meanwhile, would continue to peel the vegetables and soak the linens in boiling tubs and mend the torn seams and bring new lives into the world. Louisa wondered if anyone would ever write poetry about that.

The sun was getting higher now and Louisa turned back toward home. There was nothing that angered Anna more than sisters who disappeared when it was time to divide up the work for the day. In addition to the regular chores, they had the preparations for the play—there was no time to spare.

As Louisa came up the back path, Anna gave a little half-wave, her elbow clutching the broom to her side. "Isn't it lovely out this morning?"

"Yes," Louisa said. "You should hear the sound of all those birds as the sun is coming up. What a racket!"

"I'm sure Lizzie loved hearing them. It was thoughtful of you to take her walking with you."

"Lizzie?"

"Yes—has she not gone back into the house already?"

Louisa frowned at her sister. "Nan, I walked by myself this morning. I have not seen Lizzie since we sat in the parlor last night after supper."

Anna's eyes widened. "That's very strange, because she isn't here."

Just then Abba appeared in the doorway. "Louisa—I'm so happy you girls are back. I know you meant well, but you must tell me when you hatch these schemes. Last night was so damp, and I've been so worried."

Anna looked at Louisa and then back at her mother. "Marmee, Lizzie isn't with Louisa."

"Isn't with her? What do you mean?"

"I mean I walked alone this morning. I hadn't any idea anyone was worried about Lizzie until I walked up just now and Anna told me she isn't here."

Abba put her hand to her mouth. "You mean . . . you don't know where she is?"

"No, Marmee."

"God in heaven." Abba closed her eyes. "What could have . . . has my child been kidnapped?"

Anna shook her head. "Marmee, let's not jump to extremes. I know she is not as strong as the rest of us and that she is more timid than most, but Lizzie *is* twenty years old. She isn't a child."

Abba's eyes darkened. "I know the age of my own daughter—I was there the day she came into this world. But Lizzie is not like other girls her age. You know she is too gentle, too easily frightened to be out on her own. . . ."

"We talked last night of cakes for the party after tomorrow's performance. Perhaps she walked down to the orchard for more apples." Anna leaned the broom against the side of the house. "Louisa and I will go look for her."

Abba nodded. "Please do. I'm going to get your father out of his study." Abba turned and disappeared back into the house. Louisa and Anna set off diagonally across the open field that stretched southeast of town. The orchard began at its outer edge, about a mile from

Yellow Wood. The sisters slogged through the mud in silence, swatting at the insects stirred up by the late-morning heat.

"I have a bad feeling, Nan. Marmee's right—this *is* very strange."

Anna gave her a sympathetic glance. "You only feel that way because you were so hard on Marmee the night May asked us to go to the circus. You're afraid she was right about what Lizzie should and shouldn't do."

"If anything should happen to her . . ." Louisa looked miserable.

"Don't say, 'It will be all my fault,' because that isn't true." The sisters were almost the same height, with the same long legs and sturdy hips. They walked with one synchronized stride.

"But I told her she needed to have a little adventure. What if something *has* happened?" Louisa continued to fret. "Do you think Marmee was right?"

"No, I don't. I think Lizzie is a grown woman, even if none of us treat her as one. She is sure to be nearby, either in the orchard or down by the river, and if we let her alone I'm sure she'd be home before dinner."

"Well, for Marmee's sake we shall look now," Louisa said.

Anna put her arm around her sister's waist and replied with a gentle tease. "And for the sake of your guilty conscience."

But though they looked up and down each of the neat rows of trees, their boughs heavy with apples flecked russet and mellow green, they couldn't find Lizzie. The orchard belonged to Mr. Parsons, who was an admirer of Bronson's writing on the education of young children and had followed his career. He had promised Abba the Alcotts could have as many apples as they liked if Bronson would promise to visit and answer his questions on Plato. Anna and Louisa trekked up the hill to his barn, where the wide door stood open to let in the light. Mr. Parsons wore a heavy apron and tinkered with a tool at the gears of his cider press.

Anna knocked on the open door, and Mr. Parsons looked up and grinned when he saw he had visitors. "Good morning, girls!"

"Good morning," Anna said.

"I understand we will have the pleasure of seeing both of you perform tomorrow night. Planché, is it?"

Louisa nodded. "Yes, sir. *The Jacobite*."

"I've read it," he said, placing the tool back in its box and taking up the oil can. "But, you know, we usually have to go to Boston to see a play performed. I am looking forward to it."

Anna smiled, waiting a polite moment before changing the subject. "Mr. Parsons, have you seen our sister Lizzie around the orchard this morning?"

He thought a moment. "Lizzie—is she the one with the wavy blond hair?"

Anna shook her head. "No, that would be May—she is the youngest. You may never have met Lizzie. She does not usually go out."

"We call her our little housewife because she so likes to bake and sew and care for our father. There's nowhere in the world she likes to be except at home." Louisa felt the dread welling up in her voice.

"Well, then," Mr. Parsons said, observing Louisa with concern. "I shouldn't know her if I did see her. But I haven't seen anyone in the orchard this morning."

"Thank you, sir. We hope you enjoy the show tomorrow night," Anna said.

"I'm sure you will find her, girls. Please let me know if I can help in any way."

Anna and Louisa walked back across the field and down to the riverbank where they had gone swimming with their friends the month before. They saw no footprints in the mud, no stump that had been brushed off for sitting on.

"Could she be in town, do you think?" Anna asked. Her confidence seemed to be wavering.

"I can't imagine that she would. Last summer, when you were away in Syracuse and I had that awful cold, I was supposed to go to the grocery one day before Marmee got home, but I felt so sick. I asked Lizzie to go and she nearly cried at the thought of doing it alone. In the end we went together." Louisa shook her head. "But we'd better check nonetheless. She may be there. How can we face Marmee if we haven't looked everywhere?"

Anna nodded. They set off walking in silence down the hill toward Main Street, afraid to give voice to their private thoughts.

Their fears only deepened as they scanned Washington Square and entered each shop to inquire whether anyone had seen Lizzie. She wasn't in either the Whig or the Democratic village store, nor the tavern, nor Slade's Meat Market. The barbershop was teeming with children crowding around to spend their pocket money on root beer and peanuts, but Lizzie was nowhere to be found. When they'd made their way all around the square, they stood in front of Singer's Dry Goods. Anna strode toward the entrance but Louisa hesitated.

Anna turned back. "Come on, let's . . ." She looked up at the sign over the door. "Oh." Louisa's eyes filled with tears as she silently admonished herself. Something terrible could have happened to Lizzie and still she could only think about her own discomfort at having to see Joseph Singer. She was a selfish sister—if guilt was her fate, she deserved it, she thought.

"Lou, why don't you wait here, and I'll go inside to check?"

Louisa shook her head, determined. "No. I am coming with you."

They entered and the familiar bell sounded above their heads. Louisa hadn't been in since the morning of the circus, and the smell of cinnamon and spices was a bittersweet reminder of that day. Her heart pounded against her ribs and she didn't dare look toward the counter where a woman stood waiting to pay for her purchase.

"Hello, *Mr.* Singer," Anna called out, more for Louisa's benefit than to get his attention. She pulled Louisa by the sleeve toward where Joseph's father stood hunched over the cash drawer, his trembling hand spilling the coins as he tried to place them in their proper compartments. A stern woman held a cake of soap wrapped in paper and sighed impatiently. "If you drop my coins and they roll under the counter, I'm not going to give you any more."

Mr. Singer paused and steadied his hand, dropping the remaining money in place. "No, of course not, Mrs. Hawkins." He slowly pushed in the drawer. "There. All set. I hope you have a lovely afternoon." Mrs. Hawkins scoffed and turned away without a reply.

Mr. Singer sighed, then turned to Anna. "Hello, Miss Alcott, is it? I believe I've met your sister, here."

"Yes," she nodded. "Louisa."

"Yes, hello, Miss Louisa. Joseph isn't here today. He's gone to Bellows Falls to pick up a shipment of flannel."

Louisa exhaled, relieved he would not pop out from the back room at any moment. "Sir, we're looking for our sister Lizzie. Not May—she is the one who is Catherine's age. Lizzie comes between May and me. You haven't seen her today in town, have you?"

"No, my dears. I've had only the regular customers today." He nodded toward the door, just now closing behind the haughty Mrs. Hawkins. "Though I can't say I wouldn't trade some of them for a gentle sister of yours."

Louisa smiled at the tired-looking man who seemed to have aged so far beyond his years. She felt full of sadness for him, for Joseph—for herself. And Lizzie—where could she be?

Though Anna and Louisa dreaded the scene at Yellow Wood, they knew they had better hurry to tell their parents they had no news. Back home, Abba sat in the parlor twisting a handkerchief in her lap. May sat by her side, stroking the worn sleeve of Abba's dress. Abba looked up when she saw them walk in. "My girls, have you found her?"

Anna knelt down in front of her mother. "No, Marmee. But I know we will hear something soon."

"This is dreadful," May said. "Just dreadful."

"Your father has gone to look in all the shops."

"We just came from there," Louisa said from where she stood by the fireplace, immediately regretting drawing attention to herself. Abba looked at her expectantly. "No one has seen her," Louisa said.

"Well, where else can we look?" Abba's voice was frantic. "Where else could she be? A person doesn't just vanish into thin air."

Anna looked around the room. "Have you noticed anything missing? Her bonnet? Any of her books?"

May nodded. "Her shoes are gone but her bonnet is still here. And this is very strange: *My* pink poplin dress, the one with the yellow sash that got torn on the gate at Pinckney Street—it's not in my room."

"Well, that's it," Louisa shouted a little too loudly. "She probably took it to a seamstress to have it fixed—to have a better sash sewn on. As a surprise. A belated birthday gift." May had turned fifteen in July.

"But she hasn't any money, Louisa," May said softly.

They brooded a moment, unable to think what to do next. Then, out of the silence came the *clip-clop, clip-clop* of horses out in front of the house. Louisa ran to the window and yanked the drape aside.

"It's Mr. *Singer's* carriage." The others rushed up behind Louisa and watched as the carriage slowed and a man got out. Louisa gasped and let go of the drape. It swung shut. "It's Joseph."

"Louisa," May shrieked. "Get *out* of the way—we can't see." Louisa moved away from the window, panic prickling the skin across her shoulders.

"He has a young lady with him," Abba said.

Anna was a head taller than her mother and stood behind her. "Is it Nora Sutton?"

Louisa gave her older sister a scathing look, which Anna pretended not to see.

May shrieked again. "Nora Sutton is wearing my pink poplin. Look—there's the yellow sash!"

Louisa took a breath and looked out once more. A smile spread across her face and she felt her voice wobble in her throat as she tried to speak. "That's not Nora Sutton—that's *Lizzie*. See, Anna, she has on your old bonnet. It's Lizzie—she's all right!"

"Here they come," shrieked May, dropping the drape.

Louisa ran to the front door and threw it open. "Lizzie!" She ran to her sister and folded her in her arms, pulling her inside and ignoring Joseph. Abba, Anna, and May crowded around.

"Oh, Elizabeth," Abba cried. "You don't know how we've worried." Louisa took care to lead her sister straight to the sofa and not to look up at Joseph, who stood watching the happy scene from the threshold, his hat in his hands. Soon Anna noticed their want of manners and rushed to the door.

"Joseph, please—come in." He nodded his appreciation and stepped inside, closing the heavy door.

Anna went to the window and refastened the drapes to let in the late-afternoon sun. "So we have you to thank for rescuing our sister?"

Joseph chuckled. "I don't know that she needed rescuing, but her feet *were* tired after such a long walk. I believe she did appreciate the offer of a ride home." Anna squeezed his arm and gestured to their father's armchair. "Please—sit. I will make some tea." She scurried into the kitchen.

"Long walk?" Abba said, still reeling from the shock of seeing her timid daughter dressed for her outing. "To where?"

"Bellows Falls, Marmee." Surprised, they all turned to Lizzie. She hadn't spoken a word since she arrived. A flash of orange fur darted out from the kitchen. Ginger leapt into Lizzie's lap and nudged her face into the crook of her elbow.

"You walked to Bellows Falls?" May asked, incredulous. Lizzie nodded, stroking the cat's head. "But that's five *miles* at least."

Lizzie sat up very straight on the worn sofa and slowly untied the bonnet. Her eyes were bright, though she looked tired and pale. "I just wanted to see . . ." Her voice tightened with tears. ". . . if I could do it. And I did."

Louisa knelt down on the floor in front of her and took her hand. "Of course you did."

Lizzie looked at each of her sisters. "Home is, to me, the most wonderful place. You know that I have always been content to listen to my sisters' stories, to see the world through your eyes. But sometimes . . ." She hesitated.

". . . you want to see it for yourself," Louisa said.

Lizzie nodded. "I wanted to turn up my hair and put on a nice dress—can you believe yours fit me, May?"

"Well, you *are* petite. I don't think it will be stretched out too terribly much," May said, worried.

"At first I thought I would just walk down to the shops here in Walpole," Lizzie continued. "But when I got there I felt disappointed that I wasn't going to have more of an adventure. So I crossed the river and kept walking north. It was a lovely morning."

"Oh, Lizzie," Abba moaned. "Think of all the things that could have happened to you! The river is so high from the rain last night. What if there had been a storm? What if you had turned your ankle with no one there to help you?"

Louisa, safe now from any blame she might have shared had something bad happened to Lizzie, grew irritated. "Oh, Marmee—she's fine! Can't you see? Now, Lizzie, tell us more. What did you do when you got there?"

"Well, I walked up and down the main street. Then I noticed a little bakery with a café attached, and I just stood looking at all the cakes through the window. The baker waved me in and pointed out the tarts, telling me their names in French. They looked like little sculptures. May—you would have loved them."

Anna came back with the tea tray and poured for Joseph and her mother and sisters. She settled in the chair opposite the sofa.

"Well, I hope you went in and had one," Anna said.

Lizzie smiled. "I did! The baker gave me the biggest one. It was made with plums and little currants. And I had a coffee with cream."

May sighed. "It sounds divine. You must have looked very sophisticated, sitting there alone in the café."

Lizzie rolled her eyes. "Perhaps I did, until it came time to pay the bill."

"Oh, no—you hadn't any money!" Louisa cried.

"Well, I thought I had—I took my coin purse. I've been saving my rag money. But I forgot I gave the money to Father and asked him to give it to that family on River Road that's had the scarlet fever." Lizzie's smile vanished and her voice grew sad. "The father is dead, you know—and there are three small children. All their dolls had to be burned."

"Lizzie, you're generous to a fault," Anna said.

"Well, in this case, yes—because I hadn't any money to pay the baker, and I couldn't very well return the purchase, since I'd already eaten it! I didn't know what I was going to do. I felt the panic welling up inside me and I made a show of searching through my purse over and over, even though I knew I wouldn't find a penny in it. I was going to leave him my locket, just so he believed that I *would* come back when I had the money. But then Mr. Singer walked in and I was saved."

Joseph, who had been sitting quietly as the story unfolded, interjected. "It was my pleasure to help. If only I had arrived sooner and saved her the worry of those few minutes."

Lizzie shook her head. "It was just right. He generously paid the bill—for which I *will* repay him as soon as I can—and saw me out. That's when he asked me to ride with him back to Walpole. I'm sorry, Marmee—I know it was rude to say yes."

"Nonsense," Joseph said. "The timing was perfect and we were headed to the same place. Besides, I suspected your family might have been worried."

"Well, my feet *were* very tired. And the walk home would have been long."

"You made it a lovely ride," Joseph said. He looked directly at Louisa and met her eyes before she could turn away. "The Misses Alcott make such pleasant companions. I only wish I had occasion to see them more often."

Louisa's heart felt like an old rag wrung out too many times. How could a person be at once so kind and so cruel? Why did he insist on these insinuations that only reminded her of his betrayal? She turned back to Lizzie, determined to focus on the happy news of her safety.

Abba covered her eyes with her hand and shook her head. "I am glad this tale has a happy ending. Should we expect our Lizzie to become a woman of the world? Have you had enough adventure?"

Lizzie squeezed her mother's hand and stifled a tiny yawn. "I am so sorry I worried you, though I am glad I went. I wanted to know that I could go off for the day on my own, like any other girl my age. But I *don't* think I want to do it again."

"Well, you may, any time you like," said Louisa. "Only, please tell us first!"

Joseph stood up. "Mrs. Alcott, I thank you for your hospitality. But I should be going and let Miss Elizabeth rest."

Abba stood up and walked with him to the door. "I think we all must rest after such a scare. I am grateful to you for your help, and I know my husband will want to thank you himself when he hears what you have done for our Elizabeth."

Joseph shook his head. "Please do not think of it again—it was my pleasure." He stepped out into the sun and placed his hat on his head. Louisa sensed his gaze was fixed on her but she refused to meet it. "Good day, ladies."

The women fell into a pleasant quiet as afternoon turned to evening. It was too late in the day to start the laundry, the activity that usually consumed their Mondays and Tuesdays, but they decided they could make it up tomorrow. Abba went up to the bedrooms to collect the sheets. Lizzie stretched out on the sofa under a blanket, though the room was sweltering, and her sisters flitted about, replenishing her tea and fetching her books to keep her company. Anna declared she would mend the yellow sash once and for all and set to work, with May looking over her shoulder to watch for stitches that weren't quite as even as they could be. When Bronson arrived home soon after, his forehead creased with worry and his shoulders low, this was the scene that revived him: all four of his daughters, at home and whole, gossiping and sewing and reading as if this had been an ordinary day.

After a time Louisa noticed that Abba had been absent awfully long and wondered whether she hadn't begun the laundry after all. When Louisa saw she wasn't in the washroom, she glanced into the bedrooms. Abba sat on Lizzie's bed in the room she shared with May, looking out the window at the back lawn with the empty clothesline and the field beyond.

"Marmee, here you are." Louisa noticed the clothesline. "Don't worry—we'll finish the laundry tomorrow. I'll work double-time."

Abba nodded but didn't turn around.

"Isn't it wonderful that Lizzie is home, safe and sound?" Louisa could see her mother's shoulders were trembling. "What's the matter —are you ill?"

Abba sighed and turned to Louisa, revealing a face lined with tears. "Only in spirit."

Louisa sat down beside her. "But aren't you *happy* that everything turned out well? No one is hurt—nothing has changed."

"Everything is *always* changing," Abba said, cringing at the plaintive sound in her voice. "You couldn't possibly understand. But the way you encourage Lizzie to go off on her own so carelessly—it's as if you *want* to take her away from me." Abba's voice was hoarse from crying.

Louisa felt the guilt bloom open in her chest, just what she'd feared all day. "Of course that's not what I want! But, Marmee, Lizzie is *not* a girl anymore and May won't let you make her your pet any longer. You have to let them grow."

"You cannot know the hardships, the exhaustion, the worry I have felt all these years . . . I've always wondered if God made woman as an afterthought—and then was ashamed of his own handiwork." Abba's voice took on the lifeless quality Louisa dreaded.

Louisa took her mother's hands. "Oh, Marmee, you sound so *wretched*." Abba sometimes descended into these "spells," as the girls called them, where despair conquered her spirit for a time. Anna always insisted their mother was only temporarily ill and would soon regain her cheerful disposition. To Anna, the despair was just a physical symptom, like a cough or a fever. But Louisa knew it ran through her mother like a current, sweeping up everything in its path and plunging down. Bronson always said that, of all the girls, Louisa was most like her mother, and he didn't mean it as a compliment. Both were mercurial, passionate, willful. Louisa had seen despair like Abba's from the inside. She had inherited it the way some daughters came into a silver tray or a set of spoons.

"When my babies were born," Abba began again, as if Louisa herself was not one of those babies, "all of their needs just . . . eclipsed me. And I was so happy. It's a cruel fate that the years I put into raising you girls are rewarded by all of you drifting away. Soon, no one will need me anymore."

Louisa pulled Abba's shoulders toward her own and held her. "We will *always* need you. And what about Father? He would be lost without you."

"Husbands and wives are not what we are discussing here."

"Marmee—you must know he is utterly devoted to you!"

Abba examined Louisa carefully for a moment. "I suppose you will learn this soon enough on your own, but I might have understood my life a little better if someone had told me. For a man, love is just a season. For a woman it is the whole of the year—winter, spring, summer, and fall—and yet, sometimes it is not what it could be. What it seems it should be."

"What do you mean, Marmee?"

Abba turned back to the window. It faced the south. She couldn't see the setting sun, but its vivid pink light sliced through the clouds that hung over Mr. Parson's orchard in the distance. "We must never give if we are hoping for something in return."

If ever men and women are their simplest,
sincerest selves, it is when suffering softens the
one, and sympathy strengthens the other.

—"Love and Loyalty"

Chapter Twelve

With her gratitude over Lizzie's safe return and her worries over Abba's most recent spell, Louisa felt her thoughts should have been too full to be plagued by Joseph Singer. Yet he continued to appear in her mind fully formed, as real as if he had walked through the door of Yellow Wood. She woke at dawn unable to sleep and nearly leapt from bed in an attempt to keep the thoughts at bay. She woke Anna, and they descended to the washroom to begin the task of laundering the sheets, towels, and underclothes that lay heaped on the floor. Soon, May and Lizzie were awake and helping, and they worked quietly, hoping Abba would sleep late and wake to find the task completed.

Two hours before the audience would begin to arrive, Anna and Louisa met the rest of the cast at Walpole Academy, where they would perform the play. Paul Ferguson hammered away at the last piece of the set, while Alfred Howland worked at the opposite end, painting in the wood-grain detail of the two-dimensional china hutch that sat at the back of the "pub." May, who took her role as prompter quite seriously, had gathered the cast around her to go over the signals she planned to use one last time. Louisa escaped this annoyance by claiming a need to "study her lines." Anna sat near her, filling out cards with the word *Reserved* in her steady, feminine hand, which they would place on the chairs in the front row. Margaret sewed buttons and trim on the costumes.

Anna and Margaret chatted. Louisa appeared to be absorbed in her reading, though she listened in.

"I traveled to Boston last week to visit with my great-aunt. She is an invalid, you know," Margaret said, pulling the thread through the seam to secure it and snipping off the end with a pair of engraved embroidery scissors that hung from her wrist on a ribbon.

Anna lifted her pen from the card so as not to smudge it. "I'm sorry to hear that. I know she has been ill for some time."

Margaret nodded. "Honestly, I can't remember a time when she was well. But she bears it cheerfully enough. I, on the other hand, dread visiting, and so I walked the long way from the train station to her apartment so that I could pass the shops. You know, I have yet to find a dress that suits me and satisfies Samuel's mother."

Anna smiled. "It seems like she might be difficult to please on that account."

Margaret shook her head. "You understate the point—I don't think there is a dress or a fabric on this earth she would approve of that doesn't make me look like I'm headed for the convent."

Louisa closed her eyes and took a deep breath, working to suppress a groan. *Margaret is so tiresome,* she thought. *If I have to listen to her go on about this dress much longer I'm going to—*

"As I was walking along I saw Nora Sutton and her mother leaving a shop with the most beautiful satin silk."

"Really," said Anna. "That sounds lovely." Louisa could feel her sister's eyes sweep in her direction, hoping, she knew, that the play was fully consuming her hearing as well as her sight. "I'm sure she will make a beautiful bride."

"She is a beauty—there is no question about that. Though, of course, there is such a thing as too much beauty. It can get one into trouble." Margaret's voice took on the conspiratorial quality she embraced when she was preparing to reveal some interesting gossip.

"What do you mean?" Anna said, playing right into her game, Louisa thought.

"Were you not aware that she was previously engaged?"

Anna raised her eyebrows. "Engaged? I suppose I have heard something about that. To whom?"

"About two years ago, a man named Cecil Morris appeared in Walpole and took a job as a clerk in the town hall. He was from New York City."

"Did he have family here?" Anna asked.

"No—that was the strange part. To anyone who asked, he said he had grown tired of the noise and dust of the city. He decided one day to find a nice village in New Hampshire where he might find a wife and settle down. When he rode into Walpole in his carriage he said he knew this was the place for him."

"How interesting," Anna said.

"Telling you now, it sounds suspicious. But at the time I think we were all flattered he chose our town. The families here take a lot of pride in this place."

"As they should," Anna said.

"Word got around, and soon all the girls were talking about him. He seemed to have money, he was charming and very handsome. Of course, *I* knew there was something untrustworthy about him right from the start. But would anyone listen to me?"

"I suppose not," Anna guessed.

"No," Margaret said, shaking her head. "They wouldn't. Well, it didn't take long before he set his sights on Nora. She fell completely in love—completely lost her senses. Mr. Sutton gave his blessing and the wedding date was set. But just a few weeks before the union was to take place, Mr. Morris disappeared."

"Disappeared?"

"He said he had to travel to Boston on a business matter. Nora went to meet his train the evening he was supposed to return, but he wasn't on it. Weeks went by, the day of the wedding came and went. She heard nothing. Finally a letter came. He admitted his whole scheme—he had been married all along to a woman back in New York. He was attempting to leave her when he first came to Walpole. But the birth of his son pricked what tiny speck of a conscience he had, and he decided to return to his family."

"Poor Nora!" Anna said.

Margaret nodded. "Yes, it was unfortunate. She had made such a fool out of herself over him, flaunting her new status all over town, and all along he had no intention of following through on his pledge."

"But how could she have known? It could have happened to anyone."

Margaret pursed her lips. "Well, not anyone. Not *me*—I knew he was trouble."

"Yes," Anna said. "You mentioned that."

"Nora soon descended into a terrible state. Her nerves took over. She wouldn't leave her room. Dr. Kittredge was at the Suttons' home every day. She was convinced she had squandered her chance for a respectable life, for marriage and children. No one really blamed her, but . . . well, not everyone is as understanding as you and I are, Anna."

Anna pressed her lips together to suppress a smile. "That's true,

Margaret. Well, it is fortunate, then, that she has found herself in"—she looked over at Louisa and cringed—"her current circumstances."

"Quite," Margaret said, nodding.

The two worked in silence for a moment, Margaret fastening the last gray button onto Louisa's Widow Pottle costume.

"Of course . . ." Margaret said.

"Of course what?"

Margaret leaned in toward Anna. "Well, I didn't tell you this . . ."

"Of course not," Anna said.

"Joseph Singer didn't court Nora, and I don't believe he wants to marry her."

Louisa's eyes froze on a period at the end of a sentence and refused to move.

"Margaret, that seems like an awfully salacious thing to say. How could you know?"

"I'm very observant, as you know, Anna. I pick up on these things."

Probably by listening at doors and beneath windows under the cover of night, Louisa thought. But she held her breath anticipating what Margaret would say next.

"Joseph's father is in grave financial difficulty. Joseph has helped to improve business at the store, but his father gambles the profits away on imprudent investments as quickly as Joseph can earn it."

Anna looked stricken. "That's terrible."

"Yes, it is. As you probably could see at the Suttons' dinner party, Mr. Singer is not long for this world. His lungs are weak and he probably will not make it through the winter. So he is looking to put his affairs in order. Technically Catherine is not too young to marry, but fifteen *is* awfully early."

"Our youngest sister May is fifteen as well. That is too young," Anna said firmly.

"I agree. And so does Mr. Singer. And she is a *young* fifteen. She has been coddled and spoiled her whole life. I think he doted on her out of guilt that she didn't have a mother. But because she hasn't known sacrifice or responsibility, there's no way she could be sent out as a governess or maid. She wouldn't last a week."

"I think I understand what you mean to infer," Anna said. "Mr. Singer went to see Mr. Sutton?"

Margaret nodded. "They are old friends. Each had something to gain from uniting their families. The Singer debts are repaid, Catherine is safe from a hasty marriage, and Nora's reputation is restored."

"Except that Joseph has to marry someone he doesn't love," Anna said, glancing at Louisa, who hid her face behind the play.

"Yes, Samuel says he is quite grave about it. But he admits he can't see a better way to take care of his sister. Joseph Singer's strength of character outdoes anyone's in this town, I've always said."

"I'm sure you have," Anna said with an amused smile.

Louisa's mind reeled. Was this what Joseph had meant to explain in all the letters she had refused to read?

May clapped her hands and stood on a crate at the foot of the stage. "Everyone—it's time to get dressed!"

There was no need of any more words. . . .

—Under the Lilacs

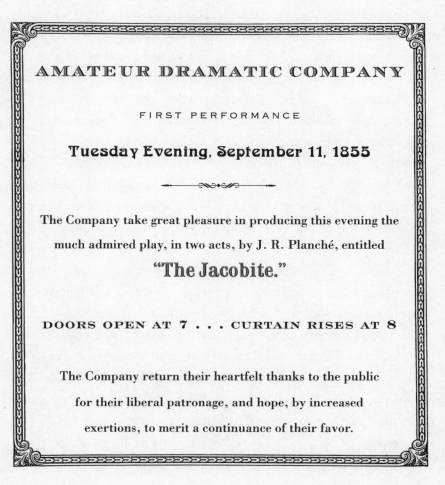

Chapter Thirteen

AMATEUR DRAMATIC COMPANY

FIRST PERFORMANCE

Tuesday Evening, September 11, 1855

The Company take great pleasure in producing this evening the much admired play, in two acts, by J. R. Planché, entitled

"The Jacobite."

DOORS OPEN AT 7 . . . CURTAIN RISES AT 8

The Company return their heartfelt thanks to the public for their liberal patronage, and hope, by increased exertions, to merit a continuance of their favor.

At seven in the evening, the cast members of the Walpole Amateur Dramatic Company began to hear the echoes of footsteps on the plank floors of Walpole Academy's great hall. They sequestered themselves in two empty classrooms—the young men in one, the young ladies in another—to put on their costumes and run over their lines one final time before the curtain rose at eight o'clock.

Louisa's Widow Pottle costume was a simple chintz dress and colored petticoat and took no time at all to put on. A linen cap that was more appropriate to the dress of the prior century, but was all that was available, concealed Louisa's heavy coiled braid. Though the others viewed their involvement as a light dalliance, Louisa had spent her evenings the last two weeks practicing her lines again and again in her room, relishing the chance to channel her frustrations into her character's improper pronouncements. Shouting "Impudent varlet!" and "Ragamuffin!" in any other context would have been a scandal, but onstage she could hope to garner some laughs. And now here was this unexpected piece of news that turned everything on its head. Joseph didn't love Nora. Even if he still planned on marrying her, this seemed a victory of sorts.

As the other girls fussed with their hair, Louisa crept quietly down the hall to the stage door. She entered and peeked through the gap between the old musty velvet curtain and the wall. Families and out-of-town guests crowded the rows of chairs, and the hall echoed with the chatter and laughter of friendly conversation as the audience anticipated the performance. She scanned the crowd of about a hundred for familiar faces. Her father and mother sat in the second row along with Lizzie. Three chairs in the front row sat empty, and as Louisa looked down the aisle to the entrance at the back of the hall, she discovered with astonishment the guest they had been reserved for.

Louisa had read in the New York paper that Fanny Kemble, the British actress she'd always admired, was touring New England to give her infamous Shakespeare readings. Incredibly, Louisa's idol now floated gracefully toward the front row in a gown of purple silk, her neck draped with jewels. Louisa never would have dreamed this famous actress would bother with a little community theater. Suddenly she was in the presence of a genius of her time, not to mention a woman unafraid of upsetting the dictates of propriety in order to live her life as she pleased. She wondered if God had put Fanny Kemble in her path at this moment to remind her that life held the promise of unlimited and surprising joys, if only one had the courage to pursue them.

Louisa glanced at the clock in the back of the hall to see that it was nearly time to begin. The stagehands entered and began to arrange the set pieces to form the interior of the Crooked Billet, the public house of the inn and the setting for the opening scene. Toward the back of the stage they leaned a large plank against a wedge to form the illusion of a cellar door left ajar. Anna and Margaret, as Patty and Lady Somerford, entered talking of Major Murray, secret lover of the Lady and currently imprisoned as a traitor to the king.

At last, from the "cellar," Louisa bellowed her first line: "I've told thee so a hundred times, fool; art thee deaf!" She tromped into the stage lights in an exaggerated stagger and the audience burst with laughter. Though the house lamps were dark, she imagined Fanny Kemble in the front row, laughing along with the rest. She felt truly buoyed for the first time in weeks. She had always loved the stage; she had always loved to make people laugh. One certainly could not have everything she wanted in life, but she could find the things she was good at and practice them with passion, with deep commitment, and try with all her heart to become the person the Almighty Friend intended her to be. It was a modern day. Marriage and motherhood were far from the only things a woman could seek to excel in. Just look at Fanny Kemble.

And then, as quickly as it began, the play ended. As they drew the curtain closed, it wobbled on the crude pulley system they had constructed—a comical reminder that indeed they were not acting in a Boston theater—and the cast gathered in a line across the stage to take its bows. Louisa held Anna's hand and walked forward, smiling broadly at the cheering audience members, now on their feet. As the stage lights dimmed, Louisa caught sight of Fanny's graceful clap— the movement of her slender arms, the rhythm of the fingertips on her left hand as they struck the palm of her right. The entire night had been a balm on Louisa's tender, battered heart. The world seemed to open to her then, unfolding in ways she hadn't seen before. Suddenly, a vision of herself a few years hence flashed through her mind. She walked down Beacon Street in Boston, three books in the crook of her arm, each with her name pressed into the spine. In her pocket, a fifty-dollar advance rustled against the fabric of her dress and she was headed back to her rented room, where she would put the kettle on the stove and draw a fresh sheet of paper from the drawer.

Back in the "dressing room" after their final curtain calls, the female cast members embraced joyously and chattered about the performance's best moments. They removed the pins from their hair, unfastened one another's costumes, and changed back into the dresses they had on when they arrived. The costumes lay in a heap on the floor.

Harriet, acting once again like the loudmouthed toad Louisa thought she resembled, shouted above the feminine rancor to gather their attention. "Everyone is invited to Birch Glen for a celebration. My mother and I have been baking cakes all week!"

The girls cheered and began in a flurry to fasten capes and bonnets, preparing to leave. Harriet looked at the pile of costumes on the dusty floor of the classroom. "Wait—Margaret worked so hard on these costumes—we can't just leave them to get damp and wrinkled. They'll have to be folded," she said in a tone that made it clear *she* would not be doing the folding.

The others nodded but Louisa held up her hand. "Why don't you let me do it, and I'll be just a few minutes behind you to the party?" She was desperate for a moment alone. She wasn't ready for the evening to end, wasn't ready to return to reality and all its confusions.

"And I'll help," Anna chimed in. "It will only take a moment."

"No, Anna," Harriet said. "You must come now. I have it on good authority that Mr. Nicholas Sutton will be an early guest. I think I know whom he will be anxious to see!"

The group broke into laughter and giddy chatter. Anna looked at Louisa, her cheeks pink with embarrassment, but her eyes full of yearning. Louisa clutched Anna's hand. "Go ahead," she whispered. "I'm right behind you. Will you tell Marmee and Father to go ahead without me? I'll be there soon." Anna nodded and kissed her sister's cheek, and the throng of girls poured into the school's hallway.

Louisa leaned against the teacher's desk and stood very still with her arms at her side, listening. She heard the lilting feminine voices take on a baritone accompaniment as the girls met up with the boys in the hallway. The audience waited to receive them, and she heard Harriet announce once again the invitation to the post-performance celebration. A few moments later a great silence descended on the entire building and Louisa gave a relieved sigh. Alone at last, she could finally relish the evening's successes.

She crouched down and swept the costumes up in her arms, carrying them over to the teacher's desk, where she could stand folding and letting her mind drift away. Margaret had done a beautiful job with the sewing. And she'd made them so quickly, too. She would be an excellent mistress of her new home with Samuel once they were married. Louisa felt happy for them but no longer felt the sting of envy. People were meant for different things in life, she reflected, and keeping a house, running a kitchen, sewing linens, and tending the chickens—these were not things Louisa could imagine herself doing, no matter how great the love that bound her as a wife to her husband. In that moment of unguarded reverie, an image of Joseph came into her mind and ran its course before she had time to cut it short.

It was the premonition of her future self she'd had onstage, ferrying copies of her books back to a room that was all her own, but this time she reached the parlor of the rooming house to find Joseph waiting on a settee, his hat resting on his lap. Waiting for her. He would see the books in her hands and break into a congratulatory smile, running his fingers over the covers and spines. He would flip them open to see the quality of the typesetting, but there would be no need to read them. He'd have read them all before. She would dash up to her room to place them on the shelf next to her desk and hurry back downstairs; they would set off for an afternoon walk, as they did most afternoons, and converse about the great moral issues on the minds of all thinking people: the question of slavery, the question of women's rights.

But reality broke into her reverie. If only it could be that simple! If only society were not so narrow in its notions of love and companionship! Louisa placed the last folded dress upon the pile, shaking her head in confusion. Surely it pleased God to see love grow thick and verdant in the light of equality and friendship. And yet it could not be.

She heard a floorboard creak behind her and spun around with a startled gasp. He stood in the doorway. Not the Joseph of her reverie, but Joseph flesh and bone and gentle voice.

"You're still here."

His pale eyes caressed Louisa's face like two hands. Her heart was at once exultant and rent anew.

Love bewilders the wisest, and it would make me quite blind or mad, I know; therefore I'd rather have nothing to do with it for a long, long while.

—*Moods*

Chapter Fourteen

It took merely a few seconds for Joseph to cross from the doorway to where Louisa stood at the front of the room, but it could have been years. Anticipation bent her like an archer's bow.

And then he was at her side. "You were wonderful," he nearly whispered. He looked tired and a little grave, two qualities she never would have imagined seeing in his face.

She felt her cheeks warming. "Wonderful as a loudmouthed old lady. I'm not sure whether to take that as a compliment." She gave him a wry smile.

He shook his head, undeterred. "I couldn't take my eyes off you." He stood very near her now and she could feel the heat of his breath. She was afraid to touch even his hand for fear of what might happen.

"Louisa . . ." he began. She focused her eyes on his shoulder, the safest place she could find, though it too had its trappings—a wide masculine slope, the promise of slick skin beneath the cloth of his shirt. He tipped her chin up with his finger so that she could look nowhere else but his eyes. "Maybe now you will give me a moment to explain—"

"I know. Margaret told me about Nora, your father . . . all of it."

"So you understand, then?"

Louisa nodded, placing her hand on his forearm. "This is what you must do, for your family's sake. It is a great burden, but you must bear it."

"Then you *don't* understand. Listen to me—I thought I had reconciled myself to marrying Nora, but when I saw you tonight, I nearly splintered in two. I have made a grave mistake."

She closed her eyes and sighed. "Oh, why did you come? Nothing has changed since you first agreed to this arrangement. There's nothing to be done about it."

His eyes grew slightly damp and his voice broke. "I cannot bear it. I won't. Do you not feel the same?"

Before she could temper her reply, she spoke. "I do." Perhaps the evening's triumphs had made her bold. The words began tumbling out—it felt futile to try to stop them. "I've thought of little else but you these last weeks."

He exhaled with relief and placed his palm on the back on her hair, drawing her face toward his. They pressed their foreheads together and she felt the sensation of contact resonate throughout her body. He brushed his thumb across her lips.

She heard a rustle of paper on the other side of the room and instinctively pulled away with a gasp. Joseph turned toward the doorway and Louisa glanced all around, but no one was there. The rustle came again and Louisa looked to see the head of a tiny mouse peeking up from beneath a pile of papers. She smiled, relieved. "We are not alone," she said, pointing. Joseph closed his eyes and shook his head, laughing at their guilty reaction to the thought of being seen together. The mouse had broken the tension between them, at least for the moment.

"Let's go outside," Louisa suggested. She didn't dare ask whether he was coming to the party at Birch Glen, and whether he would be bringing his intended wife with him. The theme of the night had been the escape from reality. Why rush back to it now? she reasoned. She placed the folded costumes in the trunk and, before she swung the lid closed, pulled a shawl from the pile. The autumn evenings had been getting cooler. She extinguished the lamp and they stood in the dark for a long moment, lacing their fingertips together. Determined to breathe, Louisa pushed past Joseph and led the way down the dark hallway toward the door.

The night air felt like a cool bath and brought her back to her senses. The thing was to keep moving, and they began to walk quickly, not along the walkway toward the street and Washington Square, as she had intended, but instead up the path that led into the woods behind the Academy and out through the dense stand of maple and elm, behind which open land stretched, patched with farms. There was no hesitation in either of their strides. A line of Whitman's lingered in her mind as she climbed the path, and she marveled at the miraculous truth of his words: *Hands I have taken, face I have kissed, mortal I have ever touched, it shall be you.*

They made their way uphill along the narrow path. Louisa walked in front, pushing low-hanging branches away, sensing the sinewy tickle of spiderwebs. They reached the last of the trail, where hunters came to take deer and pheasant. But now it was empty, save for the buttery moon hanging low in the sky.

Joseph struck out ahead, taking Louisa's hand and pulling her along. He sat down in a feathery patch of weeds so high they almost reached his shoulders, and she sat down beside him. She felt afraid to look at him the way one does not look directly at the sun. Her left hand rested on his right palm and she felt his fingertips run along the inside of her fingers, up her wrist toward her elbow. He whispered her name and she turned toward him, her breath an imperceptible pant, to see the yellow light of the moon washing over his features.

He took her face in his hands, his thumbs pressed against her jaw, and pulled her mouth toward his. The kiss was hungry, aching, long. Louisa felt she'd like to leap into his mouth, be swallowed whole between his lips. His hands coursed her shoulders and down her back, roving frantically, taking her in. Her heart began to pound and she felt she would cry out with fear. Never had she felt her mind in such opposition to her body.

In Joseph's eyes she saw only gentle affection. He had felt her stiffen and pull away and he slowed the fumbling of his fingers at her stays, taking her fully into his arms, pressing her face to his neck, stroking her hair.

"It's all right," he said. "I only wanted to be here with you, nothing more. I only wanted to sit here beneath the moon with you, share the warmth of your kiss. Only that."

She pulled away to face him and reached to the back of her head where his hand had been, slid out a few pins and released her raven curtain of hair, which fell in waves down her back. As she began to recline onto the soft ground he stopped her, slipped out of his jacket, and spread it on the weeds beneath her head. She slid his suspender off his shoulder and he lowered himself down upon her, taking her mouth to his once again.

These hearts of ours are curious and contrary things.

—*Little Women*

Chapter Fifteen

Louisa's mind felt completely empty. She rolled on her side and felt the cool silk lining of Joseph's jacket against her cheek. A black ant ascended the sleeve of her dress, which lay rumpled on the grass beside her. He was unmoved by what he had surely witnessed from his perch on a blade of grass a few minutes before. Louisa supposed it was hard to scandalize an ant.

Joseph lay still beside her, his shirt open, and she placed her palm on his sternum to feel once again the galloping stampede of his heartbeat. He was so quiet she thought he might be asleep, but when she looked she saw that his eyes were open, scanning the sky. They lay in the tall weeds, concealed from the eyes of anyone who might pass along the path, though no one would. They seemed to be the only people in New Hampshire, in the world, for the moment.

"Are you awake?" she whispered anyway, not knowing what else to say. He did not answer but brought his hand to hers and began tracing circles on it with his fingers.

She had convinced herself that they had somehow fallen out of time, that she could lie in the grass in her shift, every inch of her skin alive with sensation, forever. She thought once again of that strange poem that seemed a cord binding the two of them together. *Press close magnetic nourishing night!* All her yearning to suspend the darkness was telescoped in that line. But as her consciousness began to return and she drifted from her body back into her mind, she saw that the moon had crossed the sky and hung above the horizon. Though dawn was only an hour away, the moon was so bright she noticed how uncovered she was for the first time. She reached for her dress.

"What time do you think it is?" she asked, sitting up, suddenly anxious. Anna would be waiting for her. They all would be. She hoped perhaps they'd have concluded that she decided at the last moment to choose a night of solitude rather than face the noise of society. She had been known to do such things.

Joseph sat up too. "I don't know." She was attempting to turn the twisted dress right side out, but he clutched her hands. "Louisa, I think I know what to do. If we leave right now they'll all still be at the party." He stood and flung his shirt over his head, attempting to button it and tuck it into his trousers at the same time. "We can walk over to Bellows Falls—it isn't far—and rent a coach. We could be in Boston just after dawn, maybe take the train to New York tomorrow. My cousin Edward—the one who sends me all the books—he could help us find accommodations, I'm sure of it."

Louisa's eyes widened. "Leave here? For how long?"

"For good." He pulled her to her feet and helped her pull her dress over her head, turning to her back to fasten it. "Don't you see—it's the only way. I can't go through with this wedding. I simply can't. I want to marry *you*, Louisa."

She took a long breath as his words penetrated her mind. Her heart wrenched within her chest. "But what about your family? What about your sister?"

"I can't think of that now. We all have to make our own way in this world."

"Joseph!" Her voice was scolding. "How can you say that? Catherine is only fifteen and a girl. How is she supposed to make her way on her own? You and I both know what can happen to girls without any means of support. She could end up a servant—or worse. I cannot let you abandon her this way!"

He stood in front of her and grabbed her shoulders hard. "Listen to me!" he shouted. His voice echoed across the empty field. "I . . . won't . . . do . . . it." With each word he shook her, his voice a low growl. Louisa grimaced with fear, her eyes swimming. Joseph seemed suddenly to realize that he was hurting her and jerked his hands away, his palms splayed open in front of him. He spoke in a meek whisper. "I'm sorry." He sank to the ground and she lowered herself down beside him.

Louisa shook her head. She knew some things about rage, for her own temper could overtake her like a hurricane when she least expected. Feeling there was something she yearned for desperately but could not have, feeling she was at the mercy of forces outside her control, forces that were determining the course of her life: these were the times she felt that hollowing anger. And she felt it now, but it was tempered by a calm that had descended on her when she looked out from the stage to see the placid, scandalous Fanny Kemble perched in the front row, a living symbol of fearlessness.

"Listen to me," she said, taking his hand. They did not look at each other but instead faced out in the same direction. "If you feel you must go away, I cannot stop you. But I will not make myself your accomplice. And if you are the person I believe you to be, you won't go at all." She was quiet a moment, measuring her words carefully. "You have to help your family, and I have to help mine. As you surely know, my own father has no grasp of or interest in finances. We only came to Walpole because my cousins were offering us a home for the summer. I can make five dollars a story in Boston, and I intend to go as soon as I can."

She glanced at Joseph but he continued to look out across the field. She saw a shadow along his jaw as he clenched it tight, and she braced herself for another angry outburst, but none came.

"And I have to go alone," she said, her voice barely above a whisper. The next words were heavy in her mouth, like marbles, for she doubted their truthfulness. "I don't think I could be married, not to anyone."

"You don't mean that." His voice broke and she realized he was not fighting back rage but tears. "It wouldn't have to be the way you think."

Louisa took a deep breath and spoke the words she believed but didn't quite own in her heart. "But it would be marriage nonetheless, and therein lies the problem. Marriage is conventional because it gives order to families, order to society. It is an exchange of property, as you well know," she said, thinking of Nora Sutton and her family's money. "Marriage does not account for love. It does not account for friendship, for independence. But what we feel for each other lives in these very things: independence of mind and spirit, ideas, each of our interests and achievements." She placed her hand against his cheek and turned his face toward hers. "Do you understand? Agreeing to marry would mean agreeing to give up everything between us that matters."

"So you would have me marry *her*? Have children with *her*?" He glanced at Louisa, gauging her reaction to the insinuation: Nora, naked in his arms.

Louisa slammed shut a door inside her mind against this image. "Your family is depending on you. You have given your word. I have seen inside the deepest part of you, and I know you are not one to go back on your word."

"If you don't love me," he said, "afford me the dignity of telling me so."

Louisa looked at him, sorrow laid bare on her face. "How dare you say this—after what happened between us just now?" She touched his arm. "How can you possibly think I don't love you?"

"I don't think it. I know it. I think you don't know what love is. If you did, you would come away with me—or let me come with you to Boston. If you loved me, you would know that nothing else matters but being together."

Louisa stared at him in disbelief. "I have been waiting my whole life for the day I would have my freedom. How can you ask me to cast it away as soon as it's finally come? Besides, it seems I am the only one who might be relied upon to earn an income for my family. I think this *real love* you talk about is only an excuse for selfishness. It is the love of an impatient boy, not a grown man. A grown man knows that in life we may not always simply have whatever we want."

"Well, you certainly had what *you* wanted tonight."

Louisa let out a cry of a wounded animal and her open palm struck Joseph's cheek with all the force in her strong shoulder. He nearly lost his balance, and a wild look came into his eyes that made her recoil. Joseph leapt to his feet. She thought he might hit her back, but instead he stood stiff with his fists clenched at his sides. He felt she was grinding his heart under the heel of her boot, and it made him want to hurt her.

"As you wish, I will marry Nora. Soon, if I can. And you will see her on my arm; you will see her cradle our children." He pointed his index finger at her face. "And you will know regret. But I will have forgotten you by then."

Louisa looked at him with something almost like pity and in her exhaustion nearly chuckled at his words. It was impossible either of them would ever forget anything about the other, no matter how much relief it would bring them. Even then they both knew that this night would haunt them the rest of their days.

She gathered the shawl from the costume trunk around her shoulders and pulled herself to her feet, a dull pain radiating from every joint and muscle. "I cannot wish you love, for you do not love her. But I wish you the peace of duty fulfilled. Which, sometimes, can be a little *like* love."

And with that she turned and strode up the hill, her chin tipped high. Joseph followed, walking into the pitiless light of the descending moon.

It is easy to forgive, but not to forget,

words which cannot be unsaid.

—*A Modern Mephistopheles*

Chapter Sixteen

Louisa walked slowly up Wentworth Road toward Yellow Wood. If she was going to have to explain to her parents where she had been all night, ten extra minutes wouldn't change that. She reflected on how successful she'd been at convincing Joseph of the right path for him to take; her acting skills had come through for her again— or were they standing in the way of her happiness? In truth she felt nothing of the calm certainty she'd expressed to him; rather, it seemed an explosion had gone off inside her, and now tiny shards stuck all throughout her body, causing unrelenting pain. How would she ever bear it?

As the house came into view she saw that she would have to face the questions she feared right away. Anna and Nicholas sat on the front step engaged in intimate conversation. They did not see Louisa coming, so she scuffed her feet and coughed to garner their attention. She didn't want to take them by surprise.

"Louisa!" Anna exclaimed, immediately distressed to be seen so late at night alone with a caller, even if it was only by her younger sister. Anna believed deeply in the importance of propriety and would die a thousand deaths before she endured her own reputation being compromised. Women could not own property and sometimes could not even control when or whom they married or when they became mothers. Reputation was the only possession a woman had under her own control. It meant everything.

Nicholas stood up, equally embarrassed. "Well, Miss Alcott," he said, stiffly. "Now that I have seen you safely home I must be off, for the hour is late." Their eyes connected for a moment and something passed between them Louisa recognized. But their longing was tempered by a kind of tranquillity she did not know—for Anna and Nicholas looked forward to the time when they would be together, for good, in the conventional way that would cause no strife. Louisa felt her temper flare like a match. It was all so unfair! She turned away to let them have a private good-bye. Out of the corner of her eye she saw Nicholas clasp Anna's hand, which she held down at her side, and pull her toward him. He whispered something that made her giggle. Then she sighed.

"I plan to meet the boys in the morning. Which is in just a few hours, I'm afraid. We'll be working on the roof if the weather is good. But perhaps I will see you tomorrow evening."

"Please be careful," Anna said. "I've seen the way you climb around like monkeys on that roof."

"As you wish, my dear," Nicholas said, turning to Louisa and clearing his throat. "Good night, Miss Louisa." He tipped his hat in her direction.

The sisters waited until he had safely exited the front gate before speaking. Louisa steeled herself for what would come next. She could see in Anna's face that her initial embarrassment about her own circumstances had been overtaken by shock at Louisa's wandering around in the early morning hours. "Where the devil have you been?" Anna hissed, her hand at her throat. "I thought for certain you'd arrived home and were upstairs in bed."

Should she simply tell her sister the truth? Louisa wondered. It pained her to lie to Anna, the person she was closer to than anyone else in the world. And why should she lie? Nothing could be truer than what she felt for Joseph, and its truth made it an almost sacred thing. To lie about it denied this fact.

And yet she knew Anna would not understand. She would be devastated on Louisa's behalf, that her sister had behaved so foolishly and ruined any chance of future happiness with a proper husband. People talked. A young lady who was less than pure was not a suitable choice for a bride.

"I have been . . ." Louisa stalled. ". . . walking."

"All night?" Anna was incredulous. "Alone?"

Louisa nodded. Perhaps if she did not say the words aloud she would not actually be lying.

Anna examined her carefully, taking time to choose her words. "I don't know if I believe you."

"Believe what you like." Louisa's voice was sharp. "It matters not to me."

"And so *angry* too, when I merely asked a simple question, a question clearly called for by your waltzing up the path at this hour with no explanation. I certainly think I have cause to question whether you are truthful."

"Perhaps I should be asking what *you* are doing with Nicholas Sutton, alone at this hour?" Louisa felt anger overtake her sensibilities. She knew this feeling—once it came on, it was difficult to turn back, no matter how much she wanted to.

Anna's eyes filled with tears. That her sister would accuse her of something improper, knowing full well that Anna would never dream of violating her modesty outside of the safe confines of marriage, seemed a mean-spirited brutality. "Louisa, when the party at Birch Glen dragged on and you did not come . . . and Joseph Singer was noticeably absent . . . I began to fear . . ." She seemed unsure how to ask the question that burned on her lips. "I pray to God you have not done something that cannot be taken back."

"Don't worry," Louisa seethed. "I won't sully your good name in society."

"Please!" Anna began to cry. "You think that is what I care about? It isn't—I only worry that my sister will have her heart broken." She placed her hand on Louisa's arm. "Nothing good can come of it, Lou. Don't you see that? Nothing good. He is *engaged* to someone else. He will not marry you."

Louisa looked away, her own eyes brimming with hot tears, but her relentless temper flared. "And you are so certain *Nicholas Sutton's* aims are honorable? As far as I know, he has yet to speak to our father about his plans. Perhaps he does not intend to at all."

"Oh, Louisa, you know that is not true."

"Do I? It seems to me he can only sit with my sister in the dead of night, when no one else is around. Perhaps he is ashamed to associate with our family. We *are* but poor daughters of a philosopher who struts about town in tatters. When it comes to marriage, you are sorely naïve if you think money does not matter. It may be the only thing that really does."

Anna brushed aside a tear with her fingertips. She clamped her hands on the small of her back and squared her shoulders as she gazed down the path that led away from the house toward town, and beyond that Boston, New York. She knew there were thousands of other places, but she didn't need to see them for herself to know they were there. "All my life," she began, her voice low but strong, "I have tried to be good. That probably sounds silly to you, but it's true. I have. I've tried to be a good daughter to my parents, tried to keep our family together—and it hasn't always been easy. I never have asked for anything for myself, have barely hoped even in silence for the things other people take for granted. But this, the love of this man, a home of our own, my own daughters, sons, if God decides to provide them—I cannot hold my tongue and let the chance of having those things pass me by. I *will* become Mrs. Nicholas Sutton. I'm determined."

Somewhere beneath her resentment, Louisa wanted to reassure her sister that if anyone deserved the happiness of marriage and family life, it was Anna. But though it was petty and small of her, she could not do it—something she would soon regret for a long time. It wasn't jealousy Louisa felt. That very evening, though it seemed like an age ago, she'd made up her mind that marriage was not her own path, and nothing in her wanted to go back on that now, despite everything she shared with Joseph. If she was jealous of anything, it was Anna's ability to be satisfied with convention. She wasn't a prisoner of the restlessness Louisa felt, the endless questioning her mind pursued. Anna had a more typical worry: If she loved him, would he love her back? Would they be together as they hoped?

"I suppose I can hardly blame you for wanting to escape this poverty. There's certainly no end in sight."

No purer heart had contemplated the meaning of the role of wife than Anna. The suggestion that she was clinging to Nicholas for his money cut her to the quick. "How can you say such a thing to me?" Anna cried, tears slick on her cheeks. "I *love* him."

"Well, we can love people for all sort of reasons."

"I won't hear this—I won't." Anna shook her head, her voice growing frantic. "It is only that you are envious, because your own affair cannot end happily."

"What do you know about the way that I feel? I don't envy you—I pity you. I am going to make something of my life. I am going to sell my stories and see the world. And you want to waste your life cooking and cleaning and chasing babies around the yard because a man made you his wife. Why would I be envious of that?"

Anna looked Louisa straight in the eye. "Because you can't have it."

The sisters stood still and close. Louisa turned away first, storming into the house. Anna followed silently behind. The last thing they needed now was to wake their parents.

But Abba was already awake. Or had never gone to sleep. They could hear her talking softly to Lizzie, the sound of a rag being wrung into a bowl. She was nursing her patient and took no notice of her older daughters' late arrival.

Women have been called queens for a long time,

but the kingdom given them isn't worth ruling.

—*An Old-Fashioned Girl*

Chapter Seventeen

Wednesday was reserved for baking, and as usual Anna and Louisa rose early to help their mother. May lingered in her room to "finish her mending"—and doze in the sunny window seat. In the bed beside her, Lizzie slept late, her fever in retreat after a restless night.

Baking was a hot, arduous task and it took most of the day to make the bread and pies that would get them through the week, including Sunday dinner. The kitchen was unusually silent. While they waited for the brick oven to heat, Louisa, who was best at forceful kneading, stood at the worktable. She ground the heels of her hands into the warm dough, her arms locked in the repetitive movements. Her muscles ached with exhaustion.

Anna had scarcely said good morning to her. Louisa knew she had said some hurtful things in the night, but despite the light of day she didn't exactly regret them. Her anger had been tamped down but still burned as an ember, keeping her moving. If it was jealousy that made her hate her sister at this moment, then so be it. There was no question that Anna deserved happiness, but didn't Louisa deserve it too? Didn't everyone deserve a chance to be happy?

When the last loaf was cooling, mother and daughters sat at the oak table for a moment of rest. Louisa reflected that all three of them could benefit from a long afternoon nap. Anna's face was drawn and pale and her shoulders sagged. Louisa stifled a yawn. Abba looked the worst off, sadness burning in her dark eyes.

She clasped her daughters' hands. "My girls," she whispered. "I fear for Elizabeth. She is so frail. It seems every fever or cough she contracts is worse than the last." She stifled a sob. "I don't know how much more her body can take."

The sisters comforted their mother and ushered her into the parlor to the comfort of the horsehair sofa. They never knew how much stock to put in Abba's dire predictions. To her, Lizzie was always frail, always on the verge of leaving this world for good, though the facts didn't bear that out. Louisa had to admit, though, that Lizzie seemed more like an invalid than ever as the summer waned. Since her adventure in Bellows Falls, she had spent most of her days in bed. No matter whether their mother was overreacting, Abba needed rest. Anna and Louisa promised to finish up the work in the kitchen.

A little later, as Abba's eyes fluttered on the verge of sleep, the sisters heard a sharp knock at the front door. Abba bolted up and swung the heavy door open. Samuel Parker stepped inside, the brilliant morning sun behind him throwing his face into shadow.

"Is Mr. Alcott in, ma'am?" Samuel's shirt collar hung open. A semicircle of sweat soaked his undershirt.

Abba's knuckles whitened on the doorknob. "Good morning, Samuel. Is everything all right?"

Louisa and Anna looked into the parlor, their aprons still fastened at their backs.

"Hello, Samuel," Anna called. An oblong smudge of flour marred her left cheek. "Would you like some brown bread? It's almost cool."

He glanced in her direction, then looked back at Abba. "*Please*— Mr. Alcott. Is he home, ma'am?"

"Well, yes." Abba, flustered, fussed with folds of her skirt. "He's in his study."

Without a word Samuel pushed past her and flew down the hall to the closed door. He bolted in and slammed it behind him. The two male voices ejected a few quick, indiscernible sentences, and the door flew open again. Samuel clomped noisily down the hallway in his work boots. Bronson followed at his heels, his shirt fluttering like a sail behind him.

"What the deuce is the matter with you two?" Louisa shouted, her forehead glistening in the heat of the kitchen.

Bronson turned back to Abba as Samuel sprinted down the front path and south toward the center of town. "Stay here." He clamped his hand on her upper arm, almost violently. "All of you. I mean it. I will be back as soon as I can."

He hurried awkwardly down the path after Sam.

"Wait, my husband, wait! What is the matter? Please—tell us!" Abba yelled.

But Bronson didn't turn back.

He didn't return, in fact, until the late afternoon. Abba and her daughters obeyed his command—they did not leave the house, not even to cast the dishwater into the weeds. The women were uncharacteristically silent as they worked about the house, grateful to have something to keep their hands busy. Never had the floor been quite so clean; never had the kitchen been so well scrubbed and aired.

Each held in her mind her own private speculation of what sort of disaster had befallen the town, and they prayed vague and desperate prayers against the unknown. Louisa felt an overpowering dread. Something in Bronson's demeanor betrayed his concern for his daughters in particular, and Louisa doubted the emergency involved an elderly uncle or friend of her father's. Death called on the old and sick like a guest with an appointment, but when it came for the young it barged through the door and took everyone by surprise. A frothing anxiety burned in Louisa's chest. Something had happened to Joseph. She felt she knew it for certain, could sense that he was in pain—or worse.

Oh, why hadn't she gone away with him when she had the chance? The world seemed full of poison, fear, and harm, and she began her grieving.

The clock on the mantel ticked past three when Bronson appeared in the doorway, cloaked by the shadow of the whole house now that the sun had made its way to the other side of the sky. He held his hat in his hands and stepped over the threshold with a deep sigh. He pointed toward the horsehair sofa. Louisa sat between her mother and sister, taking their hands and steeling herself for the blow to come. Bronson knelt down before them. Louisa closed her eyes and began to pray, so she did not see him take Anna's hands in his.

"My child, forgive me for what I have to tell you. Nicholas Sutton is dead."

Later they would hear the story. Halfway down the south panel of the roof, his back turned toward the breathtaking view of the Connecticut River and the verdant hills of Vermont the third-story dormer would provide, Nicholas Sutton lost his footing and felt the slate slide beneath the soles of his boots. He reached out desperately to take hold of an ill-placed shingle protruding from the pattern, an exposed beam, but there were none. The young men had crafted a smooth, even design, and there were no imperfections he could exploit. In one horrific moment his friends watched as he disappeared over the cornice, his face twisted in terror.

Samuel and Joseph clambered down the ladder as quickly as they could, throwing their own safety into jeopardy, and scrambled around to the back of the house. Joseph felt his knees buckle when he saw the contorted shape Nicholas made in the grass. His hips were squared toward the sky, his knees pointing up, but his upper body faced down into the grass. His right cheek was visible, and part of his right eye. The socket was full of blood. Samuel and Joseph sank down beside him and Nicholas emitted a small moan.

Samuel and Joseph locked eyes—they couldn't believe he was still breathing. Samuel leapt to his feet and took off running full speed toward his father's house—the first place he could think to go. Soon he would remember that his parents had gone to the next town over for a luncheon, and he would turn toward the Alcotts, two doors down, where he felt sure Mr. Alcott would be in his study. Though it was rumored he had sent his own daughters out to work rather than take on work he felt was beneath his intellectual abilities, Walpoleans also knew well the story of Bronson's effort to free the jailed runaway slave the previous summer, where his bravery and quick thinking amid the pistol shots astonished the mob. Mr. Alcott would know what to do.

Meanwhile, Joseph knelt in the blinding morning sun on the dry, caked ground, talking softly to Nicholas. "Samuel has gone to get help, Nick. Hold steady, man. Everything will be all right."

The last part was a lie, he knew. As he said it his oldest friend, who, like an older brother, had taught Joseph how to dig the thimble-sized frogs out of the muddy stream bed behind his house when they were boys, shuddered out his last breath.

We used to have such happy times

together, before we were grown up.

—*Moods*

Chapter Eighteen

September 13, 1855

Honor to the memory of our true and noble Nicholas
Charles, only son of Charles and Clara Sutton, who died
in this town on Wednesday morning in his twenty-fourth
year. The friends of the family and classmates of the
deceased are invited to attend the funeral Saturday at
ten in the morning at the Unitarian Church.

The house was unusually quiet for a Saturday afternoon. Typically,
Bronson entertained a few of his intellectual sparring partners
from Concord or Boston while Anna, Louisa, and Lizzie looked on,
sometimes chiming in, but mostly keeping to their sewing, or in Louisa's case, escaping to the bedroom to work on a story. May would tear
through the house just on the way to or just returned from some gathering with the friends she seemed to collect like charms on a bracelet.
And Abba, when they could convince her to let the kitchen and the
wash and the garden be, would hover a moment in her rocking chair,
her chapped and aching hands resting in her lap like two old potatoes.

But on that morning the people of the town of Walpole had laid
Nicholas Sutton to rest in the cemetery behind the Unitarian Church.
After the service, the Sutton family received mourners at their home.
Bronson had insisted they all attend and he received little resistance.
Anna entered the Suttons' parlor looking especially pale in her black

dress, her hair knotted in a severe bun at the back of her head. She stood tall and did not cry, but her eyes were empty and Louisa could see she had retracted somewhere deep within herself. The neighbors greeted one another, many stopping to clutch Anna's hand a moment longer than the others', acknowledging what she alone had lost. Around midday they returned to Yellow Wood and scattered to separate corners of the house, either to contemplate the shock of the tragedy alone or to simply try to forget.

Louisa stood in the kitchen preparing a simple supper of baked apples, spider corncake steamed in molasses, and succotash. The others insisted they had no appetite, especially Anna, who ended nearly two days of silence to say so. But Louisa knew that as the nervous tension of the day subsided, they would discover they were ravenous. She reflected as she tested a half-cooked butter bean between her teeth that the grief and uncertainties that plagued the human mind drove people back into their bodies almost as a kind of refuge. Noticing the coarseness of wool against the skin, hot sun on the back of the neck, the delicious stretch of the muscle in the arch of the foot—these palpable sensations had distinct beginnings and endings, unlike the swirling chaos of the troubled mind. Louisa knew a full belly would bring unexpected comfort.

And comfort was exactly what Anna needed now. Louisa glanced out into the parlor at her sister, who sat in Abba's rocking chair gazing numbly out the window at the gray sky. Judging that the beans needed at least another quarter hour, Louisa sighed and told herself that she could no longer put off telling Anna what had been weighing on her heart since Wednesday.

She crossed the room and stood behind her sister, looking out to see what she had been watching. The leaves of the maple tree in front of the house had begun to turn. The bright green was edged with orange, as if slow flames devoured the leaves.

"Do you remember the day we went to Singer's to buy the fabric for the drapes?" Anna's voice was scarcely above a whisper, as if sorrow itself constricted her throat. She had sensed Louisa standing near, but her gaze held steady. Louisa nodded, then said softly, "I do."

"I thought to myself that day, 'I will be engaged to be married by the time these leaves turn orange.' I remember thinking that *so* distinctly. Isn't that strange?" Louisa put her hand on Anna's shoulder. "It's not like me at all to have such a thought. The hubris—to think I had control over it all, that I could *will* it to happen. And yet I was so sure I was right. As if I were having some kind of premonition. That was before I'd even met Nicholas."

"Nan," Louisa began, her voice already quavering. "The things I said to you on Tuesday night, the way I questioned his intentions . . ." She crossed in front of Anna and sank down onto her knees and took Anna's hands. "I am so ashamed. Can you ever forgive me?"

Even in her sorrow Anna's compassion broke through. "But your *heart* is broken. You only said them because your heart is broken. Of course I forgive you."

Louisa released the sob wedged in her throat and rested her cheek on Anna's lap as she cried. Not only had she said these things and thought worse, but when the shock of their father's news about Nicholas abated, Louisa couldn't help but bemoan the fact that she would now be stranded in Walpole, taking care of Anna. She felt her dream of an independent life in Boston, the place where she could finally be herself, free from obligation, free from her heartbreak, was slipping away. Louisa's heart felt hollowed out like a melon rind. Her hair was damp from her work in the kitchen, and Anna brushed it with the tips of her fingers.

"None of it was even close to true," Louisa said. "Everyone knew how much he loved you, and you him. They treated you like a widow today, as they should. Even if you weren't married in God's eyes, you were married in your hearts."

Anna's hands stopped their absent caressing. "Please," she whispered. "Say no more about it. I cannot bear it."

Louisa sat up with a start. "Of course—I'm so sorry. I only meant—"

"Please," she said again. "Please."

Louisa nodded. "Let me make you some tea."

Anna looked out at the leaves again. "I must leave this town at once. As soon as I can find a position somewhere."

Louisa's head shot up. "Leave?"

"Argue with me all you like—it won't dissuade me. That funeral today wasn't just for Nicholas. It was for me, for the life I was meant to have as his wife, the mother of his children. Each time I pass that house I will think of the corner of the garden where my corn and beans would have grown, all the unhung Christmas wreaths. If I stay here he will die over and over again, every day. Have mercy and let me go."

How quickly everything kept changing! "I will speak with our father as soon as possible. Anything you want, my dear sister, you shall have. The Almighty Friend is looking down upon you now, one of his tenderest servants. Let him give you comfort. Sorrow is only a season. You will be glad again—I know it."

Anna turned her vacant gaze on her sister and stared at eyes the same color as her own: dark like the soil. Louisa instantly knew she had taken her stalwart optimism too far. Anna's tone was low. "It is through the sheer force of will that I do not walk down to the river's edge right this second and throw myself under the current. I've thought of little else these last days—it seems to me the sweetest dream of relief. I know that *you* shall be glad again, and it pleases me to know it." Her voice turned cold as she looked away. "But take care not to speak of things you know nothing of."

One of the sweet things about pain and sorrow

is that they show us how well we are loved,

how much kindness there is in the world.

—Jack and Jill

Bronson secured by letter a position for Anna in Syracuse as a teacher at the newly built New York Asylum for Idiots, run by the famous Dr. Hervey Wilbur, where children born without all their faculties could go to learn a trade or simply how to read and write. Anna dreaded going and regretted asking to leave as her day of departure approached. But it was too late for changing her mind. And at work she could earn money to help the family, something she was beginning to realize her father might never be able to do. Bronson, Louisa, and May stood in front of the house while the driver loaded Anna's luggage into the carriage that would take her across the bridge to the train in Bellows Falls. She would ride the rest of the day, by train and then another carriage, to Syracuse. The trees along Wentworth Avenue had gone copper and vermilion, and a few leaves cascaded down around them. Louisa thought wistfully that no matter where Anna went, she would not be able to escape the reminder of these leaves. This thought was interrupted by a sound from behind her. Abba and Lizzie stood in the front window, knocking on the glass and waving to the traveler. Bronson stepped forward and put his hands on his eldest daughter's shoulders.

"You break an old man's heart today, and yet I know you must go. Take an early bed, my child. And walks each day. Give yourself time for reading and other pure amusements." He kissed her forehead. "And above all, heed your conscience."

Anna gave a solemn nod in response, and Louisa noticed with a somersault of joy in her stomach that the tiniest hint of a smile crossed Anna's lips. They had laughed many times together over their father's penchant for monologues full of wise advice. How wonderful it was to see that the old Anna resided within her, dormant beneath the heavy blanket of sorrow. *Perhaps Father is right,* Louisa thought. *She must go away so that she can return to us her old self.*

Anna hugged May next. "Good-bye, little sister."

"I hope you won't wear your widow's weeds *too* long," May said worriedly. "They make your complexion look awfully pale."

Anna sighed. "Don't worry, my dear—I will take care that my fashions don't embarrass you."

May winced and grasped Anna's hand. "Forgive me—wear what you please. And know you have all my love."

Anna laughed at her inability to stay upset with May for more than a moment. "Now get inside and help Marmee. You really will have to do your share now." May nodded and turned back toward the house.

Louisa pulled Anna close and kissed her cheeks. "Work hard. But not *too* hard." She pressed an eagle into her palm and closed Anna's fingers around it. "Buy a dress or two in Syracuse. See a play."

Anna glanced at her hand and then looked up startled at Louisa. "But this is for your writing room—your little place apart. You took an oath!"

Louisa shook her head. "It's all right—I can spare it. And don't try to argue with me. It's my money and I can do what I like with it."

Anna smiled and shook her head. "You never fail to surprise me, my dear." Bronson stood talking to the driver about the route and Anna leaned in close to Louisa so he would not hear. "Now I have a surprise for you. But first you have to promise you won't be angry."

Louisa gave her a suspicious look. "I suppose that depends on what you've done. I can *try* not to be angry. . . ."

"That's the best I can hope for. I want you to go into my sewing basket—I told May I'd leave it for her to have my ribbon and trims—there's something in there for you."

"What kind of something?"

Anna hesitated, examining Louisa's face. "Letters. Probably a dozen."

"Letters from my sister, I hope," Louisa whispered back, her eyebrows drawn together.

Anna shook her head. "They just kept coming, for weeks after the Suttons' harvest party. And then they stopped. But I didn't want you to burn them, in case . . . well, in case things changed. And they have, haven't they?"

An abrupt laugh exploded from Louisa's lips and she nodded, tears pricking her eyes. Everything had changed and then changed again. Margaret's gossip had revealed the truth about Joseph and Nora, had given Louisa an excuse to yield to him when he came to her the night of the play. But that brief succumbing, sweet as it was, had nearly caused her to lose sight of what mattered, to forget that her object was freedom, not the fleeting promise of love. She thought back on that night in the field, the terrible things they'd said to each other. Joseph had nearly begged her to let him love her, to let him walk through life by her side. But she was like an animal in a trap, gnawing off a part of herself to get free.

Anna squeezed her hand. "Louy, you should talk to him. Don't leave things the way they are."

A flicker of something like hope crossed Louisa's face, but the wounded part of her, that once-tender place now grown over with the tough skin of a scar, couldn't let her take the risk of hoping. "The way they are is the way they should be. His life is his, and my life is *mine*. And that's what I always wanted, more than anything else. That my life would be my own."

Anna sighed. "And there isn't a way you could have both? Love him *and* have your freedom?"

Louisa shook her head. "It's not possible."

Anna watched her a moment. "I wish it could be different somehow. But I suppose you will do what you must."

Just then Bronson reappeared and turned the face of his pocket watch out toward Anna. "It's time to go, my dear."

Anna nodded at her father, then leaned in to Louisa, whispering, "At the very least, fish those letters out. You certainly don't want May to find them and cause a scandal."

Louisa glanced nervously at the house, then nodded.

"I'll write you every day." Anna choked on a sob.

Louisa gave a wicked smile in reply. "Well, soon you will have to send your missives to a new address. I hope to go to Boston before long."

Now Anna smiled, a real, full smile. "Write until your fingers break. It may be the cure for everything. And don't think of this place. Pretend it was the setting in one of your stories, now finished. Perhaps one you threw in the fire."

Louisa thought for a moment of her night on the stage as the Widow Pottle, Fanny Kemble in her emeralds, Joseph's hot breath on her collarbone. "One cannot always judge things by the way they end."

"True," Anna whispered, gathering her overcoat close to her neck. "One must have faith. I want so much to believe the Psalm: '*He heals the brokenhearted and binds up their wounds.*'"

And with that she was gone. As Louisa headed back into the house, she pictured Anna speeding out of New Hampshire in the rented carriage, wrapped tight in heavy blankets to stave off the cold morning air. In the entryway she wiped her boots. May and Abba were in the back of the house, talking loudly over the clang of pots in the sink. At the foot of the armchair near the fireplace Anna's sewing basket sat, its lid askew. Louisa glanced back at the kitchen and then crossed the room to it.

The top tray, divided into sections, held a half-dozen cards wound round with various colors of thread and ribbon. A length of stiff lace had been folded into a square. Louisa pinched the center ridge of the tray and lifted it out of the basket. The deeper space below held a lone ball of yarn, a rusted pair of scissors, and the thick stack of letters. She hesitated before reaching to pull them out of the basket, as if their existence posed an actual physical threat. But once they were in her hand she almost laughed out loud. They were mere letters— paper and ink. Knowing they were in the world didn't change a thing. She stood, straightening her skirt, and stepped toward the hearth to cast them in. But then she hesitated, glancing at the flames. *Perhaps*, she reasoned with herself. *Perhaps it would be all the same if I tucked them away*. . . . She climbed the attic stairs two at a time and lifted the lid of the trunk that sat at the foot of her bed. Inside, there was a place where the lining was torn away. She tucked the letters behind the threadbare calico, placed her hand against them. Then she stood, swinging the lid shut, and began the arduous task of forgetting.

Thursday, October 4

My dear Louy,

I arrived yesterday morning and was whisked straight into the care of the head teacher, a Mrs. Hutchins, who appears to be most competent, if a little stern. We are about a mile outside of Syracuse proper in a new building just opened in August. Our quarters are plain but cozy enough: a long room with five narrow beds on each side and windows along one wall. We have an efficient little stove where we can fix our tea and I've made friends already by offering Lizzie's apple cake all around.

There is room here for as many as one hundred children, but we are not yet full. My first assignment yesterday was helping to assess a new arrival, a little pale child of ten who is both deaf and dumb. Her mother hopes she can learn to write and sew, and I intend to try to teach her if I can. It is a relief to cast myself completely into my work. Heaven knows I can use the distraction.

May let slip the news that Margaret and Sam's wedding is on the horizon. I believe they waited until my departure to begin their plans. It is thoughtful of them but I am fine and it will do me good to hear about their happy day. You must provide a full report. But don't do it in your way, skipping over all the details to the conversations afterward. I want to hear about every button on her dress, the flowers—all the trifles you despise!

Ever your loving
Anna

Dear Anna,

Only an Alcott girl would believe the cure for sadness lies in reading a painstaking recitation of the joys of others. Or maybe it is just that you yearn for a beautiful dress. Have you been shopping in town? Please spend the money I gave you on something entirely impractical. It makes me mad to know that my good little lass is going around in shabby things and being looked down upon by people who are not worthy to touch the hem of her ragged old gowns.

And now you will have to bear with my faulty account of Tuesday's events. I tried to note the "trifles" as they went by, but there were so many of them!

The affair was a small one. Besides the Parkers and the Lewises, Uncle Willis and the Wellses came, along with some other folks from town. The senior Mr. Singer, I gathered from conversation, has taken a turn for the worse and his children were with him at home. Though I am saddened to hear of this news, I must admit to a little selfish relief that I did not have to face his son.

We gathered in the parlor of the Parker manse. As you know better than I, Mrs. Parker does have unimpeachable taste for fine things, but the place is not overdone. Some of the older folks sat in chairs and the rest of us stood behind in a cluster as Samuel came in from the study looking a little pale but cheered when he greeted his old friends. As I know you will want to know, he wore the checked trousers they all seem to favor, a pale silk waistcoat in a sort of butter color, white cravat tied in the loose foppish way, and a frock coat with wide lapels. He was as dashing as you can picture it, and I think we all felt a little jealous of Margaret.

Speaking of the former Miss Lewis, she made us all wait a good bit of time, as only Margaret would see fit to do, to build our anticipation before she appeared. Anna, I wish you could have seen her! Plump and lovely, her curls swept up and arranged just above her neck. She wore a wreath of white silk orange blossoms with a little veil in the back. And the dress! Words can't do it justice, but I shall try. The bodice was silk, a solid dove gray, with a snow-white lace tucker. The skirt (with a wide crinoline that Mrs. Parker must have reviled) carried the same color in a tiny flowered pattern. The bride also wore a mink pelerine. Far too early in the year for that, in my opinion, but I suppose she couldn't help but want to show it off. Father, as you would imagine, commented later that he saw no place at a ceremony dedicated to love and commitment for skin stolen from an animal. But Marmee understood, I think, and declared it "lovely."

Bride and groom made their vows in the usual way and placed the bands upon their fingers. Then commenced my favorite chapter of the day: the feast. Chicken and duck, potatoes, squash pies, corn and beans, and ice cream with champagne. It was divine and afterward I felt I could happily die in peace. Mr. and Mrs. repaired to the apartment above the Whig store where they'll stay until they complete the purchase of the little house just out of town. The current owner is moving his family to St. Louis, and it's all taking some time. To spend the time, M and S will tour in New York City and Niagara Falls. Oh, and you will want to know: They left the party at nine. He was dashing in his top hat. She wore a white bonnet with pearls, white gloves embroidered with doves, and waved one of the pocket handkerchiefs you sent her, with lily of the valley stitched along the edge.

Have I done my duty, Nan? I hope you will be satisfied with my account. The day was incomplete without you, though I think you are just where you need to be now and speak with pride of your good works. Your prime place in Paradise has long been assured, and now you are just fluffing the pillows. If only I can work on earning my spot now—I intend to be there at your side.

Yours ever,
L

Wednesday, October 24

Dear Lou,

Oh, I am undone. Thank you for your letter—your account was just what I hoped for. I won't conceal that I did weep all the way through, for it was just as I had imagined for myself. (Except for the mink pelerine, for I agree that a fur should stay packed away until at least December.) The dress, the feast are just what I would have wanted for my own happy day. And will have, I suppose, someday. I won't give up hope that the Almighty Friend thinks of me on occasion, though His plan does seem cruel and mysterious to me now. I only want to be of use as He sees fit, and perhaps have a little happiness for myself. It isn't so very bad to want that, I don't think.

And what of your plans? Are you finding Walpole dull?

I'm off to an outing this evening. We will take some of the children to a play in town.

Bye-bye for now,
Anna

Friday, November 2, 1855

My Dear,

Dull is a gentle way to describe this town, for what I really feel is confined and imprisoned. I've nothing here but ghosts around every corner, for my beloved sister is away, friends are married and gone, and the sight of a certain former friend is a torment. Is this a pleasant place to live besides all that? Where are the plays? There are none, unless we put them on. Is anyone here writing or arguing in parlors? No—unless it is about the virtues of a particular method for pressing cider or scouring a stove. I need to get back to the city before I weep myself a river to drown in. (And now you know your sister's flair for drama has not subsided!)

The happy news is that I shall depart presently. I had delayed my plans because of Marmee. She was so sad to see you go and I worried about burdening her with too many good-byes in one season. But last evening to my surprise she sat me down in front of the fire to tell me that she asked Uncle Willis to write to a widow in Boston who lets out rooms. So I will have my independence after all, with her blessing! As long as I can earn enough money to pay my way, I may stay in the city, and I will, for I'm not afraid of hard work when the reward is so sweet.

I must fly to preparations now. I've many letters to write.

Your sister,
Louisa

. . .

Louisa spent the weeks after Anna's departure preparing for her own. She examined her scanty wardrobe in the midday sun to locate the spots and scrub them out with a horsehair brush. Her mending basket overflowed with a few mousseline and batiste dresses handed down from a cousin, which she intended to make over, and she depleted the family's candle supply significantly in a few nights as she stayed up late sewing.

A few days after Anna's first letter arrived Louisa felt the familiar tightness in her abdomen and, the next morning, saw the red bloom of blood on her drawers. Its appearance took her breath away. Through sheer force of will she had nearly erased the memory of lying with Joseph in the tall grass. In forgetting, she did not have to acknowledge that she was at risk for a far more serious consequence than a broken heart. Her body would carry no lasting reminder of her transgression. Though she usually cursed the cotton batting and ladies' belt as a burden, reaching for it now prompted a twinge of relief.

Though she had been the one to initiate the Boston plans, Abba seemed to regret that impulse as the day of Louisa's departure approached. Suddenly, destitute families across New England were crying out for donations of candles, wool stockings, pickled vegetables. A few pieces of broken crockery urgently required gluing. Fall dresses had to be aired and pressed, sprigs of rosemary tucked in the pockets to keep them fresh until the weather turned cool. Louisa strove to make her mind still, like the surface of the river, and indulge her mother's requests. It was only a matter of time now, and she could spare a few more days.

On Louisa's last Friday in Walpole, Mr. Parsons's sow got her foot caught in some chicken wire and suffered such severe injuries from her struggling that he had to put her down. A red basket containing five pork steaks appeared on the doorstep at Yellow Wood Saturday morning, along with a note from Mrs. Parsons wishing Louisa well on her journey. Abba seized the basket and rushed to the kitchen with Bronson fast on her heels. Though she had no intention of deferring to his prohibition on meat, Abba allowed him to believe she was waiting for his approving nod. Louisa and her mother patiently weathered his speech on the sins of a carnivorous diet—the suffering of the animals, the filth of the farmyard. He frowned and weighed the consequences, finally allowing that it would be wasteful and rude not to make use of the gift.

Abba broke into a full smile and praised her husband's ardent compassion, declaring they would have a feast to send Louisa off properly. Anna had sent home a portion of her first week's wages, and for once there was enough to buy a few extra treats. Abba shooed Bronson back to his study and scratched out a list of ingredients on a scrap of the butcher paper. Louisa pulled the shopping basket from the top shelf of the pantry and wrapped a wool shawl around her shoulders. She glanced out the window to assess the sky—pale but clear—and started off for Washington Square.

The heat of the woodstove fogged the windows of the grocer's tiny shop. Inside, a table overflowed with winter squashes: the strangely shaped butternut, the warted acorn. Louisa chose a heavy squash and asked the grocer for five potatoes, two pounds of butter, and a block of cheese. As she turned to leave the shop, she felt pleased with the heft of her loaded basket. It was warm for a November day and dinner would be lovely. She nearly had her freedom.

Across the square a man in an unbuttoned coat stood leaning against the door of a carriage. He touched the brim of his hat, then reached into the pocket of his waistcoat and examined his watch.

Joseph. Louisa stood frozen a moment, mortified at the thought of what they would say to each other if he saw her. With her free hand she pulled the collar of her shawl slowly up over the back of her head, hoping she could hide, wondering whether he was alone. Just before she turned away, he looked up. His eyes registered her presence but his expression remained cold. They stared at each other, neither of them moving to wave or nod in recognition. A figure emerged from behind the carriage, her purple skirt fluttering in the wind. Nora held her package to her chest. Joseph turned away to help her up, brushed her trailing hem into the cab, and closed the door behind her. As he stepped up and settled onto the open front seat, Louisa remembered the time she had sat there beside him while his sister pouted all the way to the circus. *He'll get to keep his carriage now,* she thought. *Catherine will be so pleased.* Joseph tossed the reins and eased the phaeton forward, his gaze fixed on the road.

The day of her departure finally arrived. Her manuscripts lined the bottom of her trunk and she piled the clothes and a few mementos on top. The savings she had guarded all summer were safe in the trunk's lining. It was time, finally, to leave everything else behind. Though she was afraid, the thought of Walpole shrinking in the distance propelled her forward.

She was edgy with anticipation when Bronson saw her to the coach parked in the road.

He shook his head. "Two of my girls gone this month," he said as he kissed her cheek.

"I'm going to write like mad and sell these stories to anyone who will have them as quickly as I can," Louisa replied.

"You must be patient, daughter. We cannot determine the pace of our accomplishments. That is for the Lord to do." Louisa knew her father doubted whether she could sell her *Christmas Elves* because it was so late in the season.

"Yes, Father, but I believe the Lord and I are in agreement that He intends me to be a writer. *Now*."

Bronson chuckled. "Well, I hope you are right. But in case the publishers are slow to respond, your mother wanted me to give you this."

He pressed a slip of paper into her hand. It said: "Mrs. Clarke, 13 Chestnut Street, Beacon Hill." She looked up at him, confused.

"This family just took in some sick relatives and is in need of new linens. Your mother was proud to recommend you to do the sewing. It is the womanly art at which you are *most* successful. Your stitches are almost as pleasing to look at as Anna's."

Louisa smoothed a smile over the face that threatened to break into a scowl. It was the same old theme: if only she could be more like Anna—womanly and docile—perhaps he would love her better.

"Thank you, Father. I will not need it, but if it makes Mother happy to know I have another way of earning money, I am happy to take it."

Bronson nodded and helped her into the carriage. "The peace and patience of the Lord be with you, my child."

To Louisa it sounded as if he were saying: Soon you will come to accept that your silly fancies are out of reach. Her confidence felt shaken, but as the carriage pulled away, she straightened up and gave her head a little shake. She'd had enough with the sadness and doubt. Enough with questioning her choices, with wondering what might have been—if it had been her purple hem trailing out the open door of Joseph's carriage instead of Nora's. Her future was in Boston. Her life was beginning.

BOSTON

November–December 1855

I'm not afraid of storms, for I'm
learning how to sail my ship.

—*Little Women*

Chapter Twenty

November 8

J. T. Fields
Publisher

Dear Mr. Fields,

If it is amenable to your schedule, could we please meet Wednesday, November 14, to discuss a story I think you might be interested in, "How I Went Out to Service." I have moved to Boston permanently and look forward to more time for writing and selling my work.

Yours truly,
Louisa May Alcott

Boston was just as Louisa remembered it: teeming with men's shouts and the chaos of horses in the dirt streets. And as she walked down Chauncey Place, southeast of the Common, a hearty autumn rain began to fall and turned the dust into a sudsy soup. She looked down to see the hem of her best dress soaked at least a good two inches with mud and laughed out loud at her futile efforts to arrive in the city with a shred of dignity.

She had the address of Mrs. David Reed's boardinghouse scribbled on a paper in her pocket and, in the swampy weather, was never so glad to locate a doorway in her life. Her trunk was at the station and would be sent for once she secured her room.

Louisa knocked and a stooped woman with an out-of-date bonnet wrenched the door open just wide enough to poke her head through.

"And who might you be?"

Louisa hesitated a moment before answering what should have been a very simple question. Who *might* she be, now that she was away, on her own? She *might* be anyone. The prospect of this so seized her mind that she considered inventing a new identity, a clean slate. But there is no escaping your own skin. "Louisa May Alcott. Are you Mrs. Reed?"

The woman nodded. "Proprietress."

"Ma'am, I am the niece of Mr. Willis."

"Which Mr. Willis?" Mrs. Reed asked, narrowing her eyes.

"Mr. *Benjamin* Willis."

A change came over Mrs. Reed's face. The nose that had been upturned in distaste, giving her the appearance of a pig, relaxed and she looked human once again. "Well, why didn't you say so in the first place? Mr. Benjamin Willis was a close friend of my late husband's. I take in anyone he recommends."

Louisa exhaled with relief. "Thank goodness for that!"

Inside, Mrs. Reed showed Louisa the cramped parlor full of worn furniture. The light through the large front window was good, though, and Louisa's eye marked a chair in the corner that would be excellent for reading.

"A woman living *alone* in this big city. I shall put you in the attic— you'll be safest there."

"I thank you, ma'am." From one attic to the next, Louisa thought.

"And just what is it you're here to do, if you don't mind my asking?" Who would ever confess that in fact they *did* mind? Louisa wondered.

"I'm here to see what I can make of myself. I'm a writer."

"Gracious me! What a boring thing to do with your time."

"Yes, well, I'm a boring sort of girl, I guess you could say." Louisa grinned as she climbed the stairs behind the woman's massive rump.

"And no husband, I presume?"

Louisa felt a tug behind her ribs. The excitement of the day had managed to drown out her other thoughts. She steeled herself, remembering that all was as it should be, and the reason she was here now, with the chance to show what she could do, was that she had refused the conventional path Joseph had wanted them to take together.

"No, ma'am. Not looking for one either."

The old woman scoffed. "Gracious me," she said again under her breath. Louisa reflected that perhaps she should not have mentioned her uncle's name, in which case she would have been cast out and free to go to the next boardinghouse down the lane, where she could avoid all these questions.

The attic room was on the fourth story, cramped and stuffy. But there was a fireplace, a window that looked out on the First Church steeple, a bed and sturdy chair. Mrs. Reed told her the charge would be three dollars a week, including board and firewood. She'd have to sew an awful lot of pillowcases to make that up if she couldn't sell her stories, but she knew it was a fair price and accepted. Mrs. Reed stood around, waiting to be asked to sit for tea by the stove, but Louisa was bold enough not to offer. She was exhausted by her travels and longed to part ways with this tiresome woman.

"Well, I'll let you get settled in, then."

"The man from the station should be bringing my trunk around soon."

"I'll send my niece Caroline up when it arrives. Supper is at five."

And with that Mrs. Reed turned and descended the steep staircase, her fingers like talons on the handrail.

The following Wednesday was sunny and warm, autumn's last hurrah before the blanket of winter descended. Louisa packed two new stories in a side bag and prepared to walk to the office of the publisher J. T. Fields, who had published Mr. Hawthorne's lurid and successful book *The Scarlet Letter*. Louisa nurtured a furtive wish to claim some literary success for her own, and Mr. Fields seemed just the sort of man to help her do it.

At the corner, Louisa stopped short to gawk in the window of Madame Garnier's boutique. It would be months before Walpole or even Concord would adopt some of the more modern trends, and she knew they'd be adopted in a sort of amateur way, with homemade touches that diminished their effect. Here she saw a painted silk fan with inlaid mother-of-pearl on the handle, a caul for the hair accented with beaded gold thread, and kid gloves in every pastel shade—pink, blue, buttery yellow. The most fashionable women now wore slightly shorter skirts, revealing a bit of ankle, and all manner of decorative hosiery was available. Horizontal stripes in the daytime, and in the evenings, slightly scandalous lace.

Though the vanity of fashion had no place in the Alcott household, Louisa observed that these garments were works of art—the texture of fine silk and lace and brocade, the pinprick-sized stitches made by the seamstress's deft hand. If she were to admire the blacksmith, who seemed to be Whitman's hero, for pounding the perfect horseshoe, why could she not admire the seamstress for her creation and admire the creation itself? After all, just as the horse would carry the weight of all his labors on those shoes, so too would the woman carry on her shoulders the weight of her lesser status, the expectations of who she should be.

Musing on Whitman made her think of Joseph and she found herself wondering what he was doing at that very moment. Cutting fabric behind the counter at the shop? Brushing Romeo's mane? Buying a pretty bonnet for the new Mrs. Singer? Louisa nearly groaned out loud at the last image. *It's as if I'm determined to make myself miserable,* she thought. *Well, I won't do it.*

With a deliberate shake of her head, she turned away from the shop window and carried on down the street. On School Street she finally came to the Old Corner Bookshop, above which Fields had his office.

"Good morning," Louisa said to the shopkeeper, who was just cranking out the awning that protected books in the window from damage by the afternoon sun. "Is Mr. Fields in?"

"I can't say as I know," the man said. His head was covered in tight brown curls that extended in all directions. "Sometimes he comes before I get here and lets himself in. But you can come through the store and up the back steps."

Louisa nodded and smiled, her heart too swollen in her chest with nerves for her to speak. She had written ahead to Mr. Fields to tell him she would be in the city and had some material for him. *Why should I be nervous?* she thought. *I am a published author. Of course he's going to be interested in my stories.* She threw back her shoulders in her best idea of a businessman's posture and, looking quite ridiculous, ascended the back staircase like Queen Elizabeth.

Indeed, Mr. Fields had arrived early. The main door to the offices was open. The desks in the main room were empty—his clerks did not arrive until the afternoon. The room led toward the front of the building, where an office was partitioned off by a green curtain. Long counters ran the length of the office, and books were stacked in piles taller than Louisa.

She approached the publisher's office, but she did not know how to alert him she was there. How does one knock on a curtain? She cleared her throat. "Mr. Fields?"

"Who's there?" he grunted.

"Louisa May Alcott."

"Ah, Miss Alcott, daughter of my favorite bumbling philosopher. Please come in."

Bumbling? Louisa thought, unsure of whether to take offense. It was true—her father was a bumbler. And that was far from the worst thing that could be said about him. She decided to brush the comment off.

"Yes, thank you," she said, pushing past the green curtain. "You received my letter, I hope?"

"Yes, yes," Fields said, nodding in a way that communicated he had no idea what she was talking about.

Louisa took a deep breath. "Well, I've brought the story. It is based on an experience I had a couple years ago, when I went out to service for a family in Dedham. I won't tell you their name—as you will see, their literary likeness is most unfavorable."

Fields nodded and sat back in his chair with the manuscript she'd pressed into his hand. Louisa stood uncomfortably while he read, as there was not another chair in the small office. She glanced back out into the main room. A row of gas lamps was bracketed along the walls on either side of the space. On a table in the corner, a basket of fruit stood rotting, perhaps a gift from a would-be author, ignored, gone to waste.

She turned back to Fields. His high forehead shone with perspiration in the cramped room. The noise from the street drifted in through the open window behind his desk.

Finally, he looked up and spoke. "You have been a teacher, in the past?"

"Yes, sir, I have. And a governess. But this story concerns only my time in Dedham. There I washed clothes, cooked for the family, beat the rugs. As a servant."

Fields pressed his full lips into a patient smile. "Yes," he said. "Well, I would advise you, then, to stick to teaching."

"I'm sorry, sir?"

"Stick to teaching. You have no talent for writing."

Louisa stood in the heat of the room blinking a moment before his words penetrated her mind. She felt the blood rush into her cheeks and the stays of her dress tighten as she struggled to breathe. She couldn't think of anything to say that would sound even mildly dignified. She also felt she might cry at any moment.

"Well," she choked the barely audible word and received the manuscript he handed back to her. "Good day." She made it halfway down the stairs to the street level before the tears began to flow.

Back out on the street the sky looked the color of dull homespun washed too many times. No one else seemed to be bothered by it, though. The streets were teeming with people rushing this way and that. Louisa tried to focus her eyes on individual faces—a mother and her two small daughters, covered from head to toe in silk bows, a bespectacled man with a doctor's bag, a pack of ruddy-cheeked boys with suspicious grins. She felt a pang of loneliness, as if all the rest of the world were part of a complicated waltz, moving to and fro in time, and she did not know the steps.

It occurred to her that in another two days she would have to pay Mrs. Reed the three dollars she owed for the upcoming week. She had spent some of her savings to pay the fare to Boston and to buy a kettle and a ream of paper. It wouldn't be enough merely to scrape by on her own—she needed to have something to send home to her parents.

In all her debates with herself over whether she should come to Boston to try to make her way on her own, she worried about leaving the family and feeling alone, but never once had she pondered the possibility that her stories would not sell. It seemed obvious to her that she had been put on the earth to be a writer. Nothing else held any interest for her. Teaching and housework strained her patience— they seemed the sort of occupations only a woman could do and she felt sometimes that she was very little like a woman. Sacrifice without the expectation of anything in return was the most lauded aspiration for a woman in her father's mind, but Louisa didn't think much of it as a goal, even if she could scarcely admit that point of view to herself. Why would God give a woman the talents and abilities mostly reserved for men if He did not want her to use them?

But in Louisa's experience, no matter how much one wished and prayed, God was not going to come down and pay the rent. She reached into the pocket of her dress and felt around for the slip of paper Bronson had given her. She had only two dresses for daytime, and she'd switched back and forth between them since arriving, merely spot cleaning the front and hem to avoid the trouble and expense of laundry. The paper was right where she'd left it.

Louisa told herself to bear up, for it was all in the service of her writing. If she could earn enough money, she could stay in Boston. Back at Mrs. Reed's she wrote out a message to Mrs. Clarke, offering her services as seamstress, and sent Caroline to deliver it.

By the next evening the Clarkes had sent a bundle over. The next few days she sat in her garret surrounded by fabric, her thumb full of pinpricks. Daylight found her asleep at her desk, her cheek pressed against the page where she'd managed to record five or six meager sentences. The sewing was piled on a table by the door: one dozen pillowcases, one dozen sheets, six cambric neckties, and two dozen handkerchiefs.

I wish I had no heart, it aches so.

—*Little Women*

Chapter Twenty-one

My dear sister,

Boston is just the way we left it—filthy and full of excitement, none of which I may have, it seems. I continue to write but have no good news to share. My birthday is just weeks away. Another year gone by and I worry that I will leave this world before I have done half of what I would like to. . . .

All along as Louisa struggled to earn her room and board and stay awake long enough at the end of the day to continue writing, Joseph wound between and through and around her thoughts like a long green snake. Yet there was nothing to be done about him. Life was moving on and she approached each day the way she would cope with a rotting front tooth and no dentist nearby. One learned to smile with her lips closed.

The weather turned colder as if to impress upon her that time was indeed passing, but she did her best to ignore it. The stories piled up, along with the rejections, and she sewed more pillowcases and men's shirts than she ever had in her life. She revised *Christmas Elves*. May came to Boston for the day with a friend from school to deliver the finished drawings that would accompany the text. Louisa was surprised by how delighted she was to see her sister, to hear the news of home. She was careful, though, to cut May off as she began prattling about what was going on in Walpole. Louisa was full of curiosity about Joseph and Nora's wedding—when it would happen, whether it had already taken place—but she was afraid of what knowing would do to her.

She tied up the manuscript and took it to Mr. Briggs, who had published *Flower Fables* the year before. He was happy to see that she continued to work but informed her that it was too late in the year for a book about the holidays because it couldn't possibly be out in time. Her father had been right after all, much as it pained her to admit it. Mr. Briggs said she could bring the manuscript back in the spring and he would see if he had the space for it then.

Though it nettled her pride after the encounter with Mr. Fields, she began to look for teaching opportunities. She knew she had to stay busy, for if she stopped to think about how differently things were working out than she had hoped, she feared she might collapse.

One Saturday morning while the rain fell in sheets out on the street, Louisa sat in the parlor of the rooming house reading *The Old Curiosity Shop*. It was a rare moment of leisure but also a practical matter: the main fireplace provided much more warmth than the tiny stove in Louisa's room, and she had spent the morning chilled to the bone. Just as she was losing herself in the image of Nell staring out at the windows of all the other houses on the lane, wondering whether those houses felt as lonely as the one she shared with her grandfather, the front door swung open with a gust, and a tall man wearing a somewhat crushed and weathered hat stepped into the entryway. Mrs. Reed's niece Caroline stood clutching the door against the wind.

"Telegram for Miss L. M. Alcott," he called to Mrs. Reed, who stood fumbling with a tea set in the dining room, preparing for the midday meal. Louisa's chest tightened. Good news usually did not arrive by telegram. She closed her eyes in prayer a moment before she spoke.

"I am Miss Alcott," Louisa said. The messenger turned to her, the shoulders of his overcoat glistening with rain.

"Yes, miss. Please sign here."

Her hand trembled as she wrote. He handed her the slender message and she thought about how a simple piece of paper could change a person's life. She ripped the message out of its envelope. It was from Joseph: *My father dead at six this morning.*

Saturday evening, November 24

Dear Joseph,

Your telegram arrived this morning in a torrent of rain that seemed choreographed to echo the tone of your message. I have thought all afternoon about what I could say to you that might provide a little comfort; of course, there is nothing. I will not say that God in his wisdom has called your father back, for you will hear it again and again in the coming days, and I know from some experience that the words ring hollow in those first days.

I surprise myself by taking comfort in the fact that the new Mrs. Singer will be by your side through this difficult time. She is strong and true and your father will rest easy knowing his son no longer walks alone.

Steal away a moment from your family obligations in the coming days to take up your Whitman. And look to the soil, for you will see that "the smallest sprout shows there is really no death. . . ."

Through the fullness of time, in any way I may be of use, I am ever

Yours,
Louisa

Friday, November 30, 1855

My Dearest Louisa,

Your letter came just in time to bolster me, for I was beginning
to wonder if I could endure the trial of this week. First I must
accept the death of my lifelong friend, and now my father. My sister has lost her idol. We are both mourning the passing of a man
who, while he did not always heed the call of his conscience in his
actions, had a full, good heart, and, always, the best of intentions.

One mistake I must correct: there remains only one Mrs.
Singer, and that lady rests peacefully in her grave now that her
husband has been returned to her. Nora remains a companion
and I a bachelor. Hoping to express respect for our family, she has
put the nuptial plans on hold. In fact this has caused my sister
additional distress, as, though she would never admit it, she is
anxious to see the covenant made and my father's financial affairs
settled. I do not know what to feel. Some days I am tired of fighting it and wish to submit, for the good of all those around me,
including Nora, whose pure heart deserves a happy home.

And yet there will always be a stitch in my side emblazoned
with the letters LMA. Just a few months ago I believed things
would turn out so differently. When we were together it seemed
we could have anything—be anything—we wanted. But it has
always been me against the inkwell, has it not? At times I can
scarcely resist the urge to alight on your doorway in Boston—to
try to convince you to change your mind. But the hardest lesson for
one so stubborn as I is to learn that indeed we are not the authors

*of our fate—there are greater forces at work. I've wasted too
much time believing it is so, and I hope you will forgive me.*

Faithfully,
Joseph

The following week Louisa sat finishing her noon meal at the
long knobby table in what Mrs. Reed called the dining room. The
space was scarcely more than a hallway, however, and as she ate
she was forced to scrape her chair in close to the table to let people pass. Louisa tried to eat quickly. She'd had a story simmering
since the early morning, and her mind felt cluttered with potions,
swords, lopsided hats, old violins without any strings, as if it were
some kind of gypsy cart. When she was working most feverishly, she
could go for days without eating. But then she would collapse and not
be able to start again until a week had gone by. She had promised her
mother she would take care of herself and so she forced herself to sit
and eat when she'd rather be scribbling away in the attic.

Another reason to bolt the food as quickly as possible was the
lurking Mrs. Reed. She liked to find Louisa alone and pummel her
with excruciating stories of fellow boarders' foibles and the trials she
endured as "proprietress." Just as Louisa was chewing the last unpal-
atable potato, the lady entered the room with a stack of clean plates
for the hutch in the corner and commenced to chat.

"Well, Louisa, there's nothing dainty about you, is there?" Mrs.
Reed pointed at Louisa's empty plate and asked in what was, as far as
Louisa could tell, an attempt at some kind of humor.

"The dainty ones look pretty in a sitting room, ma'am, but when a
woman is making her way in the world on her own, she must resolve
to take fate by the throat and shake a living out of her."

Mrs. Reed gaped at her, scandalized. "And where did you learn to talk this way? What a violent mind you have, child."

"It has always been so. My three sisters have pure hearts and gentle spirits, but all the boiling blood went into me, I'm afraid. I write it into my characters to keep it at bay."

"And your father—Mr. Alcott? He must not approve of this life you have chosen. Doesn't he wish you would marry?"

Louisa thought the question over for a moment and realized she didn't know the answer. Bronson was an unconventional man in many respects, and she knew she would be underestimating him if she categorized his disapproval as something so run-of-the-mill. Over the years, through his many parlor conversations with his friends— Mr. Emerson, Mr. Thoreau, Mr. Channing, Margaret Fuller, and others—he had developed a complex philosophy about human nature Louisa had never been able to untangle. But part of it held that a man must both marvel at the power of *and* learn to control the wildness within him. The wildness itself was not sinful—it connected man to the earth, gave him spirit and the ability to endure. But its presence was a test of his diligence. In Bronson's eyes, Louisa had never buckled a saddle on that wild mare rearing within her. Worse, she seemed almost proud of this fact and channeled the passion into writing tales of sensational drama rather than study her German, contemplate the mysteries of the divine, or somehow put her gifts to use for the greater good. In short, he thought her unashamedly feral. Whether marriage would remedy that fact was beside the point.

"Mrs. Reed, I think my father is happy to have the meager earnings my stories can bring. It is a difficult time for our family, and we all must work toward the cause of bread and decent bonnets."

She shot Louisa a skeptical look and closed the door on the hutch. "Nonsense. Every father wants his daughter to marry. When he comes to visit I will have a chat with him. From time to time, eligible bachelors come to stay at this house. I could arrange an introduction."

Louisa smiled sweetly, but inside she boiled. Was it too much to ask to simply be left alone? It seemed her very existence as a single woman invited speculation and offers of help, as if it were simply impossible that she truly might not *want* to be married.

And yet she felt a wave of doubt when she thought about the price of this freedom. The death of Joseph's father seemed to reveal the fissures in her resolve to separate herself from him. She thought of him often, felt weighed down by the grief he was suffering. It was so difficult to force herself not to love him. Joseph was *good*; he wanted to do right by his sister and Nora, didn't shy away from wrestling with the question of the proper course when what was righteous went against what was true. And there was nothing she could do to help him.

"Thank you, Mrs. Reed, but it is of no use. Even if my father was desperate for me to marry, and I don't believe he is, he couldn't get me into marriage with a shoehorn. It goes against my nature."

Mrs. Reed stared at the girl and shook her head. "This is a most unnatural way to live."

Louisa shrugged, pushing her chair back from the table one last time. "And now I'm off to write some unnatural tales. Good afternoon."

Another week of writing stories she feared no one would ever read came and died away, and Saturday morning arrived. Louisa fastened the buttons on the better of her two dresses and brushed the tangles out of her thick mane of hair. She parted it down the middle and wound the side sections into thick twists stretching from her temples to the nape of her neck. There she coiled the rest of the hair into a heavy chignon and fastened it in place with the mother-of-pearl comb Anna had sent from Syracuse as an early birthday present. The gift was just in time—Louisa never had been able to find the comb with the steel flowers that she had lost sometime over the summer.

Louisa wasn't the sort of girl to stand before the mirror contemplating her appearance, but this morning she hesitated a moment. She wished the glass could reflect more than just her deep-set eyes and round unremarkable chin and show her some clue of what was in her heart. How long should she wait to see whether anyone would show interest in her work? Perhaps it was time to consider the possibility that she might only be a writer for herself and her family. There were worse fates. She was fortunate in so many ways. She felt healthy and strong, she could work and take care of her family. And she could still write, for leisure, when she had the time. The only difference would be that she would do something else to make money. Governess, teacher. It was silly and selfish to ignore the truth.

She went out at half past eleven to deliver a stack of towels she'd finished the night before to Mrs. Clarke. Walking always had a calming influence on her. The metronomic swing of her legs cleared her mind and forced her to breathe, coaxing her courage out of its hiding place. The sun hung directly above the city. November's chill weakened its heat, but the glare was an assault on eyes accustomed to the soft light of the reading lamp. She made her way north across the Common to Chestnut Street. Soon she was rapping the iron knocker of the Clarkes' stately home, built about fifty years before by the Boston architect Charles Bulfinch. It sat among some of Boston's finest homes.

Polly, the Clarkes' stout older servant, answered the door.

"I'll take your coat, Miss Alcott," she said.

"No, thank you, Polly—I won't be but a moment. I came to bring the sewing." Louisa handed her the package of towels wrapped in paper.

"Is that Miss Alcott?" Mrs. Clarke said, coming in from the parlor. "Do come in, dear, and have some tea. What a dreadfully cold morning."

"I won't trouble you, Mrs. Clarke."

"Nonsense. Polly, would you please put on the tea? And bring us some of that wonderful sweet potato bread."

"Yes, ma'am." Polly turned and her white cap bobbed toward the kitchen.

"Let me hang your coat," Mrs. Clarke said, helping Louisa slip it off. She moved awkwardly with it to the front closet. It was clear she was inexperienced with a task of this sort. It was as if she wanted to show Louisa that though she was fortunate to afford servants, as well as a girl to do her sewing, she didn't take their work for granted. It seemed a silly show, and Louisa was almost flattered that it mattered to Mrs. Clarke what she thought.

"Now," she said with a satisfied sigh. "Let's go sit by the fire."

Mrs. Clarke was the wife of Ebenezer Clarke, a member of the Massachusetts General Court, and a lady of fine reputation in the city. She was known for her grand parties and the paintings she made of the birds and squirrels in the Public Garden.

They settled on the velvet armchairs that flanked the marble fireplace. "So tell me, Miss Alcott—how is the writing going?"

A little wave of panic came over her. Stupidly, vainly, she'd told everyone she met about her plans for a stellar writing career in Boston. The daughter of Bronson Alcott wouldn't establish herself in Boston just to be a seamstress. Now, of course, they all wanted to know how she was faring. She cleared her throat. "Well, I am determined to keep trying, though so far I haven't met with much success."

"Oh," Mrs. Clarke said, brushing Louisa's doubt away with a flick of her hand. "I am sure you will come by with good news very soon. You can't give up—that's the main thing."

"Oh, I don't intend to. But sometimes I wonder . . ."

"What's that, dear?"

"I wonder if I shouldn't be looking for a more steady type of employment. I will continue writing, of course, no matter what I'm doing with the rest of my time. But Anna is working in Syracuse now and I can't help but think I had better do my share as well."

"I see. Well, as you may know, my daughter Frances is a teacher at a school in Plymouth. Of course, it isn't that she has to work," Mrs. Clarke said, then reddened with the realization that she sounded like she was bragging about her wealth again. "But she loves teaching and Mr. Clarke and I feel it is very important for our children to learn the value of work and what the lives of others less fortunate than ourselves are like.

"Her letter from last week mentioned that one of the teachers is leaving to marry. Would you like me to inquire about the position for you?"

Polly brought in the tea tray and set it on the table between them. The china was so white it was almost blue, and the fronds of a fern splayed in the center of each saucer. *Ask and ye shall receive,* Louisa thought as Mrs. Clarke described the teaching position. But did she want to receive it? Coming from Mrs. Clarke an "inquiry" was more like a command. Probably, the job would be hers if she wanted it. She should be happy. It was just as she said—now was the time to think of others.

"That would be very generous of you, Mrs. Clarke. I would appreciate it."

"Not at all, dear. We cannot squander this bright mind of yours on sewing and other chores."

Or teaching a herd of children their letters, Louisa thought.

"The pay is quite good compared to most other schools," Mrs. Clarke said. "You'll have money left over to go to the theater, to buy a winter coat. The one you were wearing when you came in—is that all you have? Surely it can't be warm enough for the January winds. They cut right through you."

Louisa nodded, sculpting a smile for her face that she hoped was convincing. She could really help her family with a position like this. And, of course, who wouldn't love a few nicer dresses, a bonnet or two? But though she loved luxury, freedom and independence were luxury to her a thousand times over. The thought of losing them made her desolate.

By the time she arrived back at Mrs. Reed's, her mind was a tangled mess. She would have to decide, she knew; but at the moment all she wanted to do was escape into the mind of another writer. She started for the stairs up to her "garret" but she noticed the aroma of potatoes and glanced at the clock. It was nearly time for dinner. So her escape would be short-lived. She stole into a corner of the parlor with her old favorite, *Jane Eyre*, and drew a curtain on her troubles.

Mrs. Reed was in the kitchen making a lot of racket. The door on the woodstove screeching open, the rustle of the logs. The thud of a full iron pot lifted off the stove and set heavily on the worktable. The clatter of the mismatched bowls with chips around the rim.

But none of it penetrated Louisa's mind. Growing up in small apartments with three sisters and an endless stream of her father's friends visiting, a girl learned how to crouch inconspicuously in a corner and block out the noise so that she could plunge into the world of a story.

"Caroline," Mrs. Reed called into the hallway. "Please come help me serve." Mrs. Reed gave a frustrated sigh when the girl did not respond.

Jane was explaining to Mr. Rochester just why she thought he *wasn't* handsome, though in truth she thought him full of unconscious pride and at ease in his demeanor in the most beguiling way.

Mrs. Reed emerged from the kitchen, looking around the parlor for the girl. Steam had formed a patina on her sagging cheeks. She glanced over at Louisa and rolled her eyes. "Reading *again*," she muttered.

Mr. Rochester told Jane that he was in a talkative mood, and since it suited him, she should speak. But Jane was stubborn—why should she have to talk for the sake of talking, just because he was ordering her to do so? He sensed her annoyance and apologized.

Caroline rounded the corner near the banister. "There you are," Mrs. Reed began. Then she stopped short. "Caroline," she hissed. "What have I told you about letting strangers in off the street?"

Mrs. Reed put on her slightly more polite public voice. "I'm sorry, sir—all my rooms are full up. I can't take anybody new just now."

The smell of the stew was beginning to break into the world of Louisa's story. Her stomach gurgled and she realized she hadn't eaten a thing all day except for the bread she'd had at tea with Mrs. Clarke. One of the most challenging aspects of the philosophy of self-denial her father tried to teach his daughters was resisting the siren song of food. Louisa was no tender waif—she loved to eat and had a man's hunger.

Practiced in patience, Louisa kept her eye trained on the letters.

She wanted to think a little more about what Mr. Rochester meant by *"remorse is the poison of life."* But it was too late—her concentration was broken. The light in the room shifted. She became aware that someone was walking toward her.

"Sir, where are you going?" Mrs. Reed cried, panic in her voice. "I told you—there's no room here."

The figure blocked the light and the page darkened. When Louisa could no longer resist it, she looked up. Joseph. Louisa blinked, staring at him, astonished. His hair had grown—it curled over his collar—and his cheeks were pink from the wind. She wondered for a moment whether her hunger was playing tricks on her, whether her mind was plagued by visions. But then the mirage opened his mouth to speak.

"You've written plenty of romantic tales," he said, taking the book from her hands and gently closing it. "Didn't you know I would come?"

"Wouldn't it be fun if all the castles in the air
which we make could come true, and we could
live in them?" said Jo, after a little pause.

—*Little Women*

Chapter Twenty-two

Every inch of her wanted to fly to him right there while Mrs. Reed watched, her mouth agape, and Caroline stood twirling her hair around her finger. But good sense prevailed, at least for the moment.

She stood up. "Mr. Singer," she said in an affected tone. "What a lovely surprise. Shall we go for a walk?"

His grin was full of mischief. "Yes, I believe we shall. A long walk."

"Mrs. Reed, Caroline—this is Mr. Joseph Singer." The aunt and her niece waddled over sheepishly, unsure how to account for the fact that they had been staring openly at him since he walked in the door.

"Pleased to meet you," Mrs. Reed said, shaking his hand. Then, turning to Louisa, she said, "The stew is served in just a minute."

Louisa shrugged. "I may miss it, I may not. I'm not sure."

"You're going to miss it," Joseph said.

"I'm going to miss it," Louisa parroted. Joseph broke into a smile that made Louisa a little weak with joy. Mrs. Reed harrumphed and made appalled little noises as she turned toward the kitchen.

They pushed out onto the sidewalk, which was crowded with shoppers and matinee-goers and families walking to friends' homes for dinner. Joseph grabbed her hand and began walking ahead, his long stride wrenching her along.

"Where are we going?"

He didn't turn his head to answer but strode on until near the end of the block they came to a narrow alley between two tall buildings. He pulled her sharply to the right and she followed him down the passage. One of the buildings ended before the other, creating a space that was hidden from the street. Only there did he pull her to him, so hard she felt the collision of their bodies echo through her bones. He pressed his face into the space between her neck and shoulder. His nose was cold from the wind and it sent a shiver down her arms. She was reeling. He was *here* now. Here in her arms. But why? How? What did it mean? Her hand moved of its own volition to the back of his head, her fingers touching his hair.

"I didn't know your hair was curly," she said. "You've let it grow."

He lifted up his head and looked at her, then brushed his finger across her lips, kissed her. How lovely it was to feel the very *fact* of him pressing against her. He was no reverie or vague-faced man in a book. He was real—his breath warm on her face, his coat smelling of burning leaves. But soon her mind corralled her impulses.

"What are you *doing* here?" she asked, almost angry.

He looked at her surprised, as if her stern voice had jarred him out of some half-consciousness. He opened his coat and reached into his breast pocket.

"Tickets," he said, handing them to her. "To New York. The train leaves tonight."

"*Tonight?*"

"Louisa, we can start again. Everything that's happened . . . we can put it behind us for good. A new city, a new beginning." He ran his thumb along her jaw. "We can be together; we can tell the truth."

She closed her eyes and listened to her heart galloping in her chest. She felt ecstatic but angry. Why now? Already she felt trapped between two choices—to stay in Boston or to face the fact of her failure and go to Plymouth to teach. Now he presented her with a third option, an appallingly selfish, dangerous, beguiling option. "It's impossible," she whispered.

"My cousin—I wrote to him. He says there is an extra room we can have. It's small, but we can manage it until I can find work. Of course, we'll be married at once. Otherwise it wouldn't be . . . proper."

She felt suddenly shy and turned her face away, thinking about just how improper they'd been together when no one was watching. Her eyes followed a cat who walked along the top of a fence at the end of the alley. It twitched its white tail and Louisa thought of Lizzie. She felt a rush of longing for home. "What did you say to Nora?"

"Don't bother yourself about that. I'll talk to her. I'll write to her."

"She doesn't know you've gone?"

"Don't you see? It doesn't matter. I don't *love* her. And she doesn't love me. She'll probably be relieved."

Louisa shot him an accusing look. "You *must* know she will be devastated."

He shook his head. "It's better this way."

"And what of your sister? Surely you can't think she will go out to service."

"We will go ahead to New York and get settled. Then we can send for her."

"But won't Catherine be angry? After all, this arrangement was meant to address your father's debts and give your sister the sort of life to which she feels . . . accustomed," Louisa said, stopping herself just before the word *entitled* slipped out instead.

He pressed his lips into a grim line. "I thought I would be able to go through with it. I thought I could make the pact despite the way that I feel about you, because it is my responsibility to take care of Catherine now—and I accept that responsibility. But there is another way to honor it. We are young and I am not afraid to work. We will live simply and, in time, pay off my father's debts. My sister will just have to become accustomed to *another* way of life."

Louisa shook her head in disbelief. She had spent so many weeks trying to crush the fantasy that her unchecked mind was eager to pursue. That he would come for her. That somehow, after everything, they could find a bridge between the two worlds she loved in equal measure.

"You can stand here all day thinking of reasons why you should not come. But eventually we will miss our train." He put the tickets back in his pocket and buttoned up his coat. "After my father died, everything became clear to me. What I need to know is, do you love me? Because if you do, we can find a solution for everything else."

Louisa was overcome by the urge to tell him she would go anywhere to be with him, to feel the scalding sensation of his stare, the comfort of his friendship. He understood her in a way that made her feel she was being seen for the first time, really seen—the layers and layers of her public self falling away. Could she not sew or teach in New York as well as she could in Boston or Plymouth? This last month she had finally claimed her freedom, and what good had come of it? She wouldn't have to let the writing go, wouldn't have to give up on it altogether. But she could let her notion of what it meant to her shift, could let it recede. Would that be so terribly sad? She would gain so much in return.

His eyes were trained on hers as he waited for an answer. The lashes were almost translucent, his irises the blue-gray of chimney smoke on a chilly day. A moment elapsed and she realized she was nodding her head.

His eyes widened. "Is that . . . are you . . . ?"

She nodded again, more deliberately. Her voice felt strangled in her throat.

A noise, half laugh, half shout, exploded from his lungs. "My God, for a moment I thought my hopes were dashed." He laughed again and kissed her. The kiss took her by surprise and she felt her lips limp against his. He took her hand and pulled her back down the alley. "Go back to Mrs. Reed's," he said. "Pack your things and have your trunk sent ahead to the station. Will I look for you at five o'clock?"

"Yes," she said, surprised at the sound of her own voice. "Five o'clock."

Joseph nodded, his hand lingering in hers as he turned to walk in the opposite direction, toward the station. "God is good to us this day, Louisa. We can't forget it."

She nodded, then gave him a little wave and started back toward Mrs. Reed's. The incessant pounding of her heart overcame all the noises of the street. She passed some children playing a game in front of a large house. They shouted to one another but no sound came from their mouths. A carriage passed and the horses' hooves struck the road, but she did not hear the muffled thumping of their shoes. There was only the deafening, relentless pounding of her heart. She felt almost manic with the prospect of freedom. It was just as she had dreamed it the opening night of the play, when she spotted Fanny Kemble settling into the front row of the audience—she could have both. Her independence *and* the kind of love she'd given to her characters but never imagined she'd have for herself.

Mrs. Reed emerged from the kitchen when she heard the door creak open. She wiped her hands on her apron. "Miss Alcott, perhaps I should write to your father. I'm not sure he would approve of—"

Louisa clasped the old woman's hands between her own. "I'm leaving, Mrs. Reed. Tonight. We're to be married at once. I will send a telegram to my parents from the station."

Mrs. Reed's stern expression softened, though she forged ahead with disapproving prattle. "Eloping then? What will your parents think? Your poor mother!" Louisa felt a wave of guilt rising up within her, but she pushed it away. "I'm glad to see you've come to your senses," Mrs. Reed said.

"What do you mean?"

"There is no occupation more womanly and fine than the duties of wife and mother. All else is foolishness, and you are wise to let it go."

Louisa bristled. "You are mistaken. I still mean to be a writer. Somehow."

"Yes, yes," Mrs. Reed said, "I suppose it makes a lovely amusement when you have free time. Of course in the near term, you'll be going to housekeeping."

The woman seemed determined to antagonize her, but Louisa silently urged herself not to take the bait.

"My work is not simply an *amusement*," Louisa said steadily. "I intend to keep at it, despite my changing circumstances."

Mrs. Reed twisted her mouth into a wry smile. "Of course, dear."

"Watch—you'll see," Louisa said, straining to keep her temper in check. What difference did it make what an old widow believed? "I have to pack my things, Mrs. Reed." She fished in her pocket for the sewing money from Mrs. Clarke. "Here is what I owe you for the balance of the week. I want to thank you for your kindness these last months."

"This happy turn of events makes it all worth it," Mrs. Reed said, putting the money in her apron and turning back toward the kitchen. "Caroline can arrange to have your trunk sent ahead."

Louisa climbed the stairs to the attic room for the last time, taking a deep breath to try to soothe her rattled nerves. Perhaps she would have to put her work aside until they were settled in, but what was the harm in that? The living quarters would be cramped. Probably no space for a writing desk. They'd be needing linens, which meant more sewing, and then there was the wash. Until Joseph found work and they could afford some help, she'd have to do it herself. And the cooking too. Well, she had done it before and she could do it again. Hard work and sacrifice separated the true hearts from the weak, as her father was fond of saying.

Of course, there was also the matter of Catherine. Louisa cringed when she thought of Joseph's tiresome sister and her behavior the day of the circus. No one would argue that she hadn't been spoiled since birth as the baby of the family and the only girl. She was used to getting everything she wanted—clothing, parties, outings—and her unchecked extravagance was partly to blame for her father's financial ruin. Joseph had told Louisa that Catherine didn't like to read and could hardly cook or sew. It was no use counting on her help—she would have two to care for. A dull headache began radiating along Louisa's hairline.

Joseph's words came back to her: ". . . in time, we'll pay off my father's debts." That phrase, *my father's debts*, had lived in her mind for as long as she could remember, trailing the shame and anger of her own father's troubles. Married to Joseph, Louisa knew she would shoulder the debts of two fathers—one dead, with creditors lurking around his grave, the other convinced that work would sully his philosopher's soul. The burden of it, the endless grubbing for just enough money to get by, filled her with weariness.

No matter, she told herself, determined to shake off the worries as she entered the attic room. *The important thing is that we will be together. The problems will be easier to solve with the two of us.* She had been using her trunk as a table of sorts, and she cleared the piles of paper from its surface before unlatching the top and swinging it open. She surveyed the creaky wardrobe in which she hung her clothes. Mrs. Clarke had told her she could keep the fabric left over from the sheets she'd made. She'd done so happily and made a new dress and a set of underclothes from it. Aside from that, she'd acquired no new articles of clothing. Once the clothes were in the trunk, though, along with the worn quilt she'd brought along, and the Dickens and Brontë and Whitman, she could see that it would be a challenge to close the lid. She glanced at the manuscripts on the night table, shoved the books over to one side, and pressed down hard on the quilt. She placed the manuscripts on top, holding them in place with one hand while she drew the lid down with the other. It stopped a gaping six inches short of the latch, and despite her efforts to wrestle it into place, it wouldn't close.

What would she leave behind? The books? That seemed out of the question. Who knew how long it would take them to be able to afford books, and the thought of living without Dickens within easy reach was unsettling. The quilt took up the most space but it had belonged to Abba's mother, and Louisa couldn't see leaving that behind. Of course she could find a box for the stories, perhaps have them delivered to the station separately. But then she thought of all the mud puddles and gusts of wind between Mrs. Reed's and the station. If anything happened to those papers, all her work would be lost.

It would have to be the books, then. She'd read them so many times the words were burned in her brain. *Perhaps I have read them* too *many times,* she thought. *Too many books, too many times—perhaps now it's time to pull my head out of the books and realize that my real life is beginning.*

With the books removed Louisa closed the trunk and fastened the latch. She tried not to let her heart grow heavy and told herself that Mrs. Reed could send them to her when she got settled. Her father visited New York from time to time. Perhaps he would bring them.

Louisa heard light footsteps on the stairs and a rustling knock. "Miss?"

"Come in, Caroline." The pale girl slipped silently into the room.

Louisa looked behind her but no one else was there. "Surely you can't mean to carry this trunk by yourself!"

Caroline shook her head. "No, Miss. There is a man from the station downstairs. But . . ."

"What is it?" Louisa replied sharply. She had made her decisions—about everything she was going to leave behind—and she knew instinctively that motion was the only thing that would keep her from doubting. Any delay could be fatal. "I'm in a hurry, Caroline. What is it?"

Caroline stood shivering in the drafty attic, her eyes darting between Louisa's wrist and the floor. She made a sound in her throat like a bird before she spoke. "I thought . . . I thought before you go you might like to see this." Caroline pulled a letter from her apron and handed it to Louisa. "It arrived while you were out."

What now? Louisa snarled to herself. *Mrs. Clarke needs some more pillowcases? May wants a new bonnet and we must all slave away until she has it?* She held the letter at her side and attempted to compose herself. Her nerves were frayed—she was lashing out at all the people she blamed for putting her in this impossible situation in the first place. But it was worth remembering that she herself had chosen this path. She alone.

She took a breath and unfolded the letter.

Mr. William Warland Clapp

Editor

Saturday Evening Gazette

Dear Miss Alcott:

The Gazette is pleased to offer publication of your story "A New Year's Blessing" in the first edition of our Quarto Series, printing after the first of January, subject to the following terms: Stories to appear under the author's name; prompt submission of at least five additional stories by the first of December . . .

Louisa's left hand felt for the bed behind her and she sank down onto it, resting the letter on her lap. Caroline stood blinking at her like a barn owl.

"Is everything all right, miss?"

Louisa stared blankly at her and then back at the letter. All she could think was *L.M.A.* and *Saturday Evening Gazette*. She had been published in the paper once before, but under a pseudonym, and *Flower Fables* was made of the simple fairy tales she'd dreamed up at age sixteen. This was something different. She had wanted to know whether she could write serious stories, not just fairy tales, and here was the proof. A story—six stories in all, if she could make her deadline—in one of the most widely read papers in America.

With a sinking feeling she started to realize the enormity of the housekeeping that lay ahead for her in New York. It wouldn't be like Boston, the city she had lived in off and on for most of her life. New York was massive, and she knew she would have to start at the beginning, learning her way around, finding a decent grocer, procuring the pots and dishes and other tools she would need to set up her kitchen. She saw her beloved silence slipping away—no time for work or contemplation when there were bellies to fill and linens to scrub.

She had two weeks to dash off five more stories, or Mr. Clapp would probably rescind his offer altogether. The stories she had written over the last few weeks needed editing and she doubted whether they were good enough to submit. She might have to write something new altogether. *Maybe there is some way it can all be done,* she thought weakly. *If I don't sleep . . .*

"Oh, Caroline," Louisa said. "What am I to do?" She felt her heart splitting like a piece of wet wood, its fibers clinging to the center. How could one letter be both the best and worst news you'd ever received? She thought of Joseph standing in the station, drawing his watch from his pocket to calculate the time left until they boarded their train. A sob climbed to the top of her lungs, but she was practiced at stopping the crying before it started, and this time was no different. For there was no doubt in her mind about what she would do, no matter what it cost her.

WALPOLE, NEW HAMPSHIRE

October 25, 1881

The train slowed to a stop at the station in Bellows Falls. Louisa shook herself from her reverie, closed her book, and placed it back in her case. As she adjusted her bonnet, she stooped to peer out the window of the train car to the sunny platform, where people stood waiting to greet their guests or welcome home sojourners. The passengers filed toward the front of the car and descended the stairs.

Inside the station she hired a Rockaway carriage and held her case on her lap as it thundered across the wooden bridge that spanned the Connecticut River and pulled to a stop in the center of Washington Square. The driver offered Louisa his hand and helped her step down to the road. She asked him to hold the carriage and explained that she would be back in an hour or so, and he should avail himself of the town's charms. They gave her heart a pang as she recited them: the trail along the Connecticut and up through the woods to the farms that lay beyond, the walkway through the town square to admire the autumn leaves, resplendent with their reds and golds.

As she made her way toward School Street and the address in Joseph's recent letter, her slow pace and aching joints reminded her that much had changed since she last walked Walpole's pathways. Twenty-six years before, the town square had been surrounded on all sides by fields, full of knee-high grass that rustled Louisa's skirts, and the precise rows of orchards stretching off toward the horizon. Now the fields had been carved into plots where charming houses stood, each with its own garden and fence, each with a wreath on the door.

Louisa pressed her eyes closed, hoping that somehow she could also press away the pain in her hips that throbbed as she walked up the hill. She'd never doubted her ability to transcend the physical, to create a new reality in her mind, and she had called on this skill often in recent years as sickness took its toll on her body. She paused, ostensibly to admire the intense crimson of a sugar maple, and caught her breath. Then she set off again, tamping down the pain by remembering why she had made this journey, why she had returned to the town she had hoped to forget.

Just as Joseph had predicted the day the storm ushered the two of them away from the crowded circus and into the abandoned barn, the country did indeed lose its patience with the southern states and went to war. Louisa spent the first year lamenting the fact that she could not fight as a soldier. She was nearly thirty years old by then, a confirmed spinster and still frustrated that her writing was not generating much in the way of income. In 1862, she applied to serve as a nurse and was assigned to a temporary hospital in an old Washington, D.C., hotel, where men were hauled in each day like livestock only half slaughtered. The things she saw—heaps of legs, arms, and fingers, men turned lunatic with fear, a boy no more than fifteen, half his face shot off, still breathing enough to scream all through the night—these images were lodged in her very tissue. If she could live a hundred thousand years more, the details would be just as sharp.

She spent three weeks as a nurse and then she herself became a patient. Little rest and a poor diet had weakened her constitution and she caught typhoid. She lay raving in the infirmary for three days before Bronson came to take her home, and by then the doctors had doused her with enough calomel to replace the sickness with near catatonia. Over time she would learn that the cure was worse than the disease. The tonic made her hair and teeth fall out and seemed to settle in her joints, causing almost constant pain. In recent years during bad spells, she'd spent weeks in bed and looked forward to the relief of death.

But when she was feeling well enough, she did what she had always done—she worked. After the war, she adapted her journals and letters home into a slim volume called *Civil War Hospital Sketches*. Editors and newspapermen began paying attention to her work, and she sold her stories one after another. Bronson and her editor, Mr. Niles, urged her to write a longer story for young girls based on her childhood with her sisters. Louisa didn't want to do it. Writing about what she saw in the war hospital made her feel like she was really *living* and had finally broken free of the identity that had been thrust upon her all her life: charming authoress spinning moral tales for the young. Louisa had grown up and apart from her old self, but the people closest to her refused to recognize it.

But there was the promise of income, something poverty had taught her never to refuse. So she gave in to her father's urgings and wrote the blasted thing. The first volume of the story she decided to call *Little Women* sold two thousand copies right away. Louisa wrote the second volume in a hurry and, soon after, went off to vacation in Quebec and Maine hoping to escape the storm. The book seemed to be taking on a life of its own, and Louisa dreaded the attention. When she finally arrived back in Boston she learned she was a wealthy woman. Suddenly she was earning more money in one month than she had over many years. Finally she could do the things she had been dreaming of:

pay off the debts, keep her parents comfortable, and send May to art school in France.

But one thing she'd never thought to do was guard her privacy. After all, the details of the *Little Women* story were plucked almost entirely from her own life, and the public knew it. They seemed to believe that purchasing copies of the tale entitled them to investigate their author. Was she really just like Jo? Was she too married to a German professor? Who was the real Laurie and why hadn't Jo married him in the end? The intrusive letters and articles irritated her, and she contemplated whether the realization of her dream was worth the price. So many years she had struggled to get her work published, to establish herself as a writer of serious fiction, not just tales for young girls. So many years she worried that she was out of her mind to think she would ever know success, and now, suddenly, she had it. But at what cost?

A paper printed the location of Orchard House in Concord, where she lived most of the time with Bronson and Abba. Young girls flocked there to get a look at the real-life Jo—and were quite disappointed to see a plump old lady answer the door. It hadn't occurred to them that "Jo" would age. Soon Louisa could no longer bear the stricken looks on their faces and began to tell them that Miss Alcott had gone out of town, that she was the maid.

One particularly busy September day Louisa escaped through the back door of the house just as she saw a tour of girls coming up the path. She had a few appointments to keep, a few errands to run, and she simply could not be bothered with the nonsense. On the way to the train to Boston, she stopped to post some letters. As the heavy steel door of the letter box swung shut, a realization washed over her that nearly took her breath away: she was going to die.

This wasn't the first time Louisa had contemplated death. She'd come very close to it a few times, and after years of suffering the bad spells brought on by the calomel, the burden of constant care for her parents, she sometimes thought death would be a great comfort. But what she hadn't thought about was the fact that when she died, perfect strangers would almost surely swoop down like scavenging birds to pick through her letters and journals and find the answers to the questions she avoided. Every word she had written when she thought no one else but God was listening would now be displayed for public scrutiny and judgment.

It would be easy enough to go back through her journals and remove pages she wanted to keep private. Bronson had taught her from an early age the importance of organizing and dating the written reflections, which he believed to be the permanent record of a mind's development—like a scientist's notes. But when she thought of the years and years of letters cast across New England and beyond—to her sisters, to friends in Boston, to acquaintances made in Paris when she traveled there with a tiresome invalid woman who paid richly for her companionship—her chest tightened. There was no way to know how much she had revealed in her correspondence, no way to call it all back. Louisa had a tendency to dash off a letter when her temper flared over some injustice or oversight. Would something she wrote on impulse twenty years ago suddenly reappear?

And then the worst of it flashed in her mind: Joseph Singer. What of their correspondence of so long ago? She remembered that his letters remained in the lining of her trunk, where they had been since the day Anna left for Syracuse. She allowed herself to read them from time to time, to linger over his apologies for concealing his entanglement with Nora, his pleas for a chance to explain. After the night of the play, when Louisa and Joseph came together and broke apart once again, the letters stopped until the news of his father's death.

Louisa hadn't spoken to Joseph since the day she left him standing alone at the train station, the day she sent Caroline with her cowardly message explaining that she would not come. He never wrote her again. All these years later her heart wrenched with a fresh pang at the memory of it. It *had* been for the best, of course. She had been determined to maintain her freedom, no matter what the cost. And the cost had been higher than she ever could have anticipated. Even still, she couldn't imagine her life having turned out any other way than this—she'd had no other choice. This is what she told herself at the time, and this is what she told herself now: the fact satisfied her mind but not her heart.

It was no use questioning her decision now. Life was nearly done, and despite some private sadnesses—never having the chance to write the sort of books she wanted to write, the loneliness of spinsterhood and, unexpectedly, of fame—life had been good to her in many ways. Almost everything she'd wished for, she'd received. It was only in the having that the objects of her wishes transfigured into something different from what she'd expected. But that was no one's fault.

She could, however, do something to protect her family and Joseph's from the truth of what had passed between them that summer in Walpole. If Nora was blissfully ignorant then, why should she have to find out now? Louisa knew they had married at Christmas, just a few short weeks after she last saw Joseph in Boston. Margaret's newsy letter described the clusters of holly that adorned the tables at the wedding feast, unaware that her benign words cut Louisa to the quick. And the children they most certainly had—why should they be given cause to question their father's fidelity? The prospect of it made her sick to her stomach.

And so she sent him a letter, a stiff, formal inquiry, requesting an appointment at his convenience and offering to travel to Walpole. Many days passed and she did not hear a reply. It occurred to her that he could be dead. He might have been a soldier. If he didn't meet his end on the battlefield, he could have died a thousand other ways: typhoid, cholera, consumption, or some vague unidentifiable illness that came on without warning and swept him away. So many others she cared about had departed this world in just that way.

But soon his reply arrived. It was only surprise at hearing from her out of the blue, he explained, that had delayed his response. He would receive her, of course, any time she liked, and though he would be willing to come to Boston to save her the trip, might she not like to see Walpole again? They agreed on a date and time. When she was young, Louisa had little patience, and the anticipation of an event like this would have driven her mad. But at forty-eight and looking and feeling much older than those years, she felt that time seemed to move much faster than she did. Soon the date arrived and now she found herself on Joseph's doorstep.

Louisa raised her hand to grasp the brass knocker shaped like a pineapple, that classic New England symbol of welcome, and hesitated. She noticed her reflection in the front window, wondered, had Joseph passed her in the street, whether he would have guessed that she was the ebullient girl he'd walked with through the woods behind his house, the target of his fierce love, anger, and regret. This woman's shoulders hunched forward, as if the weight of her mere bones strained her muscles to their limit. Beneath her bonnet, a thin froth of hair only partially covered her scalp, though she'd taken pains to arrange it as best she could. The possibility that he wouldn't recognize

her—or worse, that she'd see disappointment or shock on his face—
made her want to turn back. Why open this door to the past she'd
closed so long ago? Sometimes it was better not to know the ways in
which people had changed. Let them stay the same in your mind,
preserve them as they were. She could write to him to ask about the
letters. There was no need to see each other.

Just as she was turning go, she saw a curtain move in the front
window. The oak door creaked open and he was there.

A spasm of laughter escaped her lungs and she was surprised to
find herself grinning. How little he had changed! Most of his hair was
gone, revealing a high, noble forehead tanned from working outdoors,
but his blue eyes seemed all the brighter for it. His shoulders looked as
strong as they ever had, but they slumped just a little. He smiled back
and they stared at each other, grinning like fools, for a long moment.

Joseph gave his head a shake, seeming to come to his senses, and
pressed his lips into a dignified line. "Miss Alcott, welcome. Please
come in."

She could see he wasn't sure how to address her. The first impulse
for both was a familiarity that made little sense in light of the facts—
they hadn't spoken in decades, they'd never had a proper good-bye.
But it *felt* right to grin. She could easily imagine grabbing his hand
and running down the path toward the river, walking together to see
how broad and thick the forsythia had grown. Twenty years fell off
her shoulders.

But if he addressed her in this way, propriety dictated she respond
in kind. "Thank you, Mr. Singer. It was kind of you to receive me.
I hope I'm not disturbing you." She stepped over the threshold and
followed him into a parlor cluttered with the tangibles of family life.
A yellowed child's drawing pressed into a frame hung above a piano
with an embroidered bench worn threadbare. A shelf stuffed with

books stood in a corner near twin armchairs with calico cushions, a mending basket at the foot of one chair. In the grate, a low fire burned. The last few nights had been chilly. Winter was on its way.

He motioned to the chairs. "Please—sit. Would you like some tea?"

"This chair looks as though it belongs to Mrs. Singer. Perhaps I should sit over there." She gestured toward the sofa.

"Ah," he chuckled. "I haven't had the heart to put that mending basket away, though it hasn't been touched for a year now. Nora passed on last fall."

Louisa winced at her clumsiness, then nodded. "I'm sorry to hear it—I hope she did not suffer long." Though she knew Joseph had married Nora after all, hearing him confirm it felt strange. He lived in Louisa's memory as a bachelor, as the twenty-three-year-old boy he'd been. She knew it was silly, but she felt surprise hearing that his life had continued to move forward. He had chosen correctly, she thought, glancing around at all the symbols of the family they'd built together.

"She died in her sleep. She was always the first up in the morning, bustling around, stoking up the fire, setting out the cups for tea. One day I woke up first, saw her rolled on her side, so peaceful. The doctor had warned us that her heart was weak, but I never suspected . . . I just thought, 'Let her sleep. I can manage,' and got breakfast ready myself. I went in to wake her later but she was long gone."

"Well, if we must go, that seems like a gentle way to do it," Louisa said.

"Yes. Though we'd all of us rather she had stayed here a little longer. Please excuse me a moment." He exited through a narrow passage that led to the kitchen, and in a moment she heard the sound of spoons and cups and saucers being arranged on a tray.

Hearing Joseph fumble to arrange the tea himself touched her, and she felt keenly the loneliness of his domestic life. To have known companionship, however imperfect, and then lost it seemed more of a burden than never knowing it at all. It was plain to see that he *had* loved Nora, and Louisa chided herself for feeling surprised by that fact as well. He may have felt nothing but friendship for her when they were young, Louisa knew. But she suspected that love could grow out of time and proximity just as well as it could strike in a passionate flash. Perhaps the particularities of Nora and Joseph hardly mattered; perhaps two strangers who stood together through life's long journey would find themselves in a kind of love at the end of it.

He returned to the parlor carrying the tray and placed it on the low table between them.

"What beautiful children you have," she said, pointing at two portraits hanging side by side above the fireplace, a boy and a girl.

"Only one child now, I'm afraid. Our daughter Jane drowned in the Connecticut when she was five years old." Joseph lifted the porcelain pot and poured the steaming tea into two cups. Its lid clattered and he silenced it with his palm before setting the pot awkwardly back on the tray. "But we are blessed with a son, Timothy, though at eighteen he is no longer a child."

Louisa imagined a ginger-haired girl, like her mother, walking across a field with her arms full of wildflowers, a low sun painting the sky orange behind her. And then with dread Louisa saw the cold and heedless river that swallowed the girl. Louisa knew the physical pain of grief, knew its current could be just as deadly as a river's. She wondered how it happened that joy finally returned to Joseph and Nora's life. Did their mourning separate them, or did the sight of Nora's silhouette unleash something wild in Joseph that allowed her body to save him? It didn't pain Louisa the way it once had to imagine his bare arms holding Nora, his palm resting on the small of her back. Life was so full of sorrow, and a body was a touchstone, a physical reminder that we are more than our grief, even if it owns us for a while.

And it was plain to see that he did know happiness again. Perhaps the day he first held his swaddled Timothy, in the yellow dawn light, the sadness subsided. Perhaps gratitude raked his veins and he thanked God for life and breath. Sometimes we are repaid for our concessions in ways we couldn't have imagined, she thought.

An uncomfortable moment passed as Louisa strained to think of the right thing to say. She shifted in the armchair, pressing against the cushion wedged behind her aching hip. "I'm sorry to hear of little Jane. That must have been a terrible time." Louisa took a sip of her tea. "But a boy of eighteen! Goodness, that makes me feel old." She felt a surge of emotion at the thought of this boy, who probably looked just like his father had that summer.

Joseph shook his head. "The time has flown. And what of the Alcotts? My condolences are long overdue for the loss of Elizabeth. I heard she passed not long after your family left Walpole."

Louisa nodded. "Scarlet fever. She picked it up from some children my mother was trying to help through one of her charities. My mother always meant well, but looking back I almost have to laugh— we were hardly in a position to be giving away bread. The six of us rarely had enough to eat ourselves."

Joseph gave her a sad smile. Louisa wondered if he was thinking back on the way she rebuked his offer of help the day she and Anna came to his father's store for flour. Or perhaps he was thinking of his own family's financial troubles. It was exhausting, the unending effort people made to shield the truth of their lives. The root of a good share of life's problems could be traced back to keeping secrets, Louisa thought.

"Elizabeth's passing must have been a trial," Joseph said. The afternoon had waned and the room was growing dim. He reached to the table behind him and turned up the lamp.

Louisa's voice softened and her heart ached to say the words aloud. "You had better save some of your condolences for more recent losses. Marmee died nearly four years ago. Her passing was a comfort, for she suffered long and was ready to go, though I miss her every day. But the worst was yet to come. May died not two years ago, in Germany."

Joseph looked stricken. "May? But she was yet so young."

"Just thirty-nine. A few years ago I sent her back to London to study, and there she met Ernest. He was still a very young man and though it seemed unlikely to the mean-spirited gossips, May wasn't too old to fall in love. They married at once and she returned with him to Germany. We were happy to hear of their good news, though we've never had the chance to meet her husband."

"He must be devastated. Was her illness sudden?"

Louisa's eyes swam as she reflected on this fresh grief. "We can't call 'illness' the travail that transfers life and spirit from one generation into the next. May gave birth after a long and difficult labor and had a month with her baby before she died. She named the little daughter Louisa May—Lulu."

"And the child?" Joseph asked, bracing himself for more tragedy.

"Rosy and blond and full of more energy than I know what to do with. The babe came to live with her Aunt Louisa and proud Grandfather Alcott just last year. May made her wishes known to Ernest before she died: she wanted Lulu to live with me. But we had to beg him to let his little one come to us. After all, she could be May's double with that blond hair and her pale eyes, and she is all Ernest has to remind him of his late wife. But caring for a child is a trying business, especially for a man who travels. If she had stayed in Germany, she would have been raised by the governess. Here, at least, she can be with family. She will be two years old next month."

Joseph broke into a relieved smile and stirred cream into his cup. "Ah, so there is some joy, then, despite the loss. Did you travel to bring Lulu home?"

Louisa shook her head. "I've been too weak for some time now for that. Seasickness makes me absolutely wretched. We enlisted the help of a friend who sailed to collect the child and bring her back to me. But I'll have you know I was the first one at the wharf, waiting to catch a glimpse of the ship as it came into the harbor."

"What a happy day it must have been! Did you know the child the moment you saw her?"

"There were so many babies in the arms of women as they came off the ship. I kept wondering as each one passed which one was our Lulu. At last the captain approached and he held in his arms a bab-bling little thing with yellow hair and blue eyes, just like May's. The captain placed her in my arms, and I tell you—she looked at me and she said, 'Marmar,' just as clear as a bell."

Louisa's voice wavered as her tears spilled over. She brushed them away as Joseph reached over and put his palm on her hand a moment before sitting back in his chair to muse over the happy reunion. They shared a long glance as the uneasiness that had filled the space between them fell away.

"So you are a mother now after all," Joseph said gently. "Think of everything you will teach her."

Louisa brushed away his comment with her hand. "I'm too old and sick and tired to do a proper job. I fear I will fail her when she needs me most." She hadn't realized this was what she felt until she said it out loud. She remembered Joseph had had a way of getting her to admit to thoughts she didn't know she had. Here he was, doing it again after all this time.

He looked at her carefully, noting the change that came over her demeanor with this confession. "And what of the eldest Miss Alcott? I pray that story has a happier ending, after all she went through. . . ."

A shiver snaked its way down Louisa's back at the memory of Anna rocking in her chair in front of the window, watching the leaves turn. "Thankfully, yes. After my mother and father left Walpole to return to Concord, Anna came home from Syracuse and took up acting as a hobby once again. She played in *The Loan of a Lover* opposite Mr. John Pratt. When the curtain went down, they found the role of lovers suited them. He was a poor man but proud and hardworking. He gave her two sons, my boisterous nephews. Sadly he became infirm when he was still quite a young man and left us too soon." Time had blunted Louisa's sadness for Anna's loss and she could speak of it without losing control of her emotions. She took a long breath.

"Well, what a host of difficulties the Alcotts have endured," Joseph said. "It makes my own troubles seem like nothing in comparison."

"Tragedy cannot be measured out and compared on a scale. Loss is loss. And you can never be sure how one is affected. I may speak plainly of these events, but let me assure you, my grief is quite alive just below the surface. It's only that I've learned not to let quite so many of my feelings show."

She hadn't intended to reference whatever it was that had passed between the two of them so long ago, but now that the words were out it seemed the only thing she could have meant.

Joseph locked eyes with her, the veil of formality lifting. "It has its risks—that is clear." He shifted in his chair. "But I suppose time changes the way we see these things."

"Perhaps." But Louisa wasn't sure if time had changed anything in her, other than giving her less energy to deal with more grief.

Joseph couldn't wait any longer to broach the subject. "It's wonderful to have you here, Lou—Miss Alcott. But I know you didn't come just to visit."

"Call me Louisa, please." She felt almost desperate, suddenly, to hear him say her name.

He watched her a moment, his eyes peeling away the wrinkles and the faded color of her hair. "Louisa," he said, resting on the word, drawing out its rounded vowels. "What brings you here?"

She straightened up. "I've been very fortunate to have had a little success with my writing later in life," she began.

Joseph chuckled. "I should say so."

"Why do you laugh?"

He gave an amused shake of his head, stood, and crossed the room to his desk, where he pulled open the bottom drawer and reached to the back. Beneath a pile of papers was a carved wooden box with a hinged lid. He pulled it out, set it on the desktop, and swung open the lid. He plucked up one of the folded clippings inside and his reading glasses, then stood in the middle of the room, reading, as if to a crowd. *"Miss Louisa May Alcott, who is generally regarded as the most popular and successful literary woman in America, did not at once jump into sudden fame, although the slow-developing bud bloomed into flower in a single night, as it were. . . ."* He lowered the paper and gave her a coy smile. "That was in the *Boston Herald* a few months back. It isn't the first."

Louisa felt equal parts mortification and glee. She thought it sheer vanity to read the articles that appeared from time to time—and so she never did. But she *was* proud of all her success, and not just because she had finally been able to pay off her father's lifetime of debt. A sort of astonishment dawned on her. "You saved this? Why?"

"I saved them all. That box is nearly full," he said, pointing to it, "if you'd like to hear any more."

She shook her head and put out her palms. "No—please!"

He thought for a moment before he spoke. "When you left me standing on the train platform that day in Boston, I was so angry. And hurt. Don't misunderstand me—looking back, I see now how everything was meant to turn out. But at the time I was . . ." He paused, as if he wasn't sure whether he should speak plainly. "Well, I was heartbroken. And so saving these clippings helped remind me that you had a good reason for—"

"—Joseph." The syllables of his name felt strange, like marbles in her mouth. "I cannot tell you how sorry I am for . . . what happened."

He waved away her apology. "That's all well in the past now."

Louisa could see in his face that the long-ago summer may have been well in the past, but seeing her brought all the old thoughts back to the present. She had never stopped wondering what exactly she had given up by staying behind on her own. It was a blessing he had not come back to Mrs. Reed's after she sent Caroline to the station with her letter. If Joseph had begged Louisa to change her mind, she might have conceded. And what a lovely concession it would have been! She remembered his long brown arms, the whisper touch of his finger as it traced the curve of her hip. But where would it all have gotten her? Hanging laundry on a line in Walpole. Brimming with bitterness and untold stories. She had escaped a fate full of disappointment, and she knew it.

"I should have written to you," she said. "Or tried harder to explain."

"No." Joseph waved off the suggestion. "I knew . . . I understood."

She could see in the slant of the afternoon light that his eyes swam. "Some things just aren't meant to be. I've had a wonderful life. You have had a wonderful life. Both wonderful, just in a different way than we might have imagined."

Louisa hesitated to dredge up old memories, but her curiosity overwhelmed her manners. "What did you do? Did you go on to New York after all?"

He smiled. "Well, first I sat on a bench for a few long hours after Caroline brought your letter. I debated myself a hundred different ways about whether to go back to Mrs. Reed's and try to win you over. But I think I knew your mind was made up. My *God*, you were stubborn."

Louisa gave him a sheepish look. "It's true. I like to think I have perhaps *some* charming qualities, but that is not one of them."

"Well, it charms me now, when I think back on it. You were like a full-speed train back then. Nothing was going to stand in your way."

"Those trains kill people all the time," Louisa said, with her hand to her brow.

"You don't have to tell me," Joseph said. "To answer your question, I did go on to New York that night. My cousin Edward was surprised to see that the rooms he'd secured for us would be occupied by just one very dour young man, but he took mercy on me and asked few questions. I spent three dark weeks roaming the streets of the city before I found a job working as a carpenter's assistant. The work was hard but I was happy to have something to do."

Louisa listened intently, feeling a rush of guilt at being the sole cause of his suffering.

"Catherine was planning to join me in the city, but I was scarcely making enough money to feed myself. I knew I couldn't go on that way much longer. I wasn't sure what I would do, but then Nora wrote me a long honest letter. She confessed she had suspected my heart belonged to someone else. She didn't know it was you, of course. . . ."

They exchanged a lingering glance. "She said she knew I didn't love her, at least not the way a husband *should* love his wife. But she also knew I was struggling in New York and said that, if I would come home and merely try, even just for a little while, she would give her best efforts to making a happy home for us. I was heartsick and she showed me true kindness. So I went back to Walpole."

"Of course you did, and what a good decision it was!" Louisa said, a bit too cheerfully. Part of her felt she should have been the one to comfort him, though of course it was a silly thought. He wouldn't have needed comforting if it hadn't been for the wounds she herself had caused him.

"I went reluctantly, but soon I accepted what my life became. God blessed me with her. Nora was a good wife and a wonderful mother." His eyes met Louisa's and he held her gaze a moment, as if he needed to be sure she understood what he was about to say. "The things I felt for you never went away, Louisa. They never even faded. But life moves on. The page has to turn."

Louisa nodded. She knew the truth of his words. As old and used up as she felt, merely sitting near Joseph now enlivened her spirit, and the intensity of all the old wishes rushed into her heart like a melted spring.

Louisa wondered what to do now. It seemed cruel to ask him for the letters, but she couldn't let these memories cloud up her thoughts and get in the way of her object in coming to Walpole this one last time. She knew she wouldn't be able to sleep until something was done about the letters to keep them from getting into the wrong hands. She had never been a patient woman, and age only made her less so.

"Joseph, I came today because of articles like the one you read," she said, pointing to the clipping from the *Boston Herald*. "Though I doubt very much that my life could be of interest to anyone, reporters come around Orchard House weekly, along with scads of young women, wanting to interview me, to take my picture. Most of them mean well and simply want to know about the writing. They want to know whether I'm Jo."

He smiled at this and she returned it with a little roll of her eyes.

"Well, aren't you?" he asked. "I recognized an awful lot of you in her character."

She nodded. "Yes—it's true, and I've never denied it. But some of these readers don't have the decency to respect my privacy. And I get the distinct feeling they're waiting for me to die so they can dig freely through my papers and turn little fragments of thought into full-blown stories that could hurt my family. And yours."

"Why would they care about me? Everything is so far in the past."

"Don't you see? They want to know who is the real-life Laurie. They all believe I am Jo, so they assume Laurie must be out in the world somewhere. They have investigated my sister May—they know *she* did not marry him, as her counterpart Amy did in the story."

Joseph nodded. "I always wondered why you made Laurie marry Amy in the end."

Louisa groaned and placed her face in her hands. "You aren't the only one!"

Joseph laughed. "Old wounds?"

"You write to please an audience, but they can turn on you— suddenly. They all wanted Jo to relent and marry Laurie, but it wasn't in Jo to do it. Those little girls never could understand that marriage is not the only thing a woman might do with her life."

"Let me make sure I understand. The young man who pursued you, who denied, pined for you, who walked around with a heart like a broken wing clutched up to his chest for months—you're afraid these meddlesome young readers will think I am he? I can't *imagine* why."

Her eyes met his and she gave him a sly smile. "Some of them are very narrow-minded. One must exercise patience."

Joseph chuckled at this. "So—am I? Am I Laurie?"

Louisa looked at him a long moment. "When I was in Paris the year before I wrote *Little Women*, I met a young man named Ladislas, a Pole. He was just nineteen, so full of spirit." Louisa took a breath. "When readers—and reporters—ask me who inspired Laurie, I tell them he did, for he is out of their reach. But that isn't the truth. Ladislas only reminded me of *you*. When I created Laurie, it was you I thought of."

"Well, I am quite honored," he said. "Laurie is very likeable. I think I can speak for an entire country of little girls when I say it would have been nice to see Jo experience a change of heart."

"And all I can say is that Jo would have ceased to be Jo if she had agreed to marry Laurie."

Joseph furrowed his brow. Louisa could see that though she wished to change the subject, he didn't want to let it go. Perhaps he had held these questions in his mind for a long time. "But she marries the professor in the end—how is that any different?"

"Eventually I gave in to the pressure of my publisher. He felt if Jo didn't marry *someone*, I'd be letting down my loyal readers. In his eyes, as a spinster, Jo would have been a tragedy. I could hardly agree, of course, given my own situation. If it had been up to me, she would have stayed happy and free, writing stories and traveling the world."

"Like you."

"Perhaps. But not so old and tired."

Joseph flashed a knowing smile. "One of the most shocking things about becoming an adult is the sight of your heroes growing older as well. For some reason we seem to think they should be frozen in time."

"Well, they aren't, and I have the gray hair to prove it." She paused, willing herself to lead the conversation back to her purpose, though she dreaded it. "And that's why I came here today. I have to try to protect my family, and your family, from learning anything . . . anything we'd rather keep to ourselves."

"I see."

Louisa took a breath. "I feel silly asking this question—undoubtedly they are long gone—but do you still have any of the letters I sent to you?"

He opened his mouth to answer, then closed it and walked back to his desk. He carried the wooden box from his drawer over to her chair. "See for yourself," he said.

She pulled the small stack of papers out of the box. Most were clippings from the local newspapers about her books and her involvement in suffrage speeches and conferences. Beneath those, her eye caught the familiar pattern of the stationery her uncle sent her as a Christmas gift several years in a row. The box slid forward on her lap and she heard a soft thud against the wood. She reached in and grasped an object, felt the cool steel of its three long teeth.

"My comb," she whispered, looking up at him. He nodded slightly. "How in the world did you come to have this?"

"Do you remember that day we had the picnic by the river, and we all went swimming? You left it on the rocks."

Mock mortification crossed Louisa's face. "Wasn't I the picture of impropriety. Prancing around with my hair undone."

"Thank God for that impropriety." Joseph closed his eyes. "I can see it clearly in my mind at this moment. You looked like a mermaid with that hair fanning out in the water. My God, what a beauty."

"Your memory has edited out all the facts, my friend. My sister Anna was the beauty."

Joseph looked at her a moment and shook his head. "You never *could* see it. But that only made you more appealing."

She reached into the bag she'd carried on her shoulder from the train. "These are your letters," she said, holding up the sheets of paper. "And the *Leaves of Grass* you gave me. You wrote an inscription." She opened to the flyleaf.

From J.S. to L.M.A. He is "the poet of the woman the same as of the man."

Joseph held out his hand and she gave him the book. He fingered the gold words on the cover, admired the liberty Whitman had taken with the type, depicting roots and leaves growing from the letters as if they lived.

Louisa watched the tender way he held the peculiar little book that bound the two of them together. "I finally had the chance to meet him," she said. "Just last month, in fact."

Joseph's eyes widened. "Well, fame does have *some* rewards, then, does it not?"

She nodded and gave him a playful grin. "I've met the president too, you know."

"Well, I am impressed. Was Whitman the way we imagined him? A loaf and a brute?"

"Not at all. Perhaps age has mellowed him. My father and I had tea with him in Concord. Mr. Whitman wears a long white beard. Walks with a cane." Louisa recalled the way the gentle poet had asked her father endless questions about his work, Emerson's, Margaret Fuller's. Whitman had shown no ego and offered sincere compliments to them all.

"Did you tell him you blamed his poetry for causing you to fall madly in love with me?"

Louisa smiled more broadly than she had in a long time. Joseph meant the coy comment as a joke, but hearing him say those words aloud—"fall madly in love"—pried opened her heart. All the inexpressible things they felt for each other that those verses allowed them to share, they could *talk* about them—they could own them now after all this time.

"I told him I never knew poetry—mere words on a page—could wreak havoc until I read his."

"And what did he say to that?"

"Well, my father was certainly puzzled—he didn't know what I could possibly be talking about. Whitman looked very wise and kind and said, 'Tell the truth and you can start a fire.' I felt he was looking right through me."

Joseph marveled at the poet's words for a moment, then looked nervously at Louisa. "What is it that you want us to do with these letters?" His fingers tightened around the book, as if he were afraid of what she would suggest.

Louisa glanced at the fireplace, where the spent logs emitted a pale glow. "Burn them."

Just the suggestion of it seemed to wound him as much as if the deed were already done. "Oh, I don't think I could."

Louisa held up her hand. "I know—it's awful. But please, let's not be sentimental about this."

"I don't consider it 'sentimental' to keep a token of—"

"Do you want your son to find these letters someday and *wonder* whether his father was unfaithful to his mother?"

Joseph closed his eyes and sighed.

"We are lucky that he hasn't already stumbled across them," she said softly.

Louisa caught a glimpse of herself in the mirror on the far wall and recalled the trepidation she'd felt standing at his front door when she first arrived. Joseph seemed to study her for a moment. She could see he thought she looked much older than her years, could see he was realizing her fears about what would happen after her death did not represent some far-off eventuality: She was dying.

Louisa carried on, desperate to convince him. "You have to believe me that these people will stop at nothing. My life is no longer my own. I must do everything I can to keep them from finding out about . . . what we had. They will make it into something tawdry and hurtful, and I couldn't bear that."

His heart cracked open like an egg. "All right," he said, nodding to the stack of letters in her hand. "But not the book."

She sighed. "I suppose the book on its own, should it be found, doesn't reveal very much. But you'll have to keep it here."

Joseph nodded and crossed the room to place the book on the shelf next to his desk. Louisa rose from the chair and lowered herself down in front of the fireplace. She felt the heft of the fire iron up to her elbow as she swung it into the pit. Joseph reached for a length of the cedar he and Timothy had chopped the day before when the temperature had turned cold.

He knelt down next to Louisa and laid the log on the freshly stoked coals. The wood was dry, and the flames climbed slowly along its fibers. She waited until the fire was high, then looked up at Joseph. He held her gaze. The apprehension that had clutched Louisa's lungs like a vise suddenly released its hold and her eyes filled as she experienced the pleasure of a full breath. What they felt for each other would be safe now; it belonged to them alone. He gave her a slight nod. Louisa cast the papers into the fire and nearly gasped at how quickly they disappeared. Joseph placed his hand on her arm and they watched the smoke that carried their secret billow up the chimney and out across the pale New Hampshire sky.

ACKNOWLEDGMENTS

My sincere thanks go to the graceful and brilliant Marly Rusoff and her associates, Michael Radulescu and Julie Mosow, who have worked tirelessly throughout this process. I am equally grateful for my editor, Amy Einhorn, whose masterly editorial skill and enthusiasm from day one have made this a better book, and for the work of her patient assistant, Halli Melnitsky. The team at Putnam is second to none. Thanks especially to Dorian Hastings, Catharine Lynch, Alaina Mauro, Meredith Phebus, Melissa Solis, Lisa D'Agostino, Krista Asadorian, Meighan Cavanaugh, Mary Shuck, Stephanie Sorensen, Claire McGinnis, Kate Stark, Lydia Hirt, Christopher Nelson, and Ashley Tucker.

I am indebted to the people who taught me about writing and reading like a writer: Hugh Spagnuolo, Fritz Swanson, Laurence Goldstein, Theresa Tinkle, and especially Tish O'Dowd. Any missteps in this book occur in spite of their efforts.

I am blessed with two loving and committed parents, Steve and Mary O'Connor, and my brother, Matt, a man of few words but a very big heart; thanks to all three of them for a lifetime of support. Thanks also to Bob Sr., Ann, Andy, and Megan McNees, my new family, for their enthusiasm. Gratitude to my first reader and dear friend Lori Nelson Spielman; to Erin Richnow Brown, for invaluable suggestions and encouragement; to John Lederman, for listening; and to Jennifer Brehl, for her support. Many thanks to Mary Bisbee-Beek, my friend who knows everybody; to Kate Emerson, for her photographic skills; and to Geoffrey Gagnon, for being in New York seven years ago and wanting to talk about writing. It's no exaggeration to say that this book simply would not exist were it not for my wise and true friend Kelly Harms Wimmer, my deep thanks to her. And finally, out of the tree of life I picked me a plum in my husband, Bob, who has offered continuous support: thank you for taking me to Ontario, where I had nothing to do, for happily eating lima beans, and for never doubting this would happen.

AUTHOR'S NOTE

Like many American readers, I have always loved *Little Women*. But I never knew much about its author until I stumbled on Martha Saxton's *Louisa May Alcott: A Modern Biography* one day while poking around in the library. I checked it out, and for some reason as I was reading I felt compelled to mark the sections I loved with sticky notes. I just didn't want to forget any of the details. When I finished, the book looked like it was sprouting leaves—there were sticky notes on almost every page.

I read it again. I kept renewing the book until the library wouldn't let me renew it anymore. After that I went into the library through the back door so no one would corner me and try to get the book back. Finally one day my husband rolled his eyes and said, "Why don't you just *buy* it?"

So I did buy it, along with all the other biographies of Louisa I could find. And right away I noticed something strange: Each biography portrayed her differently. One painted her as a pioneering feminist; another described a reluctant spinster; yet another imagined her as little more than an extension of her father and his philosophical work. After spending so much time reading about her, I felt I had to know—who was the real Louisa?

All the biographers had drawn their details from the same primary sources—Louisa's letters and journals, among other things. So I decided to read them myself, and they simply took me over. My husband and I had recently relocated from Providence, Rhode Island, to the somewhat out-of-the-way town of Waterloo, Ontario, for his work. Leaving my job as a teacher in Rhode Island and trying to figure out what to do with myself in our new home left me feeling unsettled. I toyed with the idea of making an honest effort to write a novel, something I had wanted to do for as long as I could remember. But I was afraid. What if I wasn't any good? What if I had nothing to say? As I read Louisa's descriptions of her own anxieties about the writing process, I felt a faint twinge of hope. I knew I had to try to write, and I knew I wanted to write about her.

The final piece of the puzzle fell into place when I happened upon an excerpt from a memoir by Julian Hawthorne, the son of Nathaniel Hawthorne. Julian had been a neighbor to the Alcotts and a childhood friend of Louisa's youngest sister, May, the inspiration for *Little Women*'s Amy. Writing about Louisa, he said, "Did she ever have a love affair? We never knew. Yet how could a nature so imaginative, romantic and passionate escape it?"

And I thought, *That's it*. Biographers note that Louisa had a habit of burning letters, though it's impossible to know how many were destroyed and what they contained. Louisa herself acknowledged a childhood infatuation with Ralph Waldo Emerson that drove her to write him adoring letters, which she never sent and which she later burned. Louisa was famous in her own lifetime, and she was careful to edit the journals and papers that biographers would use to tell the story of her life after she died.

Knowing this, I didn't have to stretch too much to imagine that perhaps Louisa *did* have a love affair but erased all traces of it. Yet when would it have happened? I remembered that the biographies mentioned that the Alcotts summered in Walpole, New Hampshire, in 1855. Only a few solid facts are known about that summer—her father Bronson kept a garden, the sisters put on a few plays with local actors, and in the fall, Louisa went off to Boston to write and Anna went to Syracuse to work in an asylum. The lack of historical information made it the perfect setting for the story: a lost summer in Louisa's life.

Next I went in search of as many details as I could cull from books on nineteenth-century New England dress, cooking, housekeeping, leisure, transportation, politics, and literature. I continuously reread Louisa's letters and journals as I worked because I wanted the Louisa in my story to sound as much like the real Louisa as possible. I made a list of all the books she loved—Dickens was her favorite writer; she deeply admired *Jane Eyre*—and

I pored over them looking for clues about what might have been on her mind. I tried to pull together the anecdotes that best showcased who she was. The picnic by the river, candlemaking with Anna, Bronson's insisting that his daughters read their journals aloud, J. T. Fields telling Louisa she should stick with teaching because she'd never make it as a writer—all of those things really happened in various forms. And as many readers will know, Ralph Waldo Emerson really did play a significant role in the Alcotts' lives as a source of friendship and financial support.

Despite its being rooted in fact, however, this story is without a doubt an invention, and I have taken plenty of liberties. In the interest of moving the narrative forward, I gathered episodes from Louisa's experiences living on her own in Boston from late 1855 through 1856 and beyond, and condensed them into a shorter period of time. Nicholas and Nora Sutton, Margaret Lewis, their families, the other young people in town, and, of course, Joseph Singer are entirely fictional characters, though that does not make them any less real to me.

Last summer, I traveled to Walpole for the first time. Until then I had been working from an old map of the town and some snapshots of Washington Square. It was wonderful and strange to walk through the town that seemed so vibrant in my imagination. I pictured the characters walking to the river, rehearsing the play in the attic of a downtown inn, and shopping for fabric in the dry goods store. I felt closer to them than ever.

I was thrilled to realize that *Leaves of Grass* was published that same summer. Emerson read it immediately and probably talked about it with Bronson. Discovering the historical coincidence of Louisa's lost summer and Whitman's great work felt like a very good omen. Nothing in American literature could bind two restless hearts in love like that volume of poetry. This seemed to bring the story together, and at that point I committed to following it where it might lead.

Most of the few images of Louisa that survive show her when she was older, after the success of *Little Women* had catapulted her to almost instant fame. In them she appears tired and much older than she actually was. Her

doctors, and, by extension, generations of Alcott scholars, believed she had been poisoned by the mercury-based calomel given to her as a treatment for typhoid. A biography published in 2009 cites the work of two doctors who attempted to settle remaining questions about Louisa's diagnosis. Their investigation of her symptoms led them to posit that Louisa had developed the autoimmune disease lupus—a fascinating idea that, alas, cannot be proved. Whatever the cause of her suffering, in her later years she was in constant pain, and this is evident in the images that appear in all her biographies—one of the few things they have in common.

But there is one picture of her as a young woman in her early twenties. She isn't smiling—most people didn't smile in pictures then because they were self-conscious about the poor condition of their teeth—yet the intensity of her gaze hints at how much life resided behind those eyes. This Louisa is young, vibrant, and full of anticipation for the joys and sorrows that lie ahead. I kept the picture on my desktop as I worked, and sometimes it seemed she was nudging me, bit by bit, toward the story she wanted me to tell.

For more details about Louisa's life and writing,
visit www.kellyoconnormcnees.com.

A NOTE ON SOURCES

I am indebted to several sources for information on Louisa May Alcott's life and work, as well as the details of life in Walpole, New Hampshire, in 1855: Madeleine B. Stern's *Louisa May Alcott*, Martha Saxton's *Louisa May Alcott: A Modern Biography*, John Matteson's *Eden's Outcasts: The Story of Louisa May Alcott and Her Father*, Susan Cheever's *American Bloomsbury*, William Anderson and David Wade's *The World of Louisa May Alcott*, Ednah Dow Cheney's *Louisa May Alcott: Her Life, Letters, and Journals*, Harriet Reisen's *Louisa May Alcott: The Woman Behind* Little Women, George Aldrich's *Walpole As It Was and As It Is*, J. C. Furnas's *Fanny Kemble: Leading Lady of the Nineteenth Century Stage*, Jane Nylander's *Our Own Snug Fireside*, and John Culhane's *The American Circus: An Illustrated History*. Any factual errors or anachronisms in this story emerged from my own flawed vision and do not reflect the painstaking work of these writers.

Little Women has never been out of print since its publication in 1868, but the Louisa I have come to know—complex, ambitious, political, and, of course, a brilliant storyteller—shows herself more fully in the many other stories and novels she wrote before and after her famous novel. Those mentioned in this book include "The King of Clubs and the Queen of Hearts," "Mrs. Podgers' Teapot," and "Love and Loyalty," all collected in *Hospital Sketches and Camp Fireside Stories*; *Work: A Story of Experience*; *A Modern Mephistopheles and A Whisper in the Dark*; "Morning-Glories," from *Morning-Glories and Other Stories*; *Little Men*; "Transcendental Wild Oats: A Chapter of an Unwritten Romance"; *Under the Lilacs*; *Moods*; *An Old-Fashioned Girl*; and *Jack and Jill*. Countless others exist, many of which were published under a pseudonym because they were deemed too sensational to be linked to Miss Alcott. Two must-reads that most certainly were *not* written for "little women" are *A Long Fatal Love Chase*, which remained unpublished until 1995, and *Behind a Mask, or A Woman's Power*, originally written under the pseudonym A. M. Barnard. I hope readers will find as much delight in their pages as I have.

Kelly O'Connor McNees is a former editorial assistant and English teacher. Born and raised in Michigan, she has lived in New York, Rhode Island, and Ontario, and now resides with her husband in Chicago. *The Lost Summer of Louisa May Alcott* is her first novel. For more information, please visit www.kellyoconnormcnees.com.